A REASON TO LEAVE

BOOK THREE

MELISSA ELLEN

BLACKWOOD SERIES

A REASON TO STAY
THE ONLY ONE
A REASON TO LEAVE
FOREVER YOURS

STAND ALONE SERIES

REDEEMING LOTTIE
CHASING HANNAH- Coming Soon

Subscribe for updates or
Follow Melissa Ellen on Facebook for the latest information
on New Releases!

Website and Newsletter:

www.melissaellenwrites.com

PROLOGUE

LIAM STONE....

I stared at her bruised face as she sat across the table from me looking on edge, void of all emotion, refusing to speak first. As much as I wanted to blame her for my being here, I couldn't. It was my own fucking fault. Not that I regretted it. I'd do it again. The bastard fucking deserved it. I'd dreamt of doing it for years, and despite landing myself here, it was worth it.

"I'm not bailing you out." She broke the silence between us, glancing at the handcuffs locked around my wrists.

"I didn't ask you to," I sneered.

"Well, just so we're clear. You're on your own. You shouldn't have come back. You should've minded your own fucking business."

Of course. Why would I ever expect her to thank me? Or, I don't know, defend my actions against her fucking asshole

1

of a husband? She was right. I shouldn't have shown back up. For some reason, I thought she needed saving. I was fucking stupid for thinking I could do just that. She obviously didn't want to be saved. And she obviously didn't want me. She was choosing *him*. Again.

"When you get out, stay away. Don't come back. I don't need you fucking things up for me."

"Fucking things up for you? I didn't think that was possible." I glared at her.

She slid her gaze from me momentarily. "I mean it. Stay. Away."

A deep hate manifested inside me. I didn't think it was possible for me to ever hate anyone this much, let alone her. But I was done—done fucking trying to be there for her, trying to help give her a better life. She was on her own. If she ended up dead, I'd no longer feel guilty. I tried. Fuck her and her fucking prick husband.

I leaned my forearms on the table, angling my upper body forward, letting my eyes penetrate hers, the hate and anger radiating off me. She shifted uncomfortably, but her stupid pride kept her from taking her eyes off me.

"Don't bother ever coming to see me again. You stay out of my fucking life. I'll stay out of yours," I promised her. "You're dead to me."

She flinched with my words and her face dropped. I had no idea why. I was giving her what she asked for. The hardness returned to her face instantly. I didn't wait for her response. I turned my head, nodding at the guard that I was ready to return to my cell. I was finished with this conversation. Finished with her.

CHAPTER 1

"K eys."

"Jim will take you."

"Keys, Rhett," I demanded again with my palm out, wagging my impatient fingers at my overbearing, slightly obnoxious, arrogant-but-still-loveable older brother.

He gave me his determined stare, not relinquishing the keys he was holding hostage in his hand. If I thought I had a chance of overpowering him and forcefully removing them from his clutches, I'd have gone for it. He was trying my patience. I was going to be late for my audition if he didn't give them to me in the next few minutes.

"Ava already said I could borrow the car."

"I didn't."

"It's *her* car." I crossed my arms over my chest.

"We're married. It's *our* car."

"I don't have time for this Rhett. I'm going to be late. Give me the keys." I tried swiping them from him, resisting the urge to stomp my feet in frustration like a spoiled brat.

Because I was *not* a spoiled brat. At least, I was doing my best these days to not be a spoiled brat. I was now a mature adult who was making a name for herself.

"Give her the keys, babe," Ava said, coming to my rescue as she waddled into the room dressed for work.

I loved my sister-in-law. For the most part, she always teamed up with me against my difficult brother, because she knew how it was to be on this side of his over-protective and frustrating demands. He kissed her temple as she made it to his side, then wrapped his arm around her waist, resting his palm on her growing belly as he pulled her into him.

"How did you sleep?" he asked her, fondly staring down at her.

The two of them were sickening. But still, it warmed my heart watching them interact. I'd never admit that out loud, though.

"Terrible," she said with a disgruntled look. "I'd say I'm looking forward to this baby being out of me, so I can have a good night's rest...but I know that won't be the case. I may never have a good night's sleep again."

"I'll make sure you do. You aren't doing this alone."

"Oh really? Did you grow breasts overnight so *you* can do night feedings?" she asked sarcastically.

"Point taken." He chuckled, kissing her head. "We'll figure something out." He turned her in his arms as he nuzzled her neck and loved on her some more.

I crinkled my nose. *Yuck.* "Helloo...still here. Still need the keys," I reminded them, wanting to get out of here before their PDA became more than I could handle. He turned back to me, annoyed by my interruption.

"Not a dent," he warned.

"Got it."

"Not a scratch."

"*Got it*. Give me the keys." I tried swiping them from his hand one more time, missing them—again—as he dangled them above my head, just out of my reach.

"Not even a dirt smudge."

"Seriously?" I huffed.

He smirked.

"Rhett"—Ava rolled her eyes at him—"just give Val the keys. I'm sure she'll take good care of it."

"Tell that to her first two cars," he muttered.

"Hey! That's so unfair! Neither one of those incidents was my fault!"

He looked at me unconvinced, shaking his head in disbelief.

"They weren't," I pouted.

It *was* true. They were so not my fault. It was *not* my fault a squirrel decided to dash out in front of my car unexpectedly.

I *had* to swerve to miss the fear-stricken momma squirrel, or her babies would've grown up as orphans. And I, for one, wouldn't have been able to live with myself knowing that. I mean, who would? It was also not my fault I had to hit a parked car to miss the poor, desperate little squirrel. Who parks their car on a residential street anyway, when there was a perfectly empty driveway to park in? You're just asking for your car to get sideswiped.

And this time around, my car was only in the shop

because some old man, who *definitely* should *not* be driving, backed into me. Never mind I was parked in a no-parking zone. That was just semantics. *He* hit *me*.

"I mean it, Val. Anything happens to this car, you'll force me to take your driving privileges away," Rhett threatened.

"You can't do that. I'm an adult. I'm twenty-one," I said firmly, standing my ground. His threat didn't scare me. Well…maybe a little. He was an unfairly determined bastard.

He cocked his disapproving eyebrow at me. "Almost twenty-one. And try me."

"My birthday is only a few days away. I'm basically twenty-one. And you can't take my driving privileges away. Right, Ava?" I turned to her for support.

She shrugged her shoulders, being no help at all.

Thanks a lot. "Whatever. Just give me the keys already. You're making me late for my audition. If I miss another one, my agent is going to drop me."

He gave me one more warning look as he reluctantly placed the keys in my hand. "Be careful. Car aside, I don't want to see anything happen to you."

"Thanks!" I stood on my tiptoes to give him a peck on his cheek. "And I will," I said, rushing out of their Malibu home.

"Don't forget, dinner with Mom and Dad on Sunday for your birthday," he yelled after me as I hurried toward the front door.

"I won't!" I waved as I darted out the door before he changed his mind and tackled me for the keys.

～

I cruised down the Pacific Coast Highway, headed back into

L.A. for my audition. I drove only slightly over the speed limit, hoping it would be enough to get me there on time. I wasn't kidding about my agent being on the verge of dropping me. She'd already warned me if I missed this one, she was no longer "wasting her time on me." She only had time for clients who were going to "take their acting seriously."

As if I wasn't. I knew she, like many who knew my last name and where I came from, thought I was just a spoiled rich girl, living off daddy's money. Never mind I'd been busting my butt the last few years to make it on my own.

Besides letting my parents take care of my tuition, and the cost of the expensive apartment my brother had forced me to live in, I'd been covering all my own expenses by working as a barista in a local coffee shop—the same job that was consistently making me miss or be late to auditions. It was a classic catch-22 situation.

I did this all while taking on a full load at school year-round, in an attempt to graduate early and kickstart my acting career—without the help of my family's connections, I might add. I wanted my career to be built on my talent, not my name.

This was the first summer I hadn't signed up for summer courses. I only had one semester left this fall before I graduated. This summer, I planned to have some fun and focus on auditions.

I rarely touched my trust fund. Only in emergencies did I dip into it. Those emergencies were usually car related—buying a new one, or repairing it...like now. My car was in the body shop, getting repaired where the old man had T-boned me. *So* not my fault...

Once I moved to California, I tried my best to hide my

upbringing from people. I know that sounds terrible. I know that sounds ungrateful. I'm not. I love my family. I appreciate everything they've done and still do for me. The problem was, all that wealth came with a certain stigma. People judged you before even knowing you. They also tended to use you—use you to make themselves look better and boost their own social standing.

I was done being used. I was done trusting that people wanted to be friends with me for me, or that guys would love me for me. I'd learned the hard way I couldn't trust people as long as they thought they could gain something from my name.

Hence why I downplayed who I was. A Blackwood. The daughter of two of New York's wealthiest socialites, Charles and Vivian Blackwood, and sister to the famed young CEO of Blackwood Industries, Rhett Blackwood.

There was only one person I confided in about my upbringing after moving from New York: my roommate, Lexie.

We originally met working together at the coffee shop, Sweet Beans. We hit it off, and she became my closest friend and only confidant besides Ava. I didn't tell her about my family right away. I actually hid it from her as long as I could.

But once she became my roommate, there was no other way to explain how I could afford my luxurious apartment on a minimum-wage salary, or why she didn't need to pay me for rent. She paid me what she could anyway. That was the type of person she was. She didn't feel right living rent free. She was my one true friend.

She was confused by my secrecy, at first, until I

explained what I'd gone through my senior year of high school and the summer that followed. I'd tried to put it out of my mind, but it still hurt me deeply—deeply enough for me to lose trust in everyone, besides my own family, and now, Lexie.

I glanced at the clock on the car dash and began to relax as I got closer to Interstate 10. I was actually going to make it on time. Finally, something was going right for me.

Boom!

What the hell was that?

"Oh, no...no, no. Please, no." I started to panic as the car began vibrating and tugged to the right. "You have to be kidding me!" I slowed the car, pulling over on the highway shoulder.

I opened the driver's door cautiously and stepped out of the car to investigate the situation. I walked around to the passenger side and saw a deflated front tire that looked more like a smashed chocolate donut.

Shit. Shit. Damn it. Shit.

Expletives ran through my head out of habit. Rhett had always been quick to lecture me about verbalizing profanity. I never quite understood his hang up about it. He once told me I was too pure at heart and beautiful of a girl to use such language. Whatever the hell that meant.

Now what?

I pulled out my phone, staring at it. *Who am I going to call?* I bit the corner of my bottom lip as I thought. There was no way I was calling Rhett. I'd never hear the end of it. And *this* was definitely not my fault. Lexie was covering my shift today, so I could make the audition, which meant she wouldn't be able to help me out either.

"Crud. Dang it. Stupid, stupid crappy tire," I huffed, kicking the deflated puddle of rubber.

"Those are some fiery words."

I nearly jumped out of my skin hearing the deep, gruff voice that came from behind me.

"I think you might've hurt its feelings."

I rotated, throwing my hands on my hips and glaring at the source of the amused voice. I hadn't even heard or seen anyone approach, due to being too distracted by my current dilemma. I was ready to fire off my smart-ass retort when I was struck by the vision of him.

My words got trapped in my throat as my eyes swept up his muscular body that was hugged by worn jeans sitting on a lean waist. His form-fitting black T-shirt did a poor job of concealing his chiseled chest and revealed strong biceps that were accented with the black ink of a tribal tattoo peeking out from his sleeve.

As my eyes traveled north, it only got better. His square jaw was lined with stubble, his eyes a beautiful, crisp grey, and his hair a messy, dirty blonde. I instantly pictured myself running my fingers through that hair and holding on tight. My core clenched at the thought as my tummy fluttered.

I made myself focus on his eyes, trying to curb the unfamiliar urges taking over my body. His eyes were doing their own inspection of me, and when they met mine, they temporarily widened with recognition, then narrowed into a seething glare as they glanced between me and Ava's fancy black Bentley GT.

What the hell is his problem?

I wondered if maybe he recognized who I was. It didn't happen as often in California as it did on the East Coast, but it did happen occasionally. He didn't seem the type to keep up with tabloids, though, with his bad-boy vibe. Also, most people didn't glare at me with distaste when they realized who I was. Their eyes normally lit up with their own greedy intentions.

His body went rigid as I continued to hold his gaze.

"Can I help you?" I spit out, annoyed by his disapproving look.

"Help *me*? It looks like you're the one in need of some help," he huffed as he glanced at my flat tire, crossing those strong arms across his rock-hard chest.

"Well, are you going to help me, or did you just stop to taunt me?" I crossed my own arms across my ample chest, suddenly feeling the need to shield myself as his eyes continued to scan my figure.

I normally boasted my body. I knew I was attractive, and I took pleasure in knowing I could get what I wanted from most men with a sway of my hips. I rarely used the tactic, though.

"Are you asking for help, princess?"

Princess? Asshole. Now I understood his loathing. He'd already pinned me as a spoiled, rich girl. There's no denying I came from money, but he didn't even *know* me. *Typical.*

"No," I said defiantly, suddenly not wanting his help, even if I needed it.

"Really?" he snorted, amused. "You sure about that?"

I opened my mouth to tell him exactly where he could go —to hell—but before I could respond, my cell phone rang, interrupting me. I glanced down at the phone and groaned. *Shit.*

"Hi, Donna!" I tried sounding cheerful to my bitch of an

agent while turning my back on the cocky, sexy jerk who still had his judging eyes on me.

"Valerie, where the hell are you?"

"I've had a bit of car trouble."

"Of course you did." I could picture her rolling her eyes through the phone. "You missed another audition. We're done."

"Wait, Donna! You can't. I was on my way there when I got a flat tire. This was not my fault."

"It never is, Valerie," she sighed. "You need to find a new agent."

"But—"

"Goodbye, Valerie, and good luck." With that, she hung up on me.

"Ughhh," I growled, releasing my frustration. I glared at the phone in my hands, trying to figure out what the hell I was going to do now.

"Should I leave you to fume alone, or do you want my help? I have places to be."

I flicked my eyes back to the sexy asshole standing in front of me, ready to take out all my anger and frustration on him. Although his words were harsh, his face suddenly seemed less so after witnessing my call. Obviously, he felt sorry for me.

I didn't want his pity, but I did need his help. I was sure someone else would've stopped to help me, but I didn't want to wait for that to happen—in case it didn't.

"Yes," I mumbled under my breath, hating to admit to this infuriating man I needed his help.

He smirked. "What was that, princess?"

Again with the princess. *Put your pride aside, Val.*

"Yes, will you please help me?" I forced out through my clenched teeth.

He smiled in satisfaction as he stepped toward the car.

"Pop your trunk. I assume you have a spare?"

"I'm not sure."

He looked at me quizzically.

"It's not my car," I said, moving to open the trunk for him.

This seemed to surprise him, but he didn't comment on it. I opened the trunk and leaned against the side of the car near the flattened tire as I watched him work efficiently.

It was a warm, summer day, and between the sun beating down on me and watching his muscles flex as he worked, I was feeling slightly overheated. Despite him being a jerk, he was hot. There was something about this brooding bad boy that had my insides fizzling.

He wasn't like the refined boys I'd dated in the past. And I say boys because compared to him, they *were* boys.

"What's your name?"

"Liam," he responded without looking up at me.

He didn't bother asking me mine, either. *Okay.* Obviously this was going to be a one-sided conversation.

"Well, *Liam*...what do you do?"

He didn't respond, just shook his head with a smirk as he finished tightening the last bolt on the spare tire. I huffed with annoyance at his dismissal of my question. He stood and gathered up the tools and the damaged tire, putting everything back in the vehicle. I walked around to the back of the car as he closed the lid of the trunk.

He grasped the hem of his shirt, wiping his hands on it then lifting the bottom to wipe the sweat off his face, exposing the washboard abs hidden below. I had to fight to keep from fanning myself. The things I wanted to do to those abs. Lick them, for one.

Whoa. Calm down, Val. Where the hell did that come from?

I heard his cocky chuckle, causing me to rip my eyes from his abs to his smirking face. It was too late to hide my shameless gawking, so I gave him a shrug with one of my shoulders, pretending to be unimpressed. I was definitely impressed. My body was definitely impressed too, feeling all needy and greedy. I leaned against the trunk, letting it support my weakening knees.

"You'll need to get the spare replaced as soon as possible. Don't drive on it for long. It's a temporary fix."

I nodded my head in understanding, still spellbound by his abs.

He watched me for a minute, as if wanting to say more. I glanced at his lips, hoping he would—then suddenly, I hoped he wouldn't. Instead, I preferred his mouth silent and on me. I'd never wanted to be kissed by a man so badly. He was only a foot from me. If I lifted my hand, I could touch his defined body.

I was like a fish being baited. He seemed all yummy and delicious, but he was bad news. He was reeling me in and I was falling for it. Hook. Line. And sinker.

Sensing my desperation, he leaned forward, his hands resting on the trunk of the car, trapping me between his strong forearms, his face inches from mine. My lips parted as I took in a small breath of air. His eyes darkened, transfixed. He leaned in, placing his face beside mine.

"I'm not your knight in shining armor, princess." His whispering breath brushed my ear. That masculine voice was soft and sultry, causing me to forget myself and ignore his warning. He said it as if he was not only trying to convince me, but also himself. My core throbbed. I felt lightheaded from the thought of feeling him pressed against me.

"I'm not a princess," I countered, my response coming out breathy and needy.

He pulled back, dragging his eyes over me before connecting with mine.

"Yes. You. Are." He delivered each word slowly and deliberately, before moving away from me. I exhaled the breath I'd unknowingly been holding.

He gave me another once-over, shook his head, then got back in his car and disappeared. Just like that. Leaving me desperate, pissed, and alone. *Jerk.*

CHAPTER 2

I walked into Sweet Beans, dropping my bag on the stool next to me as I flopped onto my own stool at the coffee bar across from Lexie. I crossed my arms on the counter and buried my head in them, blocking out the world. Life sucked.

"Audition go bad?" Lexie asked.

"I wouldn't know. I didn't make it," I grunted out through the muffling of my arms, not bothering to expose my face to her. When she didn't respond, I was forced to lift it.

Lexie was a pixie-like girl with thin, dark hair and brown eyes. But don't let her tiny figure fool you. She was tough: a rocker chick with a diamond-stud nose piercing, tattoos— mostly concealed by her clothes or her mid-length hair—and an attitude to match.

She was a walking contradiction. She was outwardly beautiful, yet rough around the edges, genuine and sweet, yet far from prim and proper. She was as loyal and feisty as they

16

came, and protective of her friends to a fault—one of the reasons I loved her so much.

If you stood the two of us next to each other, based on our outward appearances, you'd never guess we were friends. Ava loved her instantly. Rhett, on the other hand, demanded she go through a background check, regardless of the fact that I'd already known her for a year before she moved in with me. I was afraid she'd run for the hills, but she was unbothered by my brother's demands and took it in stride. In the end, she'd found a place in his heart, and he could be just as protective of her as he was of me.

"So you're saying I worked your shift for nothing." She put her hands on her hips, cocking her head down at me.

"Pretty much. Sorry." I gave her my best don't-hate-me pouty lip.

"What happened?" she sighed, releasing her arms, shaking her head as she grabbed a rag to wipe down the bar top.

"Flat tire. Broody jerk…the norm," I said, feeling defeated by the day, though it was barely halfway over.

She gave me a sympathetic smile. "You have the worst luck with cars. Maybe you should take your brother up on his offer of giving you a personal driver. You might actually make an audition *and* it'd give us a DD for when we went out," she teased.

"No. Way."

She laughed. "Okay. So, tell me about the broody jerk." She leaned forward with her forearms on the bar, flashing a big smile and inquisitive eyes at me. "I at least need to know something was worth me picking up this extra shift for you."

"Not much to tell. He was just a jerk who changed my tire," I replied, not looking directly at her, trying to keep my cheeks from flushing as I remembered his voice, lips, and firm, sweaty abs.

"What a jerky thing to do," she said sarcastically. "You know you're a horrible liar, right? Never play poker."

"What do you mean?"

She glanced at my finger, which now had my thick, golden and dark brown hair twisted around it. *When did I do that?*

"Any time you're lying, you play with your hair."

"I do not." *Shit. Do I?* I would have to be more aware of that in the future.

"You so do. Plus, your cheeks are bright red right now."

"It's hot outside."

"Right."

"Quit being a jerk and get me a water."

"Ouch. You're being bossy. He really got your expensive panties in a wad, didn't he?"

"No! He didn't get anywhere near my panties."

"So that's the problem. You wanted him to," she goaded me some more, a grin spreading across her face as she began to laugh, again.

I responded to her accurate guess by flipping her off. She laughed harder. "Okay, what did he do then?"

"He called me princess."

"Oh, no!" she said, pretending to be flabbergasted, throwing her hand over her gaping mouth. "Not princess! The nerve!"

"You can be such a bitch sometimes, Lex," I huffed.

She continued to laugh.

"It wasn't just that he called me princess. It was how he

said it, and the way he looked at me, as if I wasn't worth his time."

She stopped laughing and looked at me, remorseful. "Sorry, Val. He does sound like a jerk, and like he's not worth *your* time."

I shrugged my shoulders, not sure if I agreed. I knew he probably wasn't, but I couldn't seem to get him out of my mind. The whole time I waited at the tire shop, all I could think about was him, and how my body had responded to him.

"Cheer up, lady. We have some shopping to do this afternoon. We're going to find you a killer outfit for your twenty-first."

"What *is* the plan for my birthday?"

"Well…I was thinking we pre-game tomorrow night at the apartment, then head to the bar at midnight."

"You really think they'll let me in the bar at midnight?"

"They will at this bar. Jake's friend works the door there."

"Where are we going exactly?"

"It's a dive bar off Silver Lake Boulevard; there's a new, up-and-coming band playing I've been dying to hear. Jake says they're bad ass. They've been playing there regularly as the headliner the last few months. He's going with us, and some of his buddies will probably meet us there."

Jake was Lexie's on-again, off-again boyfriend from high school. Apparently, they were on-again. He wasn't my favorite person, only because he seemed to always be messing with Lexie's head. But I tolerated him for her.

"Sounds fun. You about ready to go?"

"Yeah, let me just wrap up here, then we can head out."

"What do you have left? I can help, since you're covering for me and all." I grinned at her.

"I knew I kept you as my friend for some reason. Go bus those last couple tables for me." She nodded toward the main seating area of the coffee shop.

Sweet Beans was in an old warehouse. It was one large, open, industrial-style space with small nooks of cozy seating, along with various sizes of eclectic tables and chairs throughout the main seating area. There was a long coffee bar, where customers could sit and enjoy their cup of joe while watching the baristas work. The consistent brewing of coffee and the wide selection of cakes and pastries left a comforting aroma in the air all day.

The place wasn't far from campus and had a constant flux of college students loitering and studying. I was one of those students. I was often here on my days off, studying or hanging out with Lexie as she worked. It'd become a second home to me.

The two of us worked quickly at finishing up her duties before leaving the coffee shop in Ethan's hands, who clocked in for the late shift. Ethan was one of the few guys we hung with outside of work. He'd grown up in the area, like Lexie, and was the epitome of a California surfer, with his toned body, golden skin, blonde hair, blue eyes, and a personality so laid back, you often wondered if he had a care in the world. Something told me the dubious amount of pot he smoked contributed to his carefree demeanor.

"See you tomorrow night!" I said as we waved goodbye to Ethan and headed out the door to Ava's car, which now had four new tires.

I decided when I dropped it back off at Rhett and Ava's

place that I'd keep that little tidbit to myself. I had the shop put four new tires on, so he wouldn't notice one was different. Fingers crossed he didn't notice all four.

∾

Lexie and I spent the rest of the afternoon shopping for our outfits for tomorrow night. She insisted I needed the sexiest ensemble we could find. I didn't disagree. It was my twenty-first birthday. I planned on having the best night of my life and looking my best while I did it.

With my crazy school, work, and audition schedule, I'd rarely had time to enjoy myself over the last few years. Not to mention, any time I wanted to go out and my brother caught wind of it, he'd insist on one of his Herculean security guys escorting me.

I don't have to explain what a buzz kill that could be for a young college girl trying to participate in some underage drinking and/or have a little promiscuous fun. In case you weren't sure…it was a *total* buzz kill. Dead. As in, my libido became nonexistent.

But not tomorrow night. Tomorrow night I was on a mission. I was going to drink my stresses away—including the latest one of losing my agent—and maybe even wake up in a random guy's bed. It had been awhile. And after my run in with the not-so-gallant Liam, it was obvious I needed to dust the cobwebs off my lady bits. It was the only reasonable justification for why he had me in such a desperate state.

We sifted through the clothes racks in one of the boutiques on Rodeo Drive. I'd decided this was an emergency, and I was dipping into my trust fund for this little shopping spree. The sales lady was less than pleasant toward Lexie, obviously deciding she didn't belong in a place of this stature.

She watched Lexie like a hawk, as if she was concerned she would steal something. I was about to come to her defense after the snobby woman wouldn't stop hovering, but Lexie stopped me, saying it wasn't worth it.

I decided she was right. I wasn't spending my money there, even if I would've gotten some satisfaction from dropping my black card on the counter in front of her. Instead, we left. Lexie was sure to give her the finger on the way out the door, leaving a horrified sales clerk with her mouth and eyes wide open.

"I thought she wasn't worth it." I said, giggling, once we were out on the sidewalk.

"Well, she wasn't worth *you* getting upset, but me shocking her pretentious ass was definitely worth it." She smirked.

"I just couldn't believe how rude she was. You'd think she'd want to make the sale."

"People can be judgmental jerks. They judge no matter if you're rich *or* poor, Val. You just have to learn to not let it get to you." She gave me a determined stare.

I knew her aim. She knew how offended I got by people's perceptions. Most people would expect me to be used to it by now. I grew up in the limelight, but my family kept me sheltered from it as much as they could for most of my life.

It wasn't until I got older that, despite their best efforts, I became more aware of the harsh critiques and unwarranted opinions, in addition to the greed and superficial attitudes. I knew it was just how things were, but it didn't mean I had to like it. I gave her a small smile. She gave my hip a friendly bump with hers as we continued to walk.

The next shop had more couth. We both felt welcome there, and they offered a better selection of dresses. I grabbed a few that appealed to me and headed to the changing room. The first few were a no-go. But the fourth dress had me feeling giddy and excited for the upcoming night. It was perfect. It had the right amount of sex appeal and class.

It was a bright red, form-fitting dress with spaghetti straps that dived into a plunging, V-shaped neckline, showing just the right amount of cleavage. The back of the dress matched the front, exposing more skin. It hugged my curves in all the right places, showing off the toned body I worked hard to keep. It stopped just above my knees, accenting my favorite part of my body: my legs.

"Val?" I heard Lexie searching me out through the closed curtain of the dressing room.

"In here," I said, popping my head out. I pushed the curtain aside and plastered a big smile on my face. "What do you think?"

"Holy shit. You look hot."

"I know. This is the one," I agreed, barely holding in my excitement as I twisted and turned to view myself from all angles in the mirror. "What about you?" I turned back to face her.

"I would have to sell my left nut to afford anything in this place."

"You don't have a left nut."

"Exactly my point."

I rolled my eyes at her. "Pick something out, Lex. My treat."

"No way. It's *your* birthday. You aren't buying me anything."

"I want to buy you something. Consider it part of my birthday present to myself. I want my best friend looking just as smoking as me," I winked.

"Your lack of self-esteem is appalling, Val." Her voice was saturated with sarcasm as she shook her head in dismay.

I laughed. "It's a Blackwood trait. So is stubbornness. We aren't leaving here until you've found something."

She narrowed her eyes at me, but it didn't deter my insistence. Lexie never accepted anything from me willingly, and usually I gave in to her defiance. But not this time. I was hell bent on buying her a knockout dress—something that would show Jake he better wise up, before she decided he wasn't worth her trouble.

"Get out there and find something," I demanded, pointing my finger toward the sales area. "If you don't, I'll pick it for you."

"Fine"— she threw up her hands in surrender —"I'm going."

She went out to the sales floor and was back in less than five minutes, holding a dress—one she'd obviously already had her eye on. It was a cute little number, with a fitted bodice and skirt covered in a snakeskin pattern. It had a high front slit in the middle of the dress and a haltered neckline. It fit her spunky personality.

"Well, what do you think?" She strutted mockingly, like a runway model, out of the dressing room.

I chuckled. "You look sexy. It fits you perfectly. Now we just need shoes."

"I figure I'll wear my black combat boots."

My nose instinctively scrunched up. "Um. No. We're getting you some stilettos."

"Hell. No. There's no way I can walk all night in heels, Val. I'll break my neck."

"It's my birthday. I want you in heels."

"I think you've been hanging out with your brother too much lately. His absurd, demanding personality is rubbing off on you."

"Ha, ha," I fake laughed. "You're a comedian. Now quit being such a baby and go change. There's a cute shoe boutique just up the road."

She let out an exaggerated sigh, before moving back into the dressing room to change. After I paid for our dresses, we wrapped up our shopping for the day with the purchase of some stilettos to match.

That evening we planned to slip on our yoga pants, order some Chinese, and catch up on some of our favorite Netflix original series. Lexie popped open a bottle of wine we had in the cabinet and poured us both a glass. My phone dinged with a new text message. I pulled it out of my purse before we took our dedicated places on each end of the couch, relaxing into the evening.

I quickly typed out my response then turned my phone to silent, laying it on the coffee table.

"Who was that?" Lexie asked.

"My brother. Checking on his precious car and insisting we have Jim be our driver tomorrow night," I scoffed, not hiding my annoyance.

"It wouldn't be a bad idea, you know. I doubt any of us will be sober enough to drive."

"Good thing there's Uber. I'm not letting my brother's paid spies keep an eye on me all night."

She shrugged, unconcerned about either scenario.

"Speaking of…we'll need to pick up some liquor tomorrow. What do you want?" Lexie asked as I navigated through the Netflix menu.

Luckily, Lexie was a year older than me, and had been supplying our apartment with a steady stash of beverages for whenever the mood struck us. I wasn't a heavy drinker, but it was nice to have it available to take the edge off a stressful day, like today. Lexie, on the other hand, partied a lot harder than me. Besides work, she had all the free time in the world to hit up bars and clubs with Jake and his crew of misfits.

"I have no idea. You know I'm an easy drunk. I'm not sure I want to be trashed before we make it to the bar."

"Shots of Patron it is," she teased.

I playfully nudged her thigh with my foot from across the couch.

"It's not a twenty-first birthday, Val, if you aren't praying to the porcelain gods by the end of the night."

"I'm not sure I agree with that. Nor does that sound appealing to me. At all."

"Suit yourself. You're probably right, anyway. Tequila makes you a mean drunk. Should I just get you some wine coolers?" she teased me some more.

"Yuck, no. And it does not."

She laughed. "Yes, it does. Do you not remember the last time you had it?" She cocked her eyebrow at me.

Obviously, I didn't. It was one of the few times I'd been so drunk, I blacked out. I swore to myself I'd never get that drunk again. And I hadn't.

"You know I don't." I rolled my eyes. "How about stuff to make dirty martinis?"

"Works for me. I can stop and get everything tomorrow after work."

"You're the best. Now be quiet. The show is starting," I hushed her jokingly.

We both turned our attention to the large, flat-screen TV and spent the rest of the night finishing off the bottle of wine, stuffing ourselves with chicken fried rice, and laughing and sobbing at all our favorite shows, until we both passed out on the couch.

I awoke in the middle of the night hot and bothered by wild, wanton dreams starring a sexy, tattooed, moody man. I sat up on the couch, glancing over at still-passed-out Lexie. I debated whether to wake her. Deciding against it, I covered her up with a blanket and went to my bedroom.

I tossed and turned the rest of the night, unable to get Liam and his abs out of my head. I also couldn't get out of my head the contradicting emotions I had for him, and he obviously had for me. It was like both of our bodies were gravitating toward each other, but our minds were telling us to do the opposite.

I'd never felt that pull before, at least not that intense. I could only imagine what it would feel like to have him touch me, to have his lips all over me.

No. Cut it out, Val. This is why you can't sleep.

I needed to stop imagining those things if I was ever going to sleep again. I rolled to my side, "fluffing" my pillow with punches of my fist, letting out my frustrations. I plopped my head back down and tried to think about less-sexy things. Like kittens. Or puppies. Or crying babies—that right there would put an end to thoughts of sex. Sex led to babies. I did not want a baby. At least, not any time soon. Unless it had a cute, single dimple on its right cheek like Liam. *Damn it! Puppies. Puppies. Kittens.*

CHAPTER 3

Saturday went by quickly, mostly because I'd slept through the morning after my sleepless night. By the time I pulled myself out of bed, Lexie was already long gone for her early morning shift at work. After making myself some coffee and eating a late breakfast, I checked my phone for missed messages.

Most were text messages from my family, reminding me once again about dinner tomorrow night for my actual birthday. There were a few selfie texts of Lexie and Ethan goofing off at the coffee shop and telling me to start getting pumped up for tonight.

I also had a missed call and voicemail from the body shop where my car was being repaired. It was *finally* ready, though they were only open until three today. I looked at the clock and it was half past noon. There was no way I would be able to pick up Ava from Malibu and make it back in time to get my car. I would have to see if she could do it on her Monday lunch break, since the body shop was closed on Sunday.

I looked at a missed text from Caleb, one of Jake's friends who I'd regretfully hooked up with a few times. Usually the hookups occurred after a night of drinking, when I had zero inhibitions left. He could be charming—at least in my hazed mind—and had a sexy smile that usually had me stripping without a second thought. He was a nice enough guy, and super cute, with his brown, spiked hair, green eyes, and lean build, but not someone I'd ever seen myself in a relationship with.

I stared at his message, contemplating whether to ignore it or respond. I groaned as I reread it.

C: Can't wait to see you tonight.

Until now, I hadn't thought about the fact that he'd be hanging out with us tonight. If history told me anything, it was that we'd end up naked and in his bed if I planned to get inebriated tonight. And I *did* plan to get inebriated. But he was not who I wanted to end up naked with.

Who did I want to end up naked with? Thoughts of Liam instantly came to my head. *Shit. Not Liam. And not Caleb.*

I decided the best thing to do was ignore the text. I needed to stop the stupidity cycle that was Caleb and me. Every time I gave into him, I just gave him false hope, and myself twenty-four hours of self-loathing. I responded to my family and Lexie, then sent a quick text to Ava about Monday before jumping into the shower.

~

By the time we got to The Republic, I was feeling good from

the pre-drinks at our apartment. When Lexie had arrived home from work, her arms were overflowing with more alcohol than we'd discussed. Ethan, Jake, and his motley crew had shown up early to drink with us. Before I knew it, I was being pressured and cheered on to take buttery-nipple shots that Lexie had attempted to make, but that tasted nothing like a buttery nipple.

Lexie and I held onto each other as we stumbled through the dark parking lot toward the entrance of The Republic. I needed her support, since I was already feeling slightly intoxicated, and she needed my support to walk in the heels I'd forced her to wear. The guys followed behind us, allowing us to enter the venue first.

The closer we got, the louder the muffled music of the band became as it filtered through the closed door. A big, stoic bouncer stood blocking the entrance. His eyes swept over us as we neared. With it being a twenty-one-and-up-only establishment, I was nervous for the first time he may not let me in once he saw my ID. After his outward inspection of us, he glanced over to Jake and gave him a nod. This was obviously Jake's friend.

"IDs ladies."

We both pulled out our driver's licenses, handing them to him. He barely glanced at them before giving them back to us.

"Happy birthday." He gave me a half-smile as he moved aside to let us pass.

"Thanks." I grinned back at him.

Lexie pulled me through the entrance, leaving Jake to pay our cover charge. "Let's get a drink!" she yelled over her shoulder as she began to pull me farther into the bar, but my stiff legs impeded her progression.

I was glued in place as the band's music hit my ears. My eyes were transfixed on the stage. It wasn't the beat of the music itself that had my attention, but rather the voice that accompanied it. That gravelly, sultry voice that was seeping into every inch of my being was one I recognized, one that had been haunting my dreams—one that induced the fluttering in my stomach.

Despite the dark, smoky room of flashing lights, I could see him clearly. Liam stood center stage, his hands wrapped around the mic, his guitar hanging from the side of his masculine body while his silky voice had all the girls screaming his name in front of him. He wore a tight black T-shirt and faded, worn jeans with black boots. Simple and sexy.

His steamy, gray eyes were currently concealed as he held them tightly shut—lost in the chorus he was singing. When his eyes finally opened, he grinned a roguish smile at the women in front of him before looking up to scan the crowd. His eyes instantly zeroed in on me, and though his words didn't falter, his smile faded. I'm sure nobody noticed the sudden change in his expression, but I did. His eyes stayed locked with mine as he continued to sing.

He was enigmatic, drawing me to him like a fly to a bug zapper. I felt my body trying to propel me forward from the darkness to the bright lights of the stage when Lexie broke my trance before I was zapped.

"Hot, right?"

"What?" I looked over at her.

"Derailed"—she nodded toward the stage—"the band."

"Oh. Yeah." I looked back at Liam who was still staring at me with an intensity that was making me heated and anxious. "Let's get that drink." I tore my eyes from him, pushing my way to the bar. Lexie followed behind me.

I waited impatiently for the bartender to make my drink, forcing myself not to look at the stage and to forget Liam was here. It was impossible. Whether I looked at him or not, his voice surrounded me, filling me with nervous energy.

"What's your deal?" Lexie asked, sidling up to me.

"What do you mean?"

"You're acting weird. Since the moment we walked in here. They won't card you again."

"I know. I'm good," I said, not bothering to correct her mistaken assumption.

She looked at my hand in my hair.

Shit. I quickly dropped it to my side. Before she could press me further, Jake came up behind us, interrupting her interrogation.

Thank God.

I had no idea what I'd even tell her. I wasn't sure why I felt so out of control when it came to Liam. Or his voice. It was driving me insane. I wasn't sure I'd make it through the next few hours without losing my mind.

"Joe reserved a table for us close to the stage, off to the side, near the front. The others are already over there," Jake hollered over the loud music.

I assumed Joe was the big guy at the door. *Great. Could this night get any worse?* I did not need a direct view of Liam, nor to be that close to him.

"You ladies head over there. I'll get your drinks," he said, smiling at Lexie.

"Thanks, babe." She smiled, wrapping her arms around his neck before devouring his mouth with her tongue.

I started to turn and leave them to it when I felt a hand squeeze my ass. I whipped around to see who the jerk taking liberties was and give him a piece of my mind, when I was silenced by Caleb's lips, sloppily smashed against my own.

Yep. It could definitely get worse. I pushed my hands between us, removing his body and lips from me.

"Hey, sweetness," he slurred as his hand failed at lightly caressing my hair. He was petting me like a damn cat.

I swatted his hand aside. He was already drunk, which meant he was getting handsy. I'd been able to keep my distance from him earlier in the night, but now that we'd both been drinking, it'd be a lot harder. Fortunately, I was feeling a lot soberer after hearing and seeing Liam.

I glanced back at the stage, finding Liam's dark gaze strangely still on me. *Why is he watching me?* I turned away from Liam, ignored Caleb, and grabbed a horny Lexie, pulling her with me to the table where the rest of our party sat.

I moved into the chair next to Ethan and tugged Lexie onto the seat beside me. That would hopefully keep Caleb at bay. The only other available seats were across from me. The band had moved on to the next song, and as the intro boomed through the sound system, I heard the screeching cries of the women in the bar hit a higher octave that had my ears ringing.

Curious, I shifted my eyes I'd been diverting from the stage to look at what could possibly have them squealing louder than they already had been. It was in that moment I finally understood the saying "curiosity killed the cat." I was that cat. And I was pretty sure I was going to die.

Liam had removed his shirt, revealing his muscular, tattooed upper body to every drunk and horny female in the room, including myself. He glanced toward me with his evil smirk and winked as he gripped his guitar in his hands. His fingers plucked the strings, joining in with the other band members. I was pretty sure my body exploded with that wink. I shifted in my seat, crossing my legs, trying to control the heat that had erupted between them.

Jake and Caleb had chosen that moment to join us at the table with numerous shot glasses and the martinis Lexie and I had ordered. I never thought I would be as relieved to see either one of those two guys as I was right then.

"We come baring gifts for the birthday girl," Jake said, handing us each our martini and a shot. I didn't even bother waiting for a toast. I threw the shot down my throat, swiped Lexie's from her hand, and proceeded to chase the first shot with hers before she could protest. I followed both by chugging my own martini.

I ignored the burning sensation in my throat as I forced the liquor down. I slammed the glass on the table and tried my best to keep the liquor from instantly coming back up as chills coursed through my body. It was inevitable. I was going to be sick tonight.

"Shit, Val!" Lexie stared at me in shock. "What the hell has gotten into you?"

One word. Liam.

"It's my birthday, right? Plus, I was thirsty. It's super-hot in here," I said, trying to conceal my lingering eyes that kept moving on their own accord to gawk at the half-naked sex god on stage.

"Uh, huh." Lexie wasn't buying my explanation. "Or *maybe*, you're just hot for the lead singer of Derailed."

"I don't know what you're talking about. I hardly noticed him," I said, catching my finger as it started to travel toward a strand of my hair. *Damn it.* I needed to get control of that finger, and my body in general.

I let my eyes browse the bar, looking anywhere but at Liam or Lexie's interrogating gaze. The place was overly packed, making it tough to move through the tiny industrial space. The floors were concrete, and the walls were cinder blocks painted in graffiti. The structure of the building was left exposed and painted black. Track lights of various colors hung from the rafters, lighting up the stage as the band played.

There was only one bar toward the front corner, opposite the entry. I had no idea how the bartenders were able to keep up with a crowd this size. There were very few tables and chairs, so I was glad Joe had reserved one for our late arrival. The restrooms were past the stage, down a narrow hall that led to a rear emergency exit.

I decided that'd be the best place for me to gather my composure. I excused myself from the table to head to the restroom.

"Do you want me to come with you?"

"No. I'll be right back," I assured Lexie. I didn't usually wander off by myself in places like this, but I needed a minute alone without her questions.

I slid off my stool, smoothed my dress down, and maneuvered through the crowd toward the long line of women

36

waiting for the bathroom. I didn't actually need a toilet, so I bypassed the line and entered the restroom to freshen up.

I remained in the ladies' room through the end of the song, until I heard the music change to prerecorded hip-hop. I hoped that meant Derailed was finished with their performance for the night. I took one last deep inhale. Exhaling slowly, I gripped the door handle and swung the door open to exit.

The dance floor was still crowded with gyrating bodies, but the stage had been abandoned by the band members and only their equipment and instruments remained. I felt relief and regret at the same time. I walked up to my table of friends and plastered on a smile.

"Better?" Lexie asked as I approached.

"Better," I confirmed.

"Good." She handed me another shot.

I took it from her without a thought and clinked it with the other shot glass in her hand. I tipped it to my lips, letting the cool, sweet liquid coat my throat. These were the shots I liked. The ones you thought were nothing but shots of juice. They were dangerous and delicious, a lot like Liam.

As soon as I set my glass back on the table, she grabbed my hand, pulling me onto the dance floor. I relaxed into the music, laughing and dancing with Lexie as I swayed my hips to the beat. It was the first time I started to enjoy myself since walking into the bar. It helped that visions of Liam and his voice were no longer overpowering my body.

The liquor started to work its magic, relaxing my muscles and easing any thoughts I had in my mind. I felt light and airy. I closed my eyes, holding my arms above my head as I spun seductively in a circle, allowing the alcohol and music to take over.

Firm hands gripped my hips and a hard body pressed into my backside. "You look hot, sweetheart," Caleb whispered into my ear as he buried his face in my neck. I slowed my movement, opening my eyes to Liam's heated stare from across the dance floor.

He sat in a secluded booth with his band members and a bunch of scantily clad groupies. His arm was wrapped around one of the girls, but his eyes were pinned on me with an angry expression. He thankfully had his shirt back on, but it did nothing to subdue my hormones. My eyes narrowed at the sight of the girl starting to kiss up his neck and nip at his ear. I had a weird surge of possessiveness plaguing me.

He moved his beer to his lips, seemingly unaffected by the desperate woman licking and sucking on him, while he continued to watch me. He took a slow pull of his beer. I started to imagine his lips on mine. I bit my bottom lip, closing my eyes, leaning my head back on Caleb's shoulder as I began to move my hips in sync with his.

I allowed Caleb to continue to rub his hands up and down my body and kiss my neck. I knew everything I was doing right then was wrong. I was using Caleb. Using him to satisfy a desire I had for someone else. But I didn't care. The alcohol flowing through my veins and the presence of Liam had any moral thoughts pushed aside.

I felt a small hand grasp at my arm, and I flicked my eyes open to Lexie. "Let's get another shot!" she yelled at me as she waved for me to follow her and Jake toward the bar.

I moved in line behind her. Caleb clasped his hand with mine, moving with me toward the bar. I should've removed my hand, but I didn't. I stupidly allowed him to continue to touch me.

I glanced back over my shoulder at Liam. He was no longer watching me. Instead, he was talking with his bandmates, with the same skank doing everything she could to get his attention. I shook it off and refocused on following Lexie and Jake.

We continued to alternate between dancing and taking shots for the rest of the night, until I no longer felt my body, and my mind was floating like I was in a dream. I did my best not to search out Liam, but my greedy eyes had a mind of their own. As the night neared its end, Lexie and I took a break from dancing and went to the restroom.

"Whoa, Val. You should probably slow down on the shots if you plan on getting laid tonight," Lexie teased me as I stumbled out of the stall.

"I'm fine," I lied, straightening myself as I concentrated on walking. She laughed, shaking her head at me. I gripped the sink counter and took a deep breath, before washing my hands, hoping the oxygen would help to clear my fuzzy brain. "Besides, I don't plan on sleeping with Caleb tonight."

"Sure as hell looks like you plan to."

"Well, I don't," I argued as I glared at her through the mirror. Because I didn't. I may be drunk, and I may have been letting Caleb touch me more than I should, but I had no plans to go home with him or vice versa.

"Whatever you say, lady. Come on. Let's go dance some more." She grabbed my hand, tugging me out of the restroom.

My footsteps faltered as we cleared the opening. I fell into Lexie, trying to catch myself before I hit the ground. She was unprepared and unable to hold me up, so we both ended up on the floor, rolling with laughter.

"Shit," I giggled as I tried rolling to my stomach, so I could push myself up off the ground.

My tight dress made it hard to maneuver. I moved to my hands and knees, flipping my head up to get my long hair out of my face. My body froze as my glassy eyes connected with a serious and disgruntled-looking Liam towering over me.

Double shit.

His arms were crossed over his chest, accentuating his tight biceps. His eyes darkened with heat and my body began to tingle. My heart throbbed in my chest. His jaw ticked. The air charged between us.

My laughter had ceased, but Lexie was still giggling and rolling on the floor, unaware we had company.

"*Hellooo, Liam,*" I slurred, grinning cheesily at him.

"Princess." His voice was as hard as his abs.

Jerk.

With Liam's response, Lexie finally became aware we had an audience. Her laughter faded as she rolled herself into a sitting position on the floor. I remained on my hands and knees, looking up at him.

"Are you just going to stand there, or are you going to help a girl in need?" I asked.

In my head, it sounded like my words came out clearly, but from Lexie's giggling and his unamused expression, I figured maybe not.

Before he could respond, the skank who'd been clinging to him all night came out of the bathroom, sauntering past us. She had the audacity to judge me as she sneered down her nose at us.

Bitch. I may be the one drunk on a dirty bar floor, but at least I had some self-respect. *Some.* This was definitely not my proudest moment.

She pulled at his arm, "Come on, baby."

Who the hell is she? A girlfriend? Doubtful. He didn't seem like the girlfriend type.

He continued to stare at me, his face impassive as she tugged at him once more to lead him farther down the hallway toward the exit. I didn't move. He didn't move. It was ridiculous. But I needed to know the choice he'd make: help me or go with her. If he chose the latter, it would tell me what I already knew: I needed to stay as far away from him as possible, regardless of what my body wanted.

We both remained still until his eyes raised, looking past me and then over at her. He threw his arm around her shoulders without a word and turned his back on me, walking away. I sat back on my heels, watching them as she groped him and pulled him into the supply room.

Classy.

She was already undoing the button and zipper of his jeans before even making it into the closet. He glanced at me, one last time, before following her inside, disappearing from my view. The expression in his eyes had me feeling alone in a crowded bar. I glanced over at Lexie, who'd been watching our silent exchange.

"Princess?" Her eyebrow raised quizzically.

She'd figured out he was the broody jerk from yesterday. I didn't have a chance to respond. Caleb and Jake were on us, pulling us up from the floor.

"What the hell are you girls doing?" Jake asked as he lifted Lexie to her feet, wrapping her in his arms.

"Val tripped, taking us both to the ground," she said smiling at him.

He grinned, shaking his head. "Should we head out?" he asked.

"No," I said firmly. "I need another shot."

"I don't think that's a good idea, Val," Lexie said, now understanding why I'd been uncharacteristically drinking heavily all night.

"I need a drink," I reiterated as I gripped onto Caleb to hold myself up.

"You only turn twenty-one once," Caleb said, reinforcing my demand. I knew it was for his own benefit—he hoped he was getting me naked tonight—but I ignored the thought.

Lexie let out a frustrated sigh. "Okay, lady lush…let's get you another shot. But then we switch to water," she commanded.

Whatever. I would argue that with her in a bit. The four of us headed to the bar for another round of shots. It was the last thing I recalled before I found myself dancing on a table with Lexie, hugging each other and laughing as we held one another up.

"Dude. You need to get your chicks out of here before I lose my job."

I spun around carelessly, finding a pissed-off Joe with his eyes narrowed at Jake.

"I'm working on it. Fucking Caleb disappeared. Probably passed out somewhere. Everyone else has already taken off."

"Get Lexie. I'll get this one," Joe said, pointing at me.

"Hey!" Lexie giggled, not putting up much of a fight as Jake grabbed at her, removing her from the table top and taking her into his arms.

"Come on, sweetheart," Joe said as he approached me, trying to gently coerce me into his thick arms.

"No!" I swatted at him like a two-year-old. "We're dancing!"

I hopped away from his reach, losing my balance. I felt myself starting to tumble over the edge of the table when strong arms gripped my waist, catching me.

I laughed at my clumsiness. And drunkenness. It made me giddy.

"I got her," a gruff, annoyed voice said over my head.

"Shit. It's you," I grumbled, refusing to look at the man holding me against his chest, cradled in his arms like a baby. He smelled yummy. And his touch had my limp, drunk body coming to life.

"Thank fucking God. I don't get paid enough for this shit." Joe shook his head as he walked away.

"Thanks, man." Jake nodded toward Liam. "Can you help me get her outside? I called an Uber. It should be here any minute.

"Sure."

Jake turned, walking away with Lexie, who was squealing with delight. I angled my head up, looking at Liam. He stared down at me. His tempting lips were only a few inches from my own. He had such full, delicious-looking lips. And now that I knew those lips could sing, it only made me want them more. He was the devil.

"Put me down," I demanded as my contradicting arms wrapped around his neck.

He smirked that ridiculous smirk. "No."

"I can walk," I slurred.

"I think you've proven otherwise, princess."

"Stop calling me princess."

He chuckled with amusement as he began to move us through the nearly empty bar toward the front exit. I buried my face against his chest.

"You smell so good. Why do you have to smell so good?"

"Why do you?"

Huh? Shit. Did I just say that out loud? I glanced up at his now-twinkling eyes. My head spun, making me dizzy.

"You're nothing but a bad-news beer," I slurred some more as I gripped his neck tighter.

"I think you mean bear."

"That's what I said."

"Right." He shook his head as his chest vibrated with muted laughter. God I wanted him. My body wanted him.

"I don't want you," I said pointedly.

"I don't want you either."

Neither one of us were very convincing. Joe held the door open as we exited the building. The cool air hit my damp skin, inducing goosebumps to prickle my body. Liam gripped me tighter to his chest. I inhaled him.

"Car's here," Jake yelled over his shoulder at Liam and me.

Jake placed Lexie on her feet and opened the rear passenger-side door. He helped her settle into the middle of the bench seat. He left the door open for Liam as he walked around to the other side of the car to get in next to Lexie.

Liam didn't release me immediately. I wondered what he was waiting for. He stared at the car as if contemplating his next move. I took in all the beautiful features of his face while he hesitated. I could see the tightening of his strong, square jaw as he struggled with his own internal debate. Tension radiated from him as he closed his eyes. I gripped him tighter, wanting to fight away whatever was making him stressed.

"It's my birthday," I whispered softly.

His eyes opened and his body relaxed.

"I know." He smiled, revealing his singular dimple. I poked it with my finger. I couldn't help it.

He laughed. "What was that?"

"I like your dimple." I grinned, relieved he was no longer tense. *I like you.*

He shook his head in disbelief. "Happy birthday, princess."

The way he spoke the word 'princess' this time, it had more fondness behind it—fondness I didn't expect. My lips parted, and his eyes dropped to them. His head leaned in closer. Our lips were close to touching. I closed my eyes, waiting for the one thing I wanted most for my birthday. His lips.

"Why do you call me that?" I whispered out of nervous anticipation.

He didn't answer. He didn't press his lips to mine. Instead, he released me from his arms, steadying me on my feet next to the car before stepping away. Losing the warmth and safety of his body had me feeling exposed and vulnerable. He was distancing himself. All this hot and cold had my intoxicated brain confused. I hugged my arms around my body, protecting myself.

Aware of my discomfort, he started to step toward me again, but halted, placing his hands in his pockets as if to keep from reaching out to me.

"You should go," he said, nodding toward the open car door, where Lexie and Jake were now sucking face—not something I was in any rush to sit next to.

"That's it?" I asked, throwing my hands on my hips. My anger flared.

"You were expecting something more?"

I stared at him in disbelief. Pissed. Regardless of my drunken state, I knew I wasn't the only one feeling the intense chemistry between us. I wanted to beg him to kiss me. To take me home. But I knew that everything about him made him Mr. Wrong. *Then why does it feel so right?*

I dropped my hands in defeat.

"No. I guess I wasn't." I turned, climbing into the car. "My name is Valerie, in case you cared," I spat.

He never even bothered asking. And for some reason that pissed me off even more. As if I mattered so little, he didn't even care to ask me my name.

"I know," he said firmly, closing the car door and tapping the hood of the car for the driver to go, leaving me confused, pissed, and desperate, once again.

CHAPTER 4

"**W**ake up, lady!" Lexie yelled, jumping onto the bed next to me.

"Ugh," I groaned, squeezing my eyes closed tighter, turning away from her while hiding my head under my pillow. "Go away you evil woman."

She chuckled, pulling the pillow from over my head, ignoring my banishment of her presence.

"No can do. We need to get you up and in recovery mode before dinner with your folks tonight."

"It's still early," I said, refusing to open my eyes. My head was pounding, and I suddenly regretted overindulging in alcohol.

"It's one already, Val. You're having dinner with your family in five hours."

"Shit. Really?!" I popped up a little too quickly, causing my aching head to spin. I threw my palms over my eyes, trying to block out the harsh light that was filtering in.

"Yes. You need some food. And a shower. You look like shit."

"I feel like shit." I dropped my hands from my face and looked around my room. There was a trash can next to me on the floor, my heels and dress were strewn on the ground in a trail to my bed, and I was currently only wearing a strapless bra and panties. I guess I didn't bother with pajamas last night. I had no recollection of how I'd even gotten home, much less into my room.

I looked over at a way-too-chipper Lexie. "What happened last night?"

"You don't remember?"

I searched my throbbing head for any memories of the previous night's events. All I could recall was Liam. A sexy, singing Liam. A shirtless Liam. An asshole Liam. A kissable Liam... *Oh. God.* My eyes widened. I touched my hand to my lips. Surely, I would remember if we kissed. I looked down at my half-naked body. I would definitely remember if he came home with me. *Right?*

"Did I? Did someone..." I struggled to get my question out.

"Come home with you?" Lexie completed my thought, giving me a sideways glance. "No. Unless you count Jake and me. He helped me get you into bed."

"He saw me half-naked?!"

"I didn't have a lot of choice, Val. You passed out pissed off and wasted after Liam got you into the car. You were dead weight by the time we got to the apartment."

Her words triggered a memory I wished had stayed forgotten: the memory of how desperately I'd wanted Liam to kiss me, *and* his rejection. My heart sank to my queasy stomach. He preferred the slutty groupie from the bar over me. I felt like a fool. A stupid, desperate fool. The only redeeming factor of the night was I didn't end up sleeping with Caleb.

I moaned, throwing myself back on the bed. "I'm such an idiot, Lex." I didn't need to explain myself. She already knew what I was referring to.

"No you're not. I'm sure you weren't the only one begging for Liam's attention last night. By the way, you never mentioned how hot your broody asshole was. I figured as much from the way you were reacting, but *damn*. If Jake wasn't in the picture…"

"Oh my gosh! Shut up. He is not *my* broody asshole," I moaned, covering my face with my arm.

She yanked it away from my face, laughing. "Are you saying he isn't the one who helped you change your tire, *princess?*" she teased me.

"Yes. But he isn't *mine*. Far from it. Obviously."

She ignored me, pulling me up out of the bed. I groaned as she got me to my feet.

"I wish last night never happened. At least I'll never have to see him again. I'm avoiding that place like the plague."

"Stop wallowing. And take a shower. I'll make you some brunch, birthday girl." She angled my shoulders, directing me toward the bathroom.

By the time I was done with my shower, I felt rejuvenated, physically and mentally. Lexie was right; I wasn't the only one mesmerized by Liam. He was obviously used to the female attention, and I wasn't going to feel ashamed of my attraction to him.

He was sexy and mysterious, with a hypnotic voice. Who wouldn't be drawn to him? You'd have to be numb from the waist down not to be attracted to those abs and that smile. I was not going to be embarrassed. Besides, I was probably barely a blip on his radar, one he'd soon forget. *Why does that thought bother me?*

Nope. Not going to think about it. I needed to forget about Liam and his alluring lips. He was a judgmental jerk, anyway. I had no room for people like that in my life. Today was my actual birthday, and I'd be having dinner with my family tonight—people that knew and loved me for who I was and didn't call me things like princess.

I wrapped a towel around my wet hair, twisting and settling it on top of my head. I slipped on some yoga pants and a tank top after brushing my teeth and walking out of my en-suite bathroom. The smell of fresh brewed coffee and bacon drifted into my room as I browsed the clothes hanging in my walk-in closet. I was searching for the perfect "I am woman, hear me roar" outfit to help reinforce my restored confidence.

My eyes lit up as I reached for my black leather pencil skirt. It fit my body like a glove, hitting just below my knees with a slit up the back. I decided to soften the edginess of the skirt with a sheer, blush, spaghetti-strapped blouse that had a low-cut neckline.

I laid each piece on my bed and admired my selections. They accomplished the tough feminism I was going for. I set my black, strappy stilettos next to the ensemble, then left my room in search of the delicious smells that had been beckoning me.

Lexie had a breakfast buffet sprawled out across the island. There was enough food to feed a party of twenty instead of two.

"Happy birthday, lady," she said beaming as I walked into the kitchen.

"Lex, this is ridiculous. There's no way we're eating all this."

She just smiled and shrugged, unperturbed. "I wanted to make sure you had all your favorites." She handed me a mimosa as I took a seat on one of the bar stools at the island.

"Ugh. Not sure I can do more alcohol right now." I eyed the spiked glass of orange juice.

"Hair of the dog. Drink it. It'll make you feel better."

I took a sip, even if I didn't believe the old saying. She made me a plate full of food that I knew I'd barely touch. My stomach was still uneasy. I pulled my foot up on the stool, bending my knee against my chest while taking a bite from a strip of crispy bacon.

"Coffee?" she asked.

"Please." She handed me a cup already prepared how I liked it. "You're the best." I grinned.

"I know."

I rolled my eyes at her. "What time did Jake leave?"

"About five minutes before I woke your lazy ass up."

"Are you guys doing anything tonight?"

"Jake and his buddies are playing pool tonight. He invited us to join. Will you be with your family all night?"

"Not likely. We'll probably just have dinner. I'll text you when we're done."

She nodded, taking a seat next to me to eat. We laughed about the previous night's events as she reminded me about some of my less-than-stellar moments. Once we finished eating our late brunch, Lexie went to take a nap. I leisurely pampered myself to get ready for dinner.

After painting my nails and drying my hair and putting it in rollers, I grabbed my phone, sitting on my bed. I had a few "Happy birthday" texts from friends and family, including Caleb. *Ugh. Caleb.* I needed to set things straight between us. I thanked them all, then set my phone on the bedside table.

I strummed my fingers on the comforter, debating how to kill some time while I waited for my curls to set. In the past, I would have cured my boredom with Facebook, Instagram, or Twitter. But now, I avoided all the social networks. They'd all been tainted for me. These days I'd adopted the motto that ignorance was bliss when it came to the hurtful things people might do or say on those platforms.

I picked up my laptop, having the urge to Google a certain popular new band. My fingers hesitated over the keyboard. *Am I really doing this? Am I really going to Google him?* Ugh. Yes. I was. Besides…I wasn't Googling *him*. I was Googling the band. Big difference. Outside of the cocky jerk of a lead singer, the band was good. *That* is why I wanted to Google them, not because of him, I tried to lie to myself. I typed out "Derailed" and hit enter before I changed my mind.

I clicked on the band's main page that came up at the top of the search. I scrolled down the landing page where it showed a picture of each band member, what they played, and very minimal information about their personal life. I had to admit, they were all pretty attractive.

It turned out Liam's last name was Stone and he was twenty-six. Not that I cared. At all. He was pictured in his signature black T-shirt, unsmiling, looking tough and mysterious with his intense grey eyes. I lingered on his photo for only a second—thirty-nine seconds, at most— before clicking on the tab that displayed their event schedule.

I mentally made note of the locations they played, dates and times. Only so I could avoid those locations at those times. Not that I frequented any of those dive bars, but one could never be too cautious.

I moved on to the photos tab in the webpage menu. Most of the pictures were of the band playing at various venues. There were also a few of them off stage at what looked like after parties. The band members were all pictured with random women slinked around them. Including Liam. My stomach started to churn, again.

I slammed the laptop shut and set it aside on the bed. I laid my head back against my headboard and closed my eyes, taking a deep breath. What had I expected to see? I already knew Liam wasn't one to remain celibate. I'd seen it with my own two eyes. *What does it matter anyway?* It's not like I planned to date him. He was a self-proclaimed bad guy. A player. Nobody I needed to be getting involved with.

I pushed all thoughts of Liam and his sexual activities deep down into the black hole of my brain, getting up from the bed to finish getting ready and head out to meet my family for dinner.

~

"Happy birthday, Val," Rhett toasted while my family raised their glasses in celebration of my birthday.

"Thank you." I clinked my glass before sipping my martini. "I guess that means you have to start accepting me as an adult now," I goaded him.

"Don't push it. You'll always be my little sister, no matter how old you get."

I rolled my eyes playfully. As difficult as my older brother could be, I knew he'd always have my back and do anything for me.

"Val, how are things going with your acting?" Mom asked, genuinely curious.

"Oh! That's right. I forgot to ask you. How did your audition go the other day?" Ava added.

My mom and Ava were the only ones in full support of my acting career. My father and brother still thought I'd do best to set my sights on a more stable and obtainable career. I hadn't mentioned to anyone that I'd lost my agent, and I wasn't telling them now. I didn't want to give Rhett and my father any ammunition. Plus, I just needed a few weeks to find another agent.

"It's good. The audition went great," I lied, catching my finger as it started to tangle around my hair.

Rhett eyed me suspiciously.

"Ava, how are you feeling? Has my nephew stopped kicking you at night?" I quickly changed the subject, needing the spotlight off me for the moment.

"No. He's as frustrating as his father," she teased Rhett.

He playfully squeezed her side before kissing her on the cheek.

"Well, here's hoping he doesn't get all of his father's traits," I joined in tormenting him. We both giggled.

Rhett shook his head at us before my dad spoke, seeming even less amused, distracting Rhett with talks of business. Even though my father had been retired for years, he still tried to keep up on the latest investments of Blackwood Industries, much to my mother's dismay.

We spent the rest of dinner catching up on my parents' travels and eating sushi, my dinner of choice. After my one birthday martini and finishing off the last of the sushi, I thanked my family for the dinner. It'd been a few months since we were all together, and dinner with them had lifted my spirits. Something I'd apparently needed.

We hugged our goodbyes before going our separate ways. My parents were heading home with Rhett and Ava, and I'd already called an Uber to meet up with Lexie. Knowing that my family would never allow me to drive if I had a drink at dinner, I'd planned ahead, not bothering to drive to the restaurant.

"Are you sure you don't want us to just drop you off?" Ava offered.

Nope. Definitely not. I'd be held hostage in the car if Rhett or my father saw where I was headed.

"No, but thank you. It's too far out of your way."

"It's not a problem, Val. We prefer to know you're safe," Rhett interjected.

"I'm good. Really. Stop worrying so much, Rhett."

I knew my assurance was useless. My brother would always worry about the women in his life. It was a good thing he was having a son and not a daughter. The poor girl wouldn't be able to date until she was forty. Luckily for me, the Uber pulled up just in time, giving me my escape.

"Text us when you make it safe." Mom kissed and hugged me one more time.

"I will. Love you," I said, hugging her back before climbing into the car. "Thanks again for dinner!" I waved at my family as the car pulled away.

I texted Lexie to let her know I was on my way. By the time I was able to meet up with them, Lexie, Jake, and his friends had already been out for a couple hours. She'd mentioned it was a low-key bar. Knowing my outfit would likely draw attention in a bar where most of the women probably wore holey jeans and rocker tees, I contemplated going home to change. In the end, I decided against it, not wanting to waste time. At least I had on a leather skirt in lieu of a flowery sundress.

I touched up my makeup in the backseat of the car while making small talk with the driver. Lexie always teased me about trying to get to know my Uber drivers. I was genuinely curious about them, though. I always wondered about their lives and what made them want to drive strangers around town.

As we pulled up to the tiny dive bar, which looked like it could barely accommodate twenty people, I thanked my driver, and he wished me a happy birthday. My phone vibrated with a new text. I pulled it out of my clutch.

L: Change of plans. How about we have a girls' night? I'll meet you somewhere.

V: I'm already here.

L: Shit...don't be mad at me. I didn't know.

Confused by her statement, I dropped my phone back

into my purse and opened the door to enter the bar. The sounds of a cranked-up jukebox overwhelmed my ears as I stepped inside. I should've taken what hearing the lyrical voice of Miranda Lambert singing "Somethin' bad is about to happen" for what it was: an omen.

CHAPTER 5

I t took only a matter of seconds standing at the entrance to know exactly what my best friend was freaking out about. Somehow this little bar with its one pool table felt smaller than it already was. It was like I was suffering the Alice in Wonderland syndrome. The walls were closing in on me, and I could barely breathe.

Liam and his buddies from the band stood casually talking and joking with Jake and his friends around the pool table. It was the first time I'd seen Liam look so relaxed, like he was genuinely having a good time.

It was short lived. Liam glanced up at me and that carefree smile disappeared. Every organ in my body faltered as his eyes perused me from head to toe. Lexie was on me instantly, blocking my view before I could even form a coherent thought or comprehend my emotions.

"Val, I'm sorry."

"What is he doing here?"

"I had no idea they would be here. They weren't supposed to be. They just showed up a few minutes ago with Joe."

I looked at my friend and could see the concern and remorse in her eyes. She was telling the truth.

"Do you want to leave?"

I shook my head no. I wasn't letting Liam run me off. If I did, I would just be admitting how much he affected me.

"It's fine, Lex. I don't care."

She looked at me with doubt written all over her face.

"*Really.* Come on," I reiterated, standing up tall, throwing my shoulders back as I linked my arm with hers to lead her to the bar. I was going to need a drink.

Considering it was a Sunday night, the bar was unsurprisingly empty. The interior was dark and grungy and smelled like a mixture of mildew and smoke. Definitely not somewhere I'd have willfully gone on my own. But with the cheap drink prices and the small crowd, I could see why Jake and his friends would choose this place.

We walked up to the old bartender with gray hair and a scraggly beard, who looked like he was barely making it from one day to the next.

"What can I get you ladies?" he asked without even so much as a smile.

"Dirty Grey Goose martini. Extra dirty, please," I responded with a smile.

He lowered his chin to his chest as he eyed me with annoyance. "I have Tito's. And I can serve it to you in an unwashed glass. Will that be dirty enough for you?"

Lexie snickered next to me.

"Uh…I'll pass. Do you have any top-shelf liquors?"

"Depends what you mean by top shelf. If you're askin' if I

have them sittin' on the shelf up top, then the answer is yes."

Good. Lord. What kind of bar is this?

"What *do* you have then?"

"I have beer."

"Great. Give me one of those. Your choice."

I was not going to place any bets on him having a beer I actually liked. He nodded and walked toward the cooler of beer bottles.

I slowly and inconspicuously glanced over my shoulder toward the pool table as Lexie and I waited for our drinks. Liam seemed to have regained his relaxed demeanor. He was laughing at his buddy when he gave me a side glance. I turned my head back toward the bartender, not wanting to hold his gaze.

"Do you want to stay at the bar or go over there?" Lexie asked as the bartender handed us our beers.

"As pleasant and delightful as this old man is, I'm not going to hide out over here, Lex. Stop making such a big deal out of this. I'm over it. Last night is ancient history. He's not as attractive when I'm sober," I said, forcing a teasing grin.

Lies. All lies. But this time I managed to keep my fingers gripped tightly around my glass bottle.

"Okay, then. Let's go, lady." She grabbed my hand, pulling me behind her as we walked toward the pool table. I scanned the group of guys and noticed, thankfully, Caleb was not here tonight. I just hoped he wasn't going to show up at any moment, making this evening that much worse.

"Where's Caleb?"

"I think he's still recovering. Why? Were you hoping to see him?" she said with a wicked smile.

"No!" I laughed. "Not at all."

As we approached the group, Lexie began to introduce me to Liam's friends, skipping over Liam, knowing there was no need for an awkward introduction. I recognized each band member from my Google search before she told me their names. I smiled at each of them as I shook their hands.

Derailed was made up of four members. There was Blaine, the drummer; Trent, the bass player; Dax, the lead guitarist; and of course, Liam, the lead singer and rhythm guitarist.

"I hear it's your birthday." Dax slid in next to me with a flirty smile after all the introductions had finished.

Most of the group had resumed their game of pool or returned to the conversations they'd been having before I'd arrived. Dax stayed close to my side, smiling at me with a glint in his eyes.

I smiled seductively back. He was cute. It was instinctual. "It is," I confirmed.

"Can I buy you a birthday shot?"

I laughed. "No. I think I've had enough shots for a while after last night. Plus, I don't think gramps over there is big on making shots. How about you just buy my next round?"

"Deal, sweetheart." He winked, causing a wider smile to spread across my face.

Feeling Liam's eyes on us, I glanced over at him. His hardened expression, which I was beginning to think was a permanent fixture on his face, was back. I ignored it and turned to continue to talk with Dax, who obviously had more interest in me than Liam.

Dax was good looking. Not nearly as sexy as Liam, but still easy on the eyes. He was lean and tall with short brown hair, hazel eyes, and a five o'clock shadow along his jaw line.

He was self-assured, which was always an attractive trait to me. I'm sure his confidence came from being in a moderately successful band.

"So, Dax, how long have you lived in L.A.?"

Before he could answer me, he was interrupted by Liam's annoyed voice, "Dax. You're up."

"One sec. Can't you see I'm talkin' to a beautiful woman here?" Dax winked at me, not bothering to look at his friend while he responded.

"Take your shot. Then you can do whatever the hell you want," Liam gritted out as he glared at his friend. Dax seemed unfazed by his friend's intensity.

"Excuse me, sweetheart. We'll finish this conversation in a minute."

I watched Dax circle the pool table before lining up to take his shot. Liam stepped around the table, his movement drawing my eyes to his body. He was too damn sexy for his own good. It amazed me how he could make a simple T-shirt and jeans look better than an Armani suit. The man did casual well.

I got a glimpse of his tattoo peeking out from his short sleeves and I pictured myself tracing it with my finger...or my tongue. Either would do. Butterflies took flight in my stomach with the thought. *Damn it.* I needed to stop picturing these things.

He stopped a few feet from me, and I could feel the familiar pull between us. Needing to break the tension, I spoke to him for the first time since I arrived. "Three days in a row. This is becoming a thing."

He turned his greys on me, annihilating the shield I'd tried putting in place when I walked into the bar.

"This isn't a thing, princess."

Asshole. That wasn't what I was implying, but the fact that he felt the need to clarify and dismiss me ever having that thought was hurtful. *Why does he dislike me so much?*

"That's not what I meant. I'm well aware there will never be a *thing* with us."

"Good."

"You're not my type," I added for good measure. His body inched closer to mine or maybe mine was inching closer to his. I wasn't sure.

"And you're not mine," he said pointedly.

No kidding, jerk. You made that clear when you rejected me last night.

Unable to stay so close to him without touching him, I abruptly moved away, walking toward Dax—someone who actually enjoyed my company. I did my best to ignore Liam and his glares as Dax and I talked and flirted. When Dax was busy playing pool, I sat with Lexie and Jake, keeping my distance from Liam.

"You girls want to play a round?" Jake asked us.

"Sure!" Lexie answered before I could say anything.

"I'm not very good. I've only played once, and I was terrible," I said, trying to dissuade them from including me.

"We can do teams. Lexie and me against you and one of the guys," Jake offered.

"You seem to be hitting it off with Dax. Why don't you team up with him?" Lexie suggested.

"I don't—"

"Hey, Dax! Val needs a pool partner. You up for it?" Lexie yelled across the bar, where Dax was getting us another round of beers.

"Of course." He smiled at me.

"I don't know how to play."

"Don't worry, I'll teach you, sweetheart." He winked.

"All right. You've been warned." I giggled, shaking my head at him.

After Blaine and Joe wrapped up their game, they passed the cue sticks to us. Dax went over the basic rules with me while Jake racked the balls at one end of the table. Dax took the first shot, breaking the triangle of balls, sending them every which way. He pocketed two solids and a stripe, calling solids for our team.

He took a few more shots, sinking more solids, but missing on his fourth shot. Jake shot next, pocketing a few stripes, before he sank the cue ball. I was up. I felt nervous tension as I approached the table. I wasn't sure if it was the fact that I was about to have to actually play, or because Liam's eyes hadn't left me since we started the game.

Dax grabbed the cue ball from the pocket and came to my side to help me place it on the table for an easy shot. I held the pool stick in my hands and bent at my waist, leaning over the table, acutely aware of Liam and only vaguely aware of Dax, who stood at my side. Dax leaned over me, forming his body with mine, resting his hand on my leather-cladded hip. The other hand slid down my arm as he helped me line up my shot.

"Okay, sweetheart." Dax's warm breath hit my ear. "You just want to glide the stick across your fingers. Keep it straight and smooth. Hit the ball, right in this spot, and you'll sink it, no problem."

His hand gripped my hip tighter as he spoke. I closed my eyes and bit my bottom lip, trying to visualize the path of the ball and ignore Dax's touch. It wasn't that his hands bothered me. What bothered me is that I wanted it to be someone else's hands.

Just as I was taking my shot with Dax's assistance, a loud bang had me jumping and nearly missing the cue ball. I nipped it just enough to send it rolling in the wrong direction.

"What the fuck, man?" Dax turned on Liam, who'd apparently slammed his beer down on the table mid-shot.

Liam's eyes narrowed at the both of us as he stood and walked away. *What the hell is his problem?*

"Sorry, sweetheart." Dax turned back to me, apologizing for his friend. "We'll make the next shot."

I nodded with a tight smile, trying to control the emotions I was feeling. "It's fine. I'm just going to run to the restroom. I'll be right back," I excused myself.

Lexie caught my eye, silently asking if I wanted her to come with me. I shook my head and headed in the direction of the restroom. I forcefully pushed the door open, rushing inside, slamming my back up against the wall. I gripped my hair in my hands at the crown of my head as I stared in the mirror, breathing heavily, my heart hammering against my ribs.

"Get a grip, Val," I reprimanded myself in the mirror.

The door swung open.

"Shit!" I jumped, grabbing at my chest, whipping my head to the opening—shocked into momentary silence. Liam walked into the ladies' restroom.

After glancing under the single stall and finding it empty, he turned his laser eyes on me, standing a mere foot away.

He was so close I could smell that uniquely musky, manly smell of his that had my body ready to submit.

"What the hell are you doing?" I asked through my strangled voice.

"Quit flirting with Dax," he demanded.

There it was. I could see it in his eyes as I focused on them. I could see the struggle in them despite his hardened expression. It was the same struggle with jealousy and possessiveness I felt when I saw him with the other woman. I wasn't letting him off easy this time. I knew I wasn't the only one feeling *things*, no matter how much we both denied it out loud.

"Why should I?" I challenged him.

He hesitated, searching for his answer. The answer we both already knew.

"Because you have a boyfriend," he gritted through his teeth.

Okay. Not the answer I expected. *Maybe I was misreading things?* No. I wasn't. This was not one sided, and I was determined to make him admit it.

"What?" I scoffed at his accusation and avoidance of the truth. "I do *not* have a boyfriend, and even if I did, what business is it of yours?" I threw my hands on my hips, staring at him expectantly. `

"The guy at the bar last night?"

"Not. My. Boyfriend."

"So, you just let all guys feel you up like that?" he growled.

"Are you kidding me, right now? You're one to talk." I pointed my finger at him, poking him in his firm chest.

He swiftly grabbed my hand in his, pinning it above my head against the wall. I gasped. A heady charge shot through my body. He leaned in, burying his face in my neck as he pressed his body against mine, gripping my hip with his free hand. I could feel his need through the material that separated us.

My chest heaved against his. Every thought focused on what it felt like to have his body pressed against mine. I was tingly and lightheaded as a current prickled my skin. My one free hand moved to the back of his neck, my fingers weaving into his hair, holding on tight.

"I'm not like the rich, pretty boys you're used to. I'm no good for you, princess," he whispered his warning into my neck.

I knew he was right. I didn't need another playboy who would break my heart. My last serious boyfriend was in high school. We'd been together for two years. I had sex with him the night of our senior prom, giving my virginity to him, and he'd been sure to let everyone know.

He never cared about me, like I did him. He only wanted bragging rights for bedding a Blackwood. He hooked up with my supposed best friend the next night at a house party. Neither of them tried to hide it. Pictures of them kissing and hanging on each other were all over Facebook, Instagram, and Twitter. It was humiliating, and it buried a deep-seated mistrust of everyone in me.

I couldn't get out of New York fast enough. Unfortunately, I had to spend the summer there. I'd kept myself locked away at home as much as possible without tipping off my family that something was wrong. Ava was the first one I confided in after moving to California. I swore her to secrecy. We both knew if my brother ever heard what happened, he'd make the guy pay for it. All I wanted to do was move on from it and start anew. I knew Ava could understand that, and she did.

Regardless of Liam's warnings, I felt safer with him than I had anyone. His words were lost on me. I knew what I felt. And I didn't care what he was saying. I was just about to tell him that when the door came flying open once again, making Liam release me and step away.

Damn it!

"Shit, sorry!" Lexie yelped. "I was just coming to check on Val. I'll leave." She whipped around to exit.

"Stay," Liam demanded, halting her retreat. "I was just leaving."

I couldn't tell if he was relieved or annoyed at the interruption. Maybe a little of both. I was definitely annoyed, and I wasn't hiding it. Lexie looked down, stepping aside as Liam walked out of the restroom.

"Sorry?" she said, unsure of whether she should be.

"Ughhhh," I let out my frustration as I sank to the dirty floor. I didn't care. I couldn't stand on my own right now. "Whoever said third time's a charm is a complete dimwit."

"What was that about?" She took a seat next to me on the nasty floor, because that's what good friends did.

"I'm not sure. I think I know. But I didn't get a chance to confirm it before you came flying in here."

"Shit. Sorry, Val. You were taking a while. I had no idea he'd be in here with you."

"It's not your fault. With my luck, nothing would have happened anyway."

"So...do you want to keep hanging out on this gross floor, or do you want to head back out there?"

I chuckled. "Maybe just hang out another minute, until I can get control of my hormones."

She laughed, wrapping her arm around my shoulders, hugging me to her. We rested our heads against each other.

"If he can't see what a catch you are, Val, then he's an idiot."

"Thanks."

Her words were sweet, but I knew, now, that was not the problem. The problem was, for some reason, he didn't think he was good enough for me. I didn't believe him. After a few more silent moments of sitting in the women's restroom, Lexie got to her feet, pulling me with her.

"Ready?"

"Ready," I confirmed. I was going to go out there and show Liam just how much I wanted him. His warnings be damned.

I walked out of the restroom with a determined stride, but my confidence stumbled, and I felt an imaginary smack to the face when we found one tiny bar missing Liam's large presence.

"Where did Liam go?" I asked Blaine, who was nearest to me, with what I hoped was an air of unconcern.

"He left a few minutes ago," he replied, taking a drink of his beer.

You have to be kidding me! My temper peaked. It looked like we did have a thing, after all. That *thing* was him making me desperate for him then leaving me pissed and alone. Well, screw him. I was done playing the desperate fool.

"You're up by the way." Blaine pointed at the pool table.

"Actually...you take my place. You make a better partner

for Dax than me. I'm going to head out for the night." I had no desire to stick around.

"Are you sure? Do you want me to come with you?" Lexie asked, overhearing my conversation with Blaine.

"No. You stay. I'm just tired and still feeling the after effects of last night. I'll see you at home," I assured her with a hug. I put in my request for an Uber on my phone. Once it was close, I told everyone goodbye and left the bar.

~

I curled up under my down comforter, ready for bed, trying to clear my mind of the night's events. I texted my mom to let her know I was home safe and sound, then put my phone on the bedside table, picking up the remote instead. I flipped on the TV in my room and scrolled through Netflix for something to watch.

My phone chimed with a new message. Expecting it to be my mom responding, I picked it up. It wasn't. It was a text from an unknown number. I read the message and knew instantly who it was from.

See you soon, princess.

"Jerk," I huffed to no one but myself.

I started to type, *screw you*, then deleted it. I typed out, *in your dreams, asshole*, but decided to delete that too. I settled on not responding at all. Giving him any reaction just gave him more power.

I put my phone down and tried ignoring it as I watched my shows. I only glanced over at it occasionally. It sat there taunting me. I picked it back up and saved Liam's number. Just in case. So I could screen his future calls and texts.

Honestly. That's the only reason why. He was obviously a creep. *How did he get my number anyway?*

I was just about to call it a night and turn off the TV when I heard the front door of our apartment open. A few moments later, Lexie came padding into my bedroom.

"Hey. You're awake still."

"Yep. Couldn't sleep."

She walked further into my room, slipping off her shoes and crawling under the covers next to me.

"Did you have a good birthday weekend? I mean besides Liam, of course." She looked at me cautiously.

I chuckled. "Yes."

She giggled with relief. "Good...soooo...Dax asked for your number." I looked at her with wide eyes. "I didn't give it to him, but I promised him I'd give you his number."

"Thanks for that. He seems like a cool guy, but not sure it's a good idea for me to start anything with him."

"Because of Liam?"

"No...maybe...I don't know. He texted me tonight."

"Who? Liam?"

"Yes."

"What did he say?"

"See you soon, princess," I said, trying to imitate his deep voice.

"What does that mean?"

"My thoughts exactly. The man is an enigma."

"You know...after you both left, Blaine and Trent were teasing Dax about getting his ass kicked later by Liam."

"Why?"

"Why do you think, Val? It's obvious to everyone that Liam was pissed about Dax having his hands on you."

"Well, I don't know why he would be. He's made it very clear he wants nothing to do with me."

"You're shitting me right now. You don't honestly believe that do you?"

I scoffed a snort for my response. No. I didn't believe that. But regardless, he was determined to stay far from me, and I wasn't going to beg. He could be a man and go after what he wanted—me—or he could hide behind his façade.

"I didn't think you believed that. Especially after what I walked in on." She raised an eyebrow at me.

"Don't look at me like that!" I pushed her shoulder as she laughed. "It's not like I was going to let him screw me in that dirty bathroom."

Or...maybe I would have. I didn't seem to have a sane thought whenever he touched me.

"Whatever you say. I'm just saying, what I saw looked pretty heated."

It was. And now it was all I could think about.

"Shut up! And get out of my room," I dismissed her playfully. "I need my beauty sleep."

"Fine, *princess*," she mocked me as she climbed out of my bed.

"I'll leave Dax's number for you on the island. You can decide what to do with it. That way I didn't break my promise to him."

I nodded. "Night, Lex. Thanks for everything this weekend."

"No problem. Sleep well, lady." She smiled before closing the door behind her.

I flipped off my TV and rolled over to my side. I tossed and turned, contemplating the meaning of Liam's text. *Was that a promise? How the hell does he know he will see me soon? Are they going to be hanging out with Jake and his friends more often? Does he plan to call and ask me out on a legitimate date?*

I needed to stop my game of twenty unanswered questions or I was never going to get to sleep. I closed my eyes tight. *Kittens. Kittens. Puppies.*

CHAPTER 6

The annoying sound of my phone alarm woke me the next morning. I slapped my limp hand on the nightstand in search of the loud offender, keeping my eyes tightly shut. It was still dark outside. *Why... Why the hell did I choose a job that required me to be up before the sun?*

I tumbled out of bed, moving through my pitch-black room, rubbing my sleepy eyes. I went through the motions of showering and getting ready for work. I skipped washing my hair, spraying it with some dry shampoo instead and twisting it into a messy bun on top of my head. It was way too early to worry about looking beautiful.

I slipped on my white shorts and a loose army-green tee. The main reason I took this job was because the manager allowed us to wear whatever we wanted. He liked the staff to feel eclectic like the coffee shop. I was grateful. There was no way anyone would be getting me in a boring, old uniform.

The only thing that unified the staff was the black aprons we wore with the Sweet Beans logo.

After applying some makeup, I sat on my bed and slipped on my brown gladiator sandals. I walked into the kitchen to grab a piece of fruit for a breakfast on-the-go. The apartment was still quiet and dark. Lexie had the late shift today, so we would only see each other in passing. I snatched an apple and a protein bar, rushing out the door. I stopped as I rounded the corner of the island, my attention pulled by the piece of paper on the counter. *Dax's number.* I picked it up, glancing at it. Not sure what I wanted to do with it, I pocketed it and left for work.

~

"Morning, Val," Ethan mumbled as I walked in the door of Sweet Beans. He was looking rough. It seemed I wasn't the only non-morning person. He was already preparing the fresh brewed coffee as I walked around the counter, pulling out a clean apron.

"Sorry I'm late. What still needs to be done?" I asked as I tied the apron around my waist.

"Will you grab the rest of the pastries from the kitchen to put in the case?"

"Sure. We missed you last night," I told him over my shoulder as I walked toward the swinging door that led to the kitchen.

"Yeah, some buddies and I decided to do some night surfing."

"That seems kind of scary."

I wasn't a fan of getting in the ocean. I was pretty certain the way I was going to die was by being eaten by a shark or an alligator or some kind of big, swimmy creature with large teeth. Therefore, the only water I swam in was contained in a pool. I didn't mind wading in it at calf level...but there was no way in hell you were getting me to go deeper than that. Especially at night.

"The waves at night are bad ass." He grinned.

I shook my head at his fearlessness, then walked into the kitchen, grabbing the rest of the fresh pastries. I finished helping him set up for the morning rush before unlocking the door.

We decided I'd take orders while he manned the espresso machine. We would make better tips that way. He was much more efficient at making the coffees, and I was much more personable. I'd come a long way with my coffee-making skills over the last few years. After my first week of working, I was positive Aaron, the owner, was going to fire me. I think he bought more coffees for disgruntled customers than he sold those first weeks.

He put me on the register and bussing duty for the next few months. Lexie took pity on me and spent extra time training me on the fancy espresso machine. It was how we first bonded and became good friends.

Monday mornings were always a mad house, even in the summer. It was the time of day when we got mostly business professionals and professors coming through the doors. They were always impatient and in a rush, unlike the college students who started to arrive mid-morning and continued through the rest of the day, until we closed.

Today was no different, and by the time my shift came to an end I was exhausted. I bussed the last of the tables before clocking out and leaving to pick up Ava for a late lunch.

~

"I'm starving," Ava complained as she ungracefully got into the passenger seat of her car. I swear her belly was growing at warp speed.

"We'll grab lunch before we go pick up my car. Where do you want to eat?"

"Anywhere that has a sampler of fried foods…and peach cobbler."

"Are you sure that's a good idea?" I gave her belly a sideways glance.

"Did you seriously just belly shame me?"

"Um…no?"

She arched an eyebrow. "Uh, huh. For that you're buying me lunch. And I'll be adding vanilla ice cream to that peach cobbler."

I chuckled. "You're grouchy."

"I'm pregnant. And hungry. You made a hungry pregnant woman wait two hours past her normal lunch time to eat."

"It's only been an hour and a half, technically."

"By the time we get to a restaurant, it'll be two."

"Okay. Okay. I'm sorry. I'll buy your lunch." I grinned at her with my peace offering.

Ava's phone chimed with a new text. She pulled it out of her purse.

"Who's that?"

"Rhett. He's asking if you've fed me and his baby yet."

"How did he even know you hadn't eaten?"

"I may have been sending him hangry texts earlier." She shrugged her shoulders unapologetically.

"You two are ridiculous. I guess he's blaming your bad mood on me, too." I rolled my eyes.

She laughed while she typed her response. "Of course, I did."

~

After we ate lunch, where Ava ordered a sampler appetizer, an entrée, *and* a dessert, we left the restaurant and headed to the body shop to pick up my car.

I slowed the vehicle, turning into the small parking lot of Frankie's Body Shop. I parked and we both stepped out of the car. Well…I stepped out. Ava more or less rolled out.

"Are you sure you're going to be able to drive?" I asked, looking at the tight space between the steering wheel and driver's seat as she waddled around the car to the driver's side.

She narrowed her eyes at me.

"Sorry!" I threw my hands up in surrender before she belly bumped me like a sumo wrestler.

"Just give me the keys." She put out the palm of her hand. I handed them over. "Do you want me to wait around until you get your car?"

"No. I'm good. Are you heading back to work?"

She shook her head. "I'm going home. I took the afternoon off. I need a nap."

I didn't doubt it after the amount of food she ate. You would've thought she was eating for five, not two. I wasn't going to voice that out loud, though. She was obviously sensitive about her size. I'd be glad once the little man finally made his appearance in the next few months and she was less testy.

I gave her a hug and thanked her for loaning me her car. I waved at her as she drove off the lot, then turned and headed inside to get my car.

The bell above the door rang as I walked inside the small room that served as the customer-service area. There was nobody in sight. Just a cluttered counter with a bell. With all the loud racket in the service-bay area of the building, I wasn't exactly sure how a dinky bell on the counter was going to page anyone. I rang it anyway. And then, I stood there...impatiently...waiting. Waiting for someone, anyone to come help me.

Well, they won't be receiving a five-star rating on customer service anytime soon.

The phone on the counter began to ring. After the third ring, I looked around to see if anyone would come answer it. I leaned over the counter, eyeing the old corded phone as it endlessly rang. Bored and with nothing else to do, I started to browse through the papers that were spread across the counter.

"Can I help you?" a loud, deep voice boomed behind me.

"Crap!" I jolted up straight, feeling guilty for being nosy. It's not like I had seen anything, really. "Yes," I replied, settling my nerves, turning to the short, stocky, middle-aged man who had a beer belly that could rival Ava's. He was wearing a stained mechanic's shirt with the name "Danny" stitched on it. "I'm here to pick up my car."

"Name?" He walked to stand behind the counter across from me.

"Valerie Blackwood. You called me over the weekend to let me know it was ready."

"That's right. The silver Camaro convertible. You banged that one up pretty good." He chuckled, amused with himself.

I glared at him. "I didn't do it."

"Whatever you say darlin'." He rifled through the mess of papers on the counter.

Seriously? Could they be any less organized?

"Ah, here it is," he said, staring at a piece of paper. "Looks like you owe four thousand."

"What?! That's more than you quoted me. That can't be right. Is that after the insurance?"

"Afraid so. We had to replace the door, remove various smaller dents, and repaint the whole car since we weren't able to match the existing paint exactly."

What the hell? This was highway robbery. "You didn't think to consult me first?" I planted my hands on my hips.

I was pissed. More than pissed. I was ready to blow a freaking gasket. It's not that I couldn't afford the bill. It was the fact that they were charging me twice the original quote. I'm sure they thought they could take advantage of me since I was a young female.

"Calm down, darlin'. I'm just the messenger. I don't do the numbers."

"Who does the numbers? I want to speak with them."

"That'd be the boss man, Frankie."

"Well, get him for me. I'm not paying this."

"No can do."

"Why the hell not?"

"He isn't here today. He'll be in tomorrow. But I won't be able to release your car to you until you're paid in full." The

shop phone started to ring, again. "One minute, darlin'."
Danny picked up the phone.

Damn it. Ava had already left and was probably half way to Malibu by now. Lexie was at work and so was Rhett. I didn't want to disturb them. Ethan had a full day shift, so that option was out too.

Who else is there? I pulled out the piece of paper in my pocket. *No. I shouldn't. Should I?* I didn't have a lot of choice. The only other person was Caleb and I was not calling him.

Screw it. I pulled out my phone and texted Dax.

Hey. It's Valerie. You busy?

As I waited for his response, I started to have second thoughts. My phone vibrated in my hand.

D: Hey, sweetheart. Just playing some Xbox with B-man. What's up?

I hesitated, trying to think of the best way to ask him for a ride. I didn't want him to get the wrong idea. Danny hung up the phone.

"Well, what's it gonna be, darlin'? You payin' or leavin'?"

I bit my bottom lip as I tried to decide. "There's nobody else I can talk to about the bill?"

"Maybe… Let me see if he's back from lunch."

Danny walked around the counter and went through the shop door into the service area in search of someone who could help me.

V: Never mind. Thought I might need a ride, but I'm good now.

D: RU Sure? I don't mind.

V: Yeah, but thanks.

D: I had fun the other night. Come watch us play tonight?

That was a definite no. For one, Liam. Secondly, I didn't

want to lead Dax on. I was already regretting texting him to start with. I started to type my response when Danny walked back in followed by a tall, masculine figure. I looked up, tightening my hand around my phone.

Great. Freaking great. Somebody in the heavens upstairs hated me, or at least liked torturing me. Liam stood just inside the doorway with his arms crossed against his chest, his face impassive, his eyes slowly dragging down my body.

His text message from last night suddenly made complete sense, along with the fact that he knew my name and phone number. He had it all at his fingertips on the shop paperwork.

I narrowed my eyes at him, crossing my own arms over my chest as I cocked my hip to the side. I was going to let him have it this time. All the built-up frustration and anger was rapidly coming to a head.

"Thanks Danny. I've got this. You can go," Liam dismissed him.

Danny looked between the two of us and chuckled, shaking his head. "Good luck, boss. She's feisty." He grinned and patted Liam on the shoulder for support as he walked out, leaving us alone in the tiny room as we stared each other down.

"You have a complaint, princess?"

"I have multiple complaints," I responded with malice. "But we'll start with the fact that you're overcharging me for the work on my car."

A fiendish smile spread across his face, revealing his offending dimple. *Ignore the dimple. Ignore. The. Dimple.* I chanted in my head. He was not going to lower my defenses with that damn dimple. Or that sexy smile. Or those hard abs that were showing through his sweaty white T-shirt. Oh. Hell. No. I was standing my ground.

"It's a fair price. There was a lot of work that had to be done. You're welcome to ask around at other shops for comparison."

"Even *if* I believed you, which I don't, you should've consulted me about the increased costs."

"Would it have made a difference?"

"That's not the point."

"What's the real problem, princess? You can't tell me you can't afford it. I've seen your Bentley. Anyone who drives a Bentley as a spare car and dresses the way you do shouldn't have a problem with the price."

"Screw. You. You're a jerk. I'm not letting you take advantage of me. And stop calling me princess."

He chuckled, dropping his arms, prowling closer to me.

"Come on, you can do better than that *princess*," he said, egging on my anger. It was as if he got some sick pleasure from riling me up.

"Fine. You're an asshole. How dare you judge me? You barely know me."

"I know enough. And I never claimed to be a good guy."

"I guess that's your one redeeming factor."

He snickered, a small smile tugging at the corners of his lips. He was standing toe to toe with me now, the air thick between us. He stared down at me, and I raised my chin, staring right back at him. I wasn't letting him intimidate me or make me swoon. Ok, mentally I wasn't. My body was doing whatever the hell it wanted, despite my brain's stance. It was already feeling heated and begging for his touch.

"Tell me what you want me to do to satisfy you, princess." His voice softened, oozing with seduction.

Kiss me. Wait. Are we talking about my body or the car? I wasn't sure anymore. He was too close. He was sending my brain into a spiral and my body was using that to its advantage.

"I want you to do what's right." I struggled to hold my voice steady.

"What if I can't?"

"You're the boss, aren't you?"

I continued to talk about the car. It was the safest route, even though I was pretty sure this conversation had taken a turn somewhere along the way—probably the moment his mouth became only inches from mine.

He grinned remorsefully. "I'd prefer to be in this situation, but I'm afraid not."

Is he trying to tell me I'm in control here? Why is he so damn confusing? Why can't he just admit it's not just me feeling something?

"Who is?" I pushed him to tell me the truth. The truth about how he really felt about me. About the potential of there being an us. He hesitated answering. His eyes scanned my face and body. He opened his mouth slightly to respond and then stopped. His lips formed a straight line and the hardness returned.

"My uncle." He took a step back, throwing his armor back up. "I'll have to talk to him about it. I can knock some of the price down. But I can't give you the original quote without him signing off on it."

We were back to the car. But he wasn't fooling me. His outward appearance and rebel attitude was a façade. He had a wall up around him, and I was determined to break through it. I turned my back to him, stepping away. I needed space to process my next move. He grabbed my wrist, stopping me.

"Valerie." His firm voice halted me more than his hand that was sending electricity traveling through my body. It was the first time he'd said my name, and it sounded so perfect coming from his lips.

"Why?" I pleaded, turning back around to face him. He knew I wasn't talking about the car. I couldn't keep doing this. I needed him to step up or leave me alone.

"I'm trying to do the right thing here."

"What if, what you think is the right thing, really isn't?" I pressed my body against him, bringing my hands to the sides of his face. I needed him to feel what I was feeling. He contemplated my words as his eyes studied me.

"I won't be gentle," he warned.

"I don't want gentle."

I wanted him. Every bit of him. All his hard, rough edges along with the softness I knew was buried inside him.

"You should. You should demand to be treated like a princess. Any man who doesn't, doesn't deserve you."

"This is what I mean. Why do you say things like that? You make me want you, and then you push me away. This is a thing. Whether you want to admit it or not. There *is* a thing between us. It's right in front of your face. *I'm* right in front of your face. Make a choice."

He lowered his forehead to mine, closing his eyes as he rested his hands on my hips. Our breaths mingled, and I waited for his answer. The seconds that passed felt like an eternity. But I knew it wasn't. An eternity would last forever; this moment wouldn't.

I inhaled his scent, memorizing it along with the feel of his hands on me. If I stood on my tip toes, I could press my lips to his, but I resisted the urge. I wanted him to make the decision.

When I felt his hands drop from body, I felt my heart break a little. He was making his choice. And it was the wrong one. He raised his head from mine and opened his eyes.

"I'll get your keys, so you can leave. I'll talk to my uncle about your bill. I know you're good for the money."

Before I could respond or tell him he was being a damn coward, he walked out of the room, leaving me by myself. I leaned against the counter, wanting to cry. But I wouldn't. I wouldn't cry over him. He didn't deserve my tears.

Danny returned to the room with my keys, shaking his head in amusement. I wanted to punch him in his little round face.

"I don't know what you did, darlin', but you sure put him in a bad mood."

"I usually do," I huffed under my breath, taking my keys from him.

"Car's out front."

"Thanks." I stomped out the door.

~

"Wow," Lexie said in shock after I got done telling her about the whole intense encounter with Liam at the body shop. I'd come straight to Sweet Beans, needing to vent to my friend. "So, what are you going to do now?"

"Nothing," I said, glancing down at my coffee mug as I spun it slowly on the bar. I looked back up to see her disapproving glare. "What? He made his choice."

"What about your choice?"

"I can't force him to be with me, Lex."

She scoffed. My forehead wrinkled, arms crossing. "What was that?"

"Nothing. It's just…if I've learned anything about you and your family, you're a stubborn bunch of bastards and don't give up easily on what you want."

"Well, maybe I don't want him as badly as you think."

"When did you get so good at lying?"

"Who says I'm lying?"

"I do. Your finger may not be in your hair right now, but I know you, Val. You like him. A lot. More than I've ever seen you like anyone. Plus, I saw your finger twitch before you stopped it." She smirked.

A smile snuck onto my face as I shook my head at her in disbelief. I took a sip of my coffee. My phone vibrated on the bar top. I picked it up and groaned.

D: Don't leave me hanging, sweetheart. I don't usually beg, but I'll make an exception for you.

"Who's that?"

I placed the phone back down and looked up at my friend. "Dax. He wants me to come to their concert tonight."

"Go."

"No."

"Why not? It's the perfect excuse for you to see Liam again."

"I'm not doing that, Lex. That's just wrong. Dax is the one inviting me. I'm not leading him on. I've learned my lesson with Caleb."

"Who cares? Just be upfront with Dax. The guy has to see what's going on. Besides, if anything is going to get Liam to step up, it'll be you showing up there to see Dax. That much is obvious after what happened last night."

"You really think this is a good idea?"

She rolled her eyes at me, putting her hands on her hips. "Go home, lady. You need to get ready for tonight."

I decided to take my best friend's advice. What was the worst that could happen? He'd already rejected me on numerous occasions. *What's one more time?* Just one more time for my heart and confidence to finally be shattered into a million pieces. That's all.

I picked my phone back up and typed out my response.

See you tonight.

Lexie's pep talk gave me the reinforcement I needed. I would just have to explain to Dax the first chance I got that I only saw him as a friend. Hopefully, he wouldn't hate me.

CHAPTER 7

This time when I heard Liam's voice filtering outside the bar, I was more prepared. It still had my heart racing, but at least I had some control over my emotions. I knew what they were and how I planned to handle them. I was under no illusion that things would go as I hoped, but I had faith that I could make him see me. Really see me. And see that I wanted him for him.

As I approached Joe at the door, his beefy head shook as a smile penetrated his steely expression. "Valerie," he greeted me. "Go on in, girl. Just stay off the tables tonight." He raised a warning brow.

I grinned. "I'll keep my feet planted firmly on the ground," I promised. At least physically; figuratively, Liam's voice already had them floating.

"Dax told me to have you sit in their booth. It's in the back corner off the stage."

"Thanks, Joe," I patted his big, brawny arm as I passed

him, entering the bar. I stopped a few feet inside the entrance to observe Derailed jamming to an instrumental bridge of the song. Liam's back was to me as he faced Dax, focused on playing his guitar.

Watching him lost in the music had me more determined to get to know the man behind the façade. I inhaled deeply then pushed my way through the crowd to get a glass of water. I decided tonight I should keep a sober mind. I didn't want to give Liam any reason to make excuses.

I slid into the circular booth that was reserved for the band and felt oddly self-conscious as women eyed me with suspicion and distaste. I'm sure they were all wondering why the hell I had a table to myself close to the stage. I ignored them, throwing my shoulders back and sitting up tall.

I looked back at the stage, where Liam was now wrapped around the microphone singing. Dax caught my gaze and gave me a sexy grin and a wink. I smiled back and gave him a small wave before returning my attention to Liam.

He didn't look at me directly, but I knew he was aware of my presence—the same way I was always aware of his when we were in the same room. At the end of the song, the crowd screamed and cheered, begging for more.

All the Derailed members but Liam stepped away from their instruments and moved off the stage. The room darkened even more, and the multiple stage lights were reduced to one spotlight focused on Liam.

The girls in the crowd began to shrill and shriek as he started singing a slowed-down, acoustic version of Radiohead's "Creep." It was the first time I'd heard him sing a cover song. His smooth, velvety voice pierced my soul, warming my body from the inside out.

The anguish and desperation lacing his voice as he sang couldn't be faked. It was real. The lyrics of the song and the pain he felt as he sang them had me wanting to protectively hug him to me. *What had happened to make him think so little of himself?*

I was so enchanted watching him that I hadn't even noticed his friends join me at the table until Dax's arms slid around my shoulder. He leaned in, giving me a small peck on the cheek, distracting me from Liam.

"Glad you made it, sweetheart," he whispered in my ear.

Shit. I needed to make my intentions for the night clear. Now. "Thanks for inviting me, Dax." I gave him a small smile, prying my eyes from Liam. "Look...I...I hope you don't take this the wrong way. And I hope you don't hate me after I tell you this—"

"It's fine, Val." He smiled. "Don't worry your pretty little head. I already know."

"You do? I mean...you know what exactly?" My eyebrows pinched together.

"I know you aren't here because you wanted to see me," he said, glancing toward Liam with a smile on his face. He was making this easy on me.

"How...? And why would you invite me then?"

He let out a heavy sigh. "Look, Liam and I go way back. I like to think I know him better than anyone. Even better than himself sometimes. He's a good guy who got dealt a shit hand and a bad rap. And for the first time, I'm seeing an opportunity to make him realize it."

I nodded, knowing he meant I was that opportunity.

"So you invited me, thinking he just needed a little push."

"Fuck the little push. He needs to be pummeled hard.

Right in his fucking face, sweetheart. It's the only way."

I laughed. "How do you suppose we do that?"

He leaned in, nuzzling his face into my neck. "We're already doing it," he whispered in my ear.

I grinned. "You're not worried about him kicking your ass?"

"It'll be worth it, if it means my friend will fight for something that's worth a damn versus taking the scraps thrown at him."

"You're a good friend."

"I like to think so. I just hope he sees it that way before he puts me in the hospital."

I shook my head, laughing at him.

"Besides, I'm not going to act like this is hard work. I'm going to have fun doing it, sweetheart. You're not exactly an ugly duckling. If it weren't for Liam—"

"Stop it!" I pushed at his chest playfully, my laughter increasing.

"That leather skirt last night was fucking hot. But seeing you in these tight-ass jeans and fuck-me heels has every man in here thinking about having those legs wrapped around them."

I blushed. That was my intent when I chose the outfit—skinny jeans, tall stilettos, and a low-cut blouse.

"Every man except the one who matters." My smile faltered as I looked back at Liam.

"Trust me, sweetheart. He's one of them. He's at the top of the fucking list."

I turned back to Dax. "I hope you're right about all this."

"I am. Have a little faith, sweetheart."

I nodded and looked back over toward the stage as the

song came to an end and the crowd of girls screamed. Liam's eyes were on me as Dax gave me another small peck on the cheek.

"I'll see you in a few. We have to get back out there." Dax slid out of the booth with Blaine and Trent.

~

I watched Derailed play the rest of their set, thoroughly enjoying their music. They were better than I remembered from the other night—not that I remembered a whole lot of that night, beyond Liam's voice. I yelled and cheered them on and did my best to contain my temper and jealousy when the girls at the front of the stage would reach for Liam or throw their panties and bras at him. *I mean, really? Who does that?*

It wasn't their desperate tactics that had me feeling the most frustrated. It was the attention he gave them while he sang. The smiles, the winks, the seductive looks. I knew it was all part of the show, but it still had me wanting to drag him off the stage and lock him up for myself.

I knew I had no actual right to feel that way. Liam hadn't chosen me. He'd rejected me on more than one occasion. But after my talk with Dax, I felt like he was mine—even if he hadn't done anything to make me believe it. In fact, he'd done everything to show and tell me he wasn't.

As the band started the intro to their last song of the night, my anxiety levels increased. I had no idea what was going to happen next. I only hoped it didn't blow up in my face. Or Dax's.

He told me to trust him, but I barely knew the guy.

Putting my trust and faith in his hands was hard. If I hadn't witnessed the genuine concern for his friend, it would've made me doubt him. But the fact that he was willing to risk his own wellbeing for his friend's warmed my heart and gave me newfound respect for Dax.

The song ended, and my heart stopped. In a few seconds, Liam would be sitting with me at the table. The crowd went wild with chants for an encore. The band thanked them, telling them to be sure to come back for the other nights and times they played.

Recorded music began to play through the sound system over the bar, while the guys put away their instruments. I waited impatiently in the booth for them to join me. My heart was now beating so hard, I thought it was going to break through my chest and run away. If I was smart, I'd follow it straight out the door, versus going through with this insane plan of Dax's and Lexie's.

The band was surrounded by female groupies when they stepped off the stage. I wondered if I should leave the booth and do the same, but my nerves had my body cemented to the fake leather bench seat. Besides, I didn't want to appear jealous or desperate. Even if I was.

A few minutes later, Dax and the guys broke free from the herd of girls, only pulling a select few along with them. Including Liam.

To say seeing him link hands with another girl hurt my pride and confidence was a vast understatement. But I plastered on a fake smile as Dax approached, knowing I needed to be in this for the long haul. The group was following behind Dax, and I could see the look of concern on his own face. Maybe he was having second thoughts. If he was, he pushed those thoughts aside as soon as he slid in the circular booth next to me.

Blaine and Trent slid in behind him with their own women, followed by Liam and some ditzy brunette who was already stripping him with her eyes. I refrained from rolling my eyes as I sat on the end of the seat, directly across from Liam. Neither of us bothered to greet the other. He was staring me down as he slipped his arm around the brunette. My eyes followed his movement. My fists clenched. *What the hell am I thinking?* There was no way I could do this.

Dax's hand gripped my knee below the table, squeezing it as a sign of support as he leaned in to whisper in my ear. "Are you okay?" His voice was low, barely loud enough for me to hear over the music.

I remained focused on Liam, whose eyes had narrowed, watching his friend. I gave Dax a small nod of my head and forced a smile.

A staff member appeared at the table, delivering us all drinks. She placed a dirty martini in front of me. I looked up at her, confused.

"I didn't order this."

"The guys ordered for you."

I looked at Dax, "How did you know what I liked?"

"I didn't order it. Liam did."

I glanced back over at Liam, surprised he'd known my preferred drink. I pushed the glass away. "I'm good, thanks," I said curtly.

He gave me a sardonic smirk. "Suit yourself, princess." Then he turned to the brunette, whispering in her ear, coaxing her to giggle and press her chest into him as she slid her hand up his torso.

It was freaking torture. I felt myself drifting to a dark place, reminded of how I'd felt after seeing the pictures of my boyfriend and friend during my senior year. I couldn't do this. I am *not* doing this. I had too much damn respect for myself. Screw him and screw this plan. It was a stupid plan.

I stood abruptly from the booth to leave. Dax grabbed at my hand, his eyes pleading for me to stay. I ignored him and yanked my hand away, headed for the restrooms. I needed a minute to myself to think. I wasn't sure if I was staying or leaving, but as I rounded the corner into the hallway that led to the bathrooms, I saw the emergency exit at the end of the hall, drawing me to it.

I needed to breathe. I needed air. My legs carried me rapidly straight through the door and into a dark alley. The cool air hit my face as I burst out into the open. I inhaled a deep breath. The door slammed shut behind me, and I stepped to the side, leaning my back against the wall. I closed my eyes, fighting back the tears that were making an undesired appearance.

"Ughhhh!" I screamed out into the dark, needing to release the anger and hurt. *Why did I think I could do this?*

I wasn't strong enough for this. I knew I should probably leave and give up on Liam. It was the safest thing for my sanity and my heart. But the thought of never seeing him again felt unbearable.

I buried my face in my hands, having no idea what to do. The door smashed open, making me jump. "Shit!" I screeched.

Liam flew through, his body heaving and tense. "What the hell are you doing out here, Val?" His gruff voice only added to my anger.

"I needed air," I said, removing my eyes from him. I couldn't even look at him. I could still see him with that stupid brunette who was probably inside waiting for him.

"Then you should've went out front where Joe could keep an eye on you. Not alone in a dark fucking alley," he scowled.

"What the hell do you care? Shouldn't you be back inside with your groupie?"

"Don't push me, princess." He moved in front of me, his body in line with mine.

I glared up at him. "Go. Away."

"No."

"I want to be alone."

"I don't care. I'm not leaving you out here by yourself."

He moved his hands flat against the wall, caging me in. My breaths came out short and heavy. I closed my eyes, hoping the loss of visual stimulation would help me regain my steady breathing. It didn't. I could smell his enticing scent. I could feel the heat radiating from his body and his warm breath sweeping across my sensitive skin. The desire to touch him was bone deep. I tightened my fists at my sides.

"Tell me what's wrong, princess," he whispered softly.

I opened my eyes, finding his face soft. His eyes searching. His lips too near.

"I can't believe you're even asking me that. You know. Please don't pretend like you don't. It only makes it that much harder."

"Harder to do what?"

"To walk away. If I thought you didn't know, I wouldn't be able to walk away. It'd only give me false hope."

He tilted his head back to the sky. I watched his chest rise with a deep inhale before he dropped his head back down to look at me. His eyes hooded over. His breathing became labored. His right hand lowered, sliding under my hair, cupping the back of my neck. Tingles prickled down my spine. His eyes focused on my lips for a moment and then locked on my eyes.

"What are you doing?" I quivered, trying to control the nerve endings that were igniting inside me.

"I'm going to kiss you now, princess," he whispered as his thumb grazed the edge of my jaw. Before I could even comprehend his words, he claimed my mouth, kissing me fiercely.

My earth shattered as waves of lust rolled through me. An indescribable sensation took possession of every inch of my body. He nipped at my bottom lip as his hands descended, gliding down my body. His tongue brushed along the seam of my mouth and I opened, allowing him passage as my hands fisted in his hair.

His palms cupped my bottom, lightly lifting me to my toes. I used the momentum to jump into his arms, wrapping my legs possessively around his hips.

He pushed my back against the brick wall, flattening us against each other. He growled as I rotated my hips up into him, needing the friction I was desperate for. I dropped my hands to grasp his broad shoulders as his lips dropped, roving and sucking my neck, allowing me to catch a rapid breath.

"Liam," I moaned his name, wanting to claim him. Wanting him to claim me. His delicious assault came to an icy halt. His body tensed. His face was still buried. Nerves took over.

"Shit," he groaned.

Oh, no. Please, no. Please don't push me away. I begged internally. If he did, I'd be broken. Everything I was feeling in that moment was like nothing I'd ever felt before. Having felt and experienced his lips and what they did to my body, there was no way I could move on from this. From him.

He lifted his head to look at me, still holding me close. His eyes weren't distant, but he was definitely frustrated.

"We aren't doing this."

"What?" I breathed out my confused fear.

"I'm not doing this in an alley. Not with you."

My mind raced, trying to understand what he was saying. His hand moved to my face as he held me one armed, still pinned against the wall. He brushed the hair from my eyes and kissed me gently before pulling away to look at me. "I want to take you home."

I nodded. Understanding and relief washed over me.

My stomach was in knots and on edge the whole drive home. We'd both shown up to the bar in our own cars. He decided to follow me, and the whole way to my apartment, I prayed he didn't change his mind.

It wasn't until we were parked and getting out of our vehicles that I felt a miniscule amount of relief. I didn't think I would fully believe he wasn't going to leave me until I had him locked inside my apartment with my legs and arms wrapped around him in a vise grip.

He met me at the side of my car and clasped my hand in his as we walked inside my extravagant apartment building. I was nervous about him seeing where I lived. He seemed a little uneasy also, which only increased my own anxiety. I already knew something about my wealth bothered him, and he didn't even know yet how wealthy my family was.

I squeezed his hand tighter, ready to fight to keep him if he tried to get away. He looked at me and grinned, revealing his dimple I loved, knowing exactly what I was doing.

"Don't worry, princess. I'm not going anywhere but your bed."

I smiled back, but still kept my tight grasp on him. Just in case. I preferred to always take precautions.

My fear was unwarranted. We barely made it inside my apartment before his hands and lips were all over me. He lifted me into his arms effortlessly as he continued to kiss me.

"Where's your room?" his husky voice asked between invasions of my mouth.

I pointed in the direction of my bedroom, unable to form words. My mind was focused on one thing, and displaying my mastery of the English language was not it.

He kicked my door closed with his foot as we passed through the threshold of my bedroom. He laid me on the bed, releasing me for the first time as he stood beside me.

His eyes steadily slid over my body with admiration. I took the opportunity to appreciate every inch of his body also. I followed the slow movement of his hands as they reached for the hem of his shirt, lifting it over his head, revealing his rippled chest. My stomach did a tiny somersault.

I mimicked his movement, pulling off my own shirt. His eyes widened, along with his smile—a smile I'd rarely seen before, but would do everything in my power to see all the time from now on, even if it meant walking around naked.

He removed his phone, keys, and wallet from his jeans, setting them beside me on the nightstand, as if it was the most natural thing in the world for him to be here with me in my room. His movements were entirely too slow. And were driving me wild. I wanted him in me. Now. And I had no idea how he was maintaining his control.

I huffed my impatience. After the last few days, I was beyond sexually frustrated. He grinned mischievously, slowly undoing the top button and zipper of his jeans, then dropping them from his waist. He was commando, and every bit of his manhood was present.

I bit my lip in anticipation as he slowly crawled over me. My eager hands slid up his body, locking around his neck as his face hovered above me. He was naked. And he was pressed against me. And for some insane reason, I *wasn't* naked. Before I could right the situation, he kissed me, causing my eyes to flutter shut and my mind to slip off into the abyss.

He licked, kissed, and nipped his way down my body, releasing my breasts from my bra before continuing his course to where I was already hot and aching for him. His lips danced around my navel as he unbuttoned and unzipped my jeans, pulling them from my body along with my lace panties.

His warm breath hit where I wanted him most, sending my hips upward with a whimper. He kissed the side of my hip, pinning them back to the bed, before moving his assault to my apex. Licking. Sucking. Bringing my body to the brink. It felt entirely too good, but I still wanted more. I wanted him inside me, but he was hell bent on making me beg. And I wasn't too proud to do just that. I was desperate for him.

"Please," I let out my breathy plea, fisting the sheets at my side.

"I'm going to take my time with you, princess, so don't bother begging. We're doing this my way."

"Your way is going to kill me."

I felt his mouth grin against my skin as he kissed his way back north before landing on my boobs. He groped and teased them with his tongue. Every move he made was deliberate, firm, yet gentle, despite his earlier warnings that he wouldn't be. He was savoring my body, overwhelming it with desire and desperation. Obviously, his new favorite pastime.

I felt him press against my core as his face appeared over mine, holding himself at my entrance. I wanted to push my hips up to relieve the aching inside, but tamped down the need when he spoke.

"Tell me you're on birth control," he pleaded huskily, brushing my hair to the side of my face as his other hand laid splayed on my hip, pinning it in place.

I nodded, biting my bottom lip. "But that doesn't protect me from other things."

"I'm clean. I've been tested, and I've always used a condom. And I will if you want me to. But I want to feel you, Valerie. All of you."

I wanted him to feel me. And I wanted to feel him too, without anything between us. I'd always used a condom in the past but despite my better judgement, I suddenly realized

I never wanted to use one with him. The thought scared me and made me feel safe at the same time.

I brushed the back of my fingers along the scruff that covered his jaw, studying him. He was giving me something he'd never given anyone before me. I wasn't naive enough to think he hadn't been with numerous women. But they'd never had this Liam. This Liam was mine. This Liam was gentle, caring, and raw.

"Okay," I agreed.

He hastily pressed his lips against mine as his hips thrust forward inside of me, sending a wake of ecstasy through my body. I dug my fingers into his broad shoulders as my body formed to his, adapting to the pleasure that overtook it.

We moved in tandem, our bodies synchronizing. I wrapped my arms and legs around him, pushing my body upward to get closer. He moved to one forearm, wrapping the other around my waist, rolling us, keeping us connected. I pressed my hands to his firm chest, sitting up as I straddled him, circling my hips, feeling empowered by him.

"Fuck, princess," he let out a guttural growl, sitting up to take my breast into his mouth. I clung to him as we both found the release he'd been depriving us of for days. Days that felt like years. I panted his name as my body quaked, and he growled his own release.

I went limp in his arms as he held me, rolling me back to the bed. He laid over me like a security blanket. His head lifted from the crook of my neck, where he had it tucked while we came down from our high.

He had a shit-eating grin plastered on his face, revealing that cute dimple that had me instantly ready for round two. I grinned back. He kissed the tip of my nose, before peeling his body from mine and falling onto his back. I frowned at the loss of his weight.

"I should go."

Wait. What?

I didn't respond. I wasn't even sure I'd heard him right. If he was saying what I thought, then his need for a brisk departure burned. He rolled to his side, looking down at me. His smile dropped when he saw the look on my face.

"What's wrong?"

"Why are you trying to leave?"

"I don't do overnights."

Right. The hard, distant Liam was resurfacing.

"Wow." I shook my head with incredulity. "So, now what? I'm just like all the slutty groupies you sleep with?"

His jaw ticked and his eyes darkened. "No."

"What's next? If I'm lucky, you'll screw me in the storage closet after the next concert?" My voice raised an octave. I was seething.

"Stop," he warned me. I could tell he was struggling to keep his guard up, so I pushed him more, forcing him to lower it.

"Then don't treat me like the other women you've been with."

"I wasn't."

"You were." I looked at him pointedly. "The moment you decided you were leaving. If you leave, you're cheapening everything that just happened between us. And I won't be able to forgive you for that."

He closed his eyes and let out a heavy sigh before reopening them. "You want me to stay."

I nodded, even though it wasn't a question.

"Then I'll stay," he said, caressing my face.

He leaned in and kissed me gently. A kiss that was laced with an apology. I pulled him closer, deepening the kiss. He rolled to his back, pulling me with him. I rested my head on his chest and threw my leg over his as he held me close. We relaxed into the silence, letting the earlier anger dissipate. Then my brain decided to return.

"Liam?" I asked barely above a whisper.

"Yes, princess?" His fingers trailed lightly up and down my back.

"The day I met you on the highway...did you already know who I was?" I hesitated asking, but curiosity had me wondering if he knew me from the tabloids.

"Yes."

"How?"

"The day you dropped your car off at the shop was the first time I saw you. You were the most gorgeous woman I'd ever seen. I had to know your name. I looked at the paperwork after you left."

I lifted my head, surprised by his admission. He was staring at the ceiling, but his eyes turned to me with my movement.

"Why were you so cold toward me?"

"Pillow talk wasn't part of the deal," he said, attempting to shut down my line of questioning.

"It is now."

"Go to sleep, princess. Unless you prefer me to leave."

The humor in his voice told me his threat wasn't real, but I knew I'd pushed him enough for one day. I let it go. For now.

The thought that he might have an issue with my upbringing and judged me for it was simmering in the back of my mind. My heart was already falling, but my brain was warning me to be cautious. That deep-seated mistrust was pushing to the forefront.

I rolled away from him to my side, suddenly needing to distance myself. His hulky arms wrapped around me, pulling my back into his chest.

"Where do you think you're going?"

"I didn't think cuddling was part of the deal either," I snapped.

He chuckled, finding my sudden bad mood amusing. "It is now, princess." He kissed the crown of my head, instantly relaxing my body and mind.

I closed my eyes, forcing myself to get out of my head. I breathed in his scent and let his steady breathing lull me to sleep.

CHAPTER 8

I hummed my happiness in my sleepy state as dreams of Liam's hard, naked body and grinning face sizzled in my brain. I reached my hand blindly across the bed, feeling for that particular body. My eyes shot open.

I turned my head to the empty side of the bed, where Liam should have been. Gone. I looked at the nightstand for his things. Gone. He'd left me. Alone. No goodbye. No sweet kiss. No "I'll call you later." Just gone. Like it never happened.

"That mother...that son of a...ugh," I growled, slamming my arms against the mattress. "Jerk!"

"Everything okay, princess?" Liam's voice interrupted my angry rant and thoughts of plotting his murder.

I shot up ramrod straight into a sitting position, the bed sheet dropping around my waist. He was leaning his perfect, half-cladded body against the open doorframe, holding a coffee mug in his hand, a smile on his face and an amused gleam in his eyes.

"You're still here?" I asked, more as a rhetorical question, unable to believe he was standing there, looking content and gorgeous in only his jeans.

"I am."

"You're shirtless."

His eyes ignited as they focused on my chest. "So are you, princess," he responded hungrily, pulling his bottom lip between his teeth, releasing it slowly.

I looked down, realizing I was still naked and my perky boobs were on display for his viewing pleasure. "Oh." I blushed, grabbing the sheet, tucking it under my armpits to conceal myself.

"Nuh, uh..." He shook his head. "Don't cover those beauties up."

His voice came out husky as he stalked toward me. He set his coffee down on the table before crawling over me, forcing my back onto the mattress as he positioned himself between my legs.

"I thought you left." I looked up into his captivating greys as he drifted above me, holding himself on his forearms.

After seeing his personal items and jeans gone, I didn't think to look for his shirt or shoes—both of which were still laying on the floor, just out of my view.

"No. But I need to go soon. I have to get to the shop."

"I don't want you to go yet." I traced my finger along the black lines of the tattoo that stretched across his bicep. I wondered about the story behind it.

"I don't want to either." He gave me a swift kiss.

"When can I see you again?"

"I'm not sure," he said, frowning. "We leave tomorrow morning for a show out of town."

I turned away from him, discontented with his answer. If I hadn't memorized his event schedule for the next week—okay two weeks—I would've thought he was brushing me off.

"What about tonight?" I asked hopefully, looking back at him.

"I have practice with the guys after work."

"Okay." My delivery of the word was short and tight.

I was trying not to let his busy schedule hurt my confidence, but that was easier said than done. I didn't want to be *that* girl. Needy after one night of mind-blowing sex. I wasn't even sure what *this* was.

"Come watch us."

"I don't want to distract you," I lied.

"I want you there."

"Since when?" I gave him a half-hearted smile, thinking about how he'd always seemed so bothered by my presence in the past.

"Since, now." He pulled the sheet away from my naked body as he brought his mouth to my collar bone.

He kissed his way across my clavicle from right to left, melting all my fears away. I weaved my fingers into his hair, closing my eyes. If he kept doing this, there was no way I was letting him leave for work.

"Don't start something you can't finish," I warned him.

"Trust me, princess...I can finish," he growled playfully.

I laughed. As he moved down my body, my laughter was replaced with heavy breathing. My thoughts were replaced with dreams. My body was revived with a new appreciation for the mechanics of his tongue.

He finished. I finished. We both *definitely* finished. A few times.

∾

"Been doing some horseback riding?" Lexie goaded as I slowly and uncomfortably walked into the kitchen, sated and sore after Liam's departure for work. "Or should I say bareback riding?"

I'd definitely done some riding, and Liam was definitely hung like a horse, but I didn't comment on that. Instead, I just gave her my eat-shit-and-die look. She snickered behind her coffee mug.

"From the heavy panting and moaning I heard over the last twelve hours, and the fact that I saw Liam's backside disappearing out the front door this morning...I'm going to take a wild guess that things went as planned last night."

"You're a real Sherlock Holmes, Lex. If this coffee gig doesn't work out for you, you have options." I gave her a sarcastic smirk.

"Ouch." She feigned hurt as she grabbed at her heart. "I would've expected you to be in a better mood this morning."

"I am. I just need coffee. And food. And something for the pain between my legs." I grabbed a coffee mug and granola bar before gently taking a seat next to her at the bar.

"What's your plan today?"

"Probably start the search for a new agent. What about you?"

"I have the day off and so does Jake. We're going to hang at his place."

"I guess things are going better for the two of you?"

A sheepish smile crept onto her face as she shrugged. "He is definitely trying harder."

"Good. I just hope it isn't short lived."

She rolled her eyes, letting out an exasperated sigh. "Don't worry about me, Val. I can take care of myself."

"Doesn't mean you should have to. And you're my friend. It's my duty to worry about you. The same way you do about me." I gave her a no-arguments-allowed look.

"Thanks. But I really think this time is different."

"I'm going to take your word for it. But if you need me to kick his butt, just let me know. And by kick his butt, I mean have my brother's henchmen take care of him," I said, grinning slyly.

She snort-laughed. We both knew I was only half joking. Jake could be a committed and doting boyfriend when he wanted to be, but it was always a phase. A phase that ended with Lexie secretively crying herself to sleep after he decided she was too much of an inconvenience for him.

"Do you want to hang out tonight?" She changed the subject from her and Jake.

"Actually...Liam asked me to come watch them practice," I said, trying for nonchalance, not looking at her eyes, which I knew would be probing.

"Interesting..."

"What?" I looked over at her.

"Nothing." She shook her head, staring down at her food.

"No, not nothing. You can't just say that and not tell me what's so interesting."

"I'm just a little surprised. I didn't expect you two to be seeing each other again so soon. That's all."

"Why is that?" I asked defensively.

"Oh come on, Val. We both know he is the quintessential hit-it-and-quit-it guy."

I looked down at my granola bar and coffee, suddenly not feeling so hungry.

"I'm sorry. This is all coming out completely wrong. I'm saying it's interesting, because he's obviously into you. It's a good thing." She gave me a wry smile as she nudged my shoulder.

"Well, I wouldn't be so sure about that. I basically had to guilt him into staying overnight and inviting me to watch him practice."

"Give yourself and him some credit, Val. He doesn't come across as the type of guy who can easily be guilted into anything if there weren't some feelings there. Besides, I doubt it was guilt making him want to spend more time with you. You're a total package."

"I am, aren't I?" I agreed, grinning and winking at her.

"I need to remind myself not to stroke your ego too much. It's really starting to go to your head." She laughed.

The rest of the day I focused on finding a new agent. It became an increasingly challenging task as the day slowly dragged on. Thoughts of my night with Liam kept possessing my mind, making me anxious for the hours to pass, so I could see him again. And a small inkling of what Lexie had said about Liam was floating around too, only adding to my anxiousness.

I hadn't heard from him since he left that morning. I knew he was working and likely busy, but I was driving myself mad waiting for some sort of communication from him. He'd promised to send me the address to his uncle's place—apparently, that was where they had always practiced since becoming a band—but as the hours passed with no word from him, I started to wonder if maybe I'd unexpectedly become a one-night stand.

I glanced at my phone for the umpteenth time to make sure it was still on and fully charged. I double and then tripled checked to make sure I didn't have it on silent, turned it to the highest volume—just in case—then set it back down on my desk. I strummed my fingers on the desk as I tried to refocus my attention on finding an agent. I submitted my headshots and material to a few more potential agents before giving up for the day.

It was barely after two in the afternoon. I crawled into my bed and picked up a book I'd been reading, hoping it could distract me from my thoughts. My eyes felt heavy as I began to read. I fought the urge to sleep but lost the battle.

My phone chimed loudly, startling me awake. I hastily twisted at my waist, reaching my arm behind me to hunt out my phone. I lost my balance, rolling straight off the edge of the bed and landing on the floor with a thump. I groaned, crawling to my knees to get up off the floor while removing the sheets that were twisted around my legs.

I picked up my phone off my desk just as it dinged a second time. Both texts were from Liam. The first was simply an address, but the second had me grinning from ear to ear.

L: Two cold showers and I still can't get you out of my mind.
V: Work going well, then? ;)

L: Work sucks. All I can think about is tasting you again...and again...

I blushed as the heat rose throughout my body. A simple text was all it took.

V: I'm glad your day has been as productive as mine.

L: You dreaming about me, princess?

V: Maybe...

V: Get some rest. You're gonna need your energy for tonight. See ya soon.

I fell backwards onto my bed, clutching my phone to my chest. *Just a few more hours.* A few more hours before I'd see him. This man was going to be the death of me. I could already see it. My obituary will read: Valerie Blackwood, spontaneously combusted from sexual frustration.

~

My GPS assured me I'd arrived as I pulled to the curb outside an older, modest home in the Atwater Village neighborhood. There was a narrow strip of concrete drive that led to the back of the old, muted gray craftsman-style home, already lined with cars parked bumper to bumper.

Assuming the British lady's voice would not lead me astray, I shut off my car and took a deep breath. I had no idea why I was stalling. I'd been impatiently waiting for this moment all day. Now that it was here, I was panicking. I closed my eyes while I gave myself a little internal pep talk.

He likes me. Otherwise, he wouldn't have invited me. He is just a guy. A hot guy who makes my ovaries go into overdrive and my body want to explode—

Tap. Tap.

"Shit!" I jolted, grabbing at my chest from the knock on my window.

I turned to a peering old man bent down, looking into my car, signaling for me to roll down my window. I clicked my keys in the ignition to accessory and cracked my window open slightly.

"You lost, honey?" the old man asked with a kind smile.

He was dressed from head to toe in a pair of dark coveralls that were stained from the day's work. I glanced at his chest, where the name 'Frankie' was stitched over his left pec. I shook my head and rolled up my window, stepping out of the car.

"You must be Uncle Frankie." I smiled at him as I put out my hand to shake his.

"You must be the girlfriend." He grinned back, shaking my hand.

I blushed, delighted by the thought, but at the same time feeling embarrassed for not correcting him. "Valerie, but you can call me Val."

"Beautiful name for a beautiful girl." He winked. The old charmer. "Well come on, sweetheart. You can have a seat with me while the boys wrap up their session." He waved his arm for me to follow.

Frankie led me along the side of the house, up the driveway toward the music that was echoing through the neighborhood. The sound of Liam's voice had my body wanting to push past Frankie and break out in a full-on sprint. But I maintained a casual pace behind him, stopping where a single lawn chair and cooler sat facing the garage in the driveway.

"Take a seat, hon." Frankie directed me to the old lawn chair.

I obliged, lowering myself into the chair, unable to take my eyes off Liam, who currently had his back to me. Frankie walked away, grabbing another chair, unfolding it and placing it on the other side of the cooler.

Liam turned, his eyes brightening as they focused on me, flashing that grinning dimple I loved so much. He winked before starting to croon again into the mic. Frankie reached into the cooler, pulling out a bottle of beer. "Would you like one?" he offered, holding up the beer to me.

"I'm good. Thank you, though," I smiled, hoping I didn't offend him. "I'm a lightweight. Probably best I steer clear of alcohol since I'm driving," I explained further.

"Beautiful and smart." He twisted the cap off the bottle, toasting the air toward me. "Sounds like he lucked out in the girlfriend department." He gave me another kind smile that reached his eyes.

I laughed nervously at him referring to me as the girl-friend again. Liam and I hadn't really defined what was happening with us, and I was worried that he might not appreciate me allowing his uncle to think we were more than whatever we were.

I leaned in toward Frankie, trying to figure out how to explain our relationship to him. "I'm sorry, I don't want to give the wrong impression…but I'm not actually his girl-friend…at least…I'm not sure if I am…I—"

"No worries, sweetheart." He patted my hand. "I'll let you

in on a little secret. I'm not actually his uncle, either." He winked at me with a playful grin.

My eyes widened with curiosity, but before I could inquire further, the deafening music stopped, creating a quieter atmosphere. I looked toward Liam and the rest of the guys as they joked around with each other, discussing the song they'd just played. Liam removed his guitar, laying it aside, and walked toward me.

"Hey there, princess." He grasped my hands, pulling me from my chair.

His use of the word 'princess' now sent a fluttering to my heart. He wrapped my arms around his waist and pulled me closer as he placed his forehead on mine, smiling down at me. "I guess you found the place okay."

"Yep. And your uncle has been keeping me company."

"Don't listen to a word he says. He's a crazy old man filled with nothing but lies," he teased.

Frankie huffed, pretending to be offended by Liam's assessment.

"You see how he treats me, darlin'?" He looked at me for sympathy as he shook his head. "Is that any way to treat your favorite uncle?"

"Just cuz you're my only uncle doesn't make you my favorite," Liam teased him some more.

"Watch it kid," he playfully scowled at Liam. "I may be old, but I can still kick your ass."

Liam threw his head back, releasing a booming laugh. I smiled cheesily, feeling his chest vibrate against me with his laughter. I liked this Liam. This Liam was light and happy. Something I could get used to. Something I could fall for. Hard. The thought scared and excited me at the same time.

He smiled back down at me. "See what I mean? Lies."

"I don't know...if I had to place a bet, I'd put my money on your uncle." I grinned up at Liam.

"I knew I liked this girl." Frankie nodded his head toward me.

Liam laughed some more before dropping a kiss on my lips and releasing me all too soon.

"We have a few more songs to run through and then we'll be done. Don't let him turn you against me in the meantime." Liam held his hand in mine as he teasingly glanced over at his uncle.

"You don't need any help with that, man. You can do that all on your own," Dax said, coming up behind us, slapping Liam on the shoulder. "How's it going, Val?" Dax asked as he leaned in, giving me a quick kiss on the cheek.

Liam's face hardened with a warning look. Dax stepped back, throwing his hands up in surrender with a mischievous smile as he winked at me. I shook my head at his risky move and then tightened my hold on Liam's hand, drawing his eyes back to me. Trent and Blaine followed behind Dax, greeting me from a distance before they all went back to practicing the last couple of songs of the set for their show this week.

I chatted with Frankie between songs, learning he was a retired vet who inherited the body shop from his father. He had no kids of his own, and the way he talked about Liam made me think he thought of him more as a son than a nephew—or I guess a nephew. I was still curious about his comment from earlier. I wasn't sure if he was joking with me to help me feel less nervous or if he was being serious.

"Liam tells me you had some issues with the cost of

repairs to your car. I apologize about that. We normally would've called you. But I had a bit of a sick spell, and it got overlooked. I'll honor the original price, though."

"Oh. Right. About that. I might've overreacted a little." I shifted my eyes down to the ground momentarily, remembering my reaction to seeing Liam there. "I know it's a fair price. I'll pay the full amount. I'm sorry to hear you were sick. I hope everything's okay?"

"Nothing to worry too much about. And I insist on you only paying what we quoted you. I won't take any more than that."

"I insist on paying you in full."

He chuckled. "I get the feeling you usually get your way."

"Your feeling would be accurate. Mostly." I grinned at him.

He shook his head as he continued to chuckle. "How bout we compromise and split the difference?"

I pretended to mull it over before nodding my head, "Deal." I put out my hand for us to shake on it. He shook my hand, squeezing it with a fond pat with his other hand before releasing it.

Shortly after our negotiation, the guys finished their practice. Pulling out their own folding chairs, they joined us in a circle on the driveway as they drank a few beers. I listened and watched with fascination as they joked and laughed, telling various stories about one another.

Frankie added his own animated stories about the four of them and their crazy antics. Liam held my hand in his lap the whole time, never releasing it once, causing my body to be on a constant euphoric high.

As the night fell, the conversation slowed and the guys

decided to head out. They were leaving in the morning and needed to prepare for their trip out of town. After saying our goodbyes, Frankie, Liam, and I stood in the driveway, watching the guys depart. Liam wrapped his arms around me from behind, resting his chin on the top of my head as Frankie raised his beer bottle in the air toward Dax's truck as it reversed down the driveway.

"Well, I guess it's time for this old man to turn in," Frankie said, turning toward us as the headlights disappeared. "Val, it was a pleasure to meet you. Don't be a stranger."

I moved to loosen Liam's hold on me, stepping toward Frankie to give him a hug. "It was really good to meet you too, Frankie. I'll stop by the shop soon to give you that check."

He nodded at me as we ended our hug, giving Liam a pat on the shoulder before turning to walk into the house. Being alone with him for the first time since I'd arrived had me suddenly feeling nervous again.

"So…" I glanced down at my feet, fidgeting with the hem of my shirt like a shy school girl, not sure if I should leave or stay. Not sure if he *wanted* me to leave or stay.

"So…" he replied softly. He stepped forward, pressing his body back against mine as he weaved his fingers through my hair, cupping the back of my head in his palm.

My heartrate increased with his touch. I tilted my head back for a better view of his handsome face and breathtaking eyes.

"I'm glad you came."

"Me too." I stalled, waiting for some kind of signal of what he wanted.

"You're cute when you're nervous."

"I'm not nervous," I lied.

He smiled, shaking his head incredulously as he retrieved my hand that was tangled in my hair, removing it and holding it tight in his own. "Do you want to come up?"

"Is that what you want?"

"I wouldn't have asked if it wasn't, princess."

"Then, yes."

He lowered his head, pressing a firm kiss to my lips before breaking us apart, pulling me to follow him up a set of stairs on the side of the garage. He opened a door that led into a small garage apartment. I followed him inside, stepping past him as he closed and locked the door behind us. I looked around the open studio apartment, taking it all in.

It was minimally furnished with all the basic necessities. There was a small kitchen and bathroom to the right, which stretched across the back of the open space. A couch, coffee table, and large flat-screen TV were situated off to the left of the door. There was a bed in the far corner, opposite the makeshift living room. The whole place could fit in my over-sized closet.

"So this is where you live?"

"Yep." He moved around me, hastily picking up some scattered clothes and trash. "Sorry. I didn't get a chance to clean up. I know it's probably not as impressive as what you're used to."

I stepped toward him, grabbing his arm, stopping his efforts. "Don't," I said firmly.

He halted his movement, looking at me confused.

"Don't change anything for me. Don't try to live up to

some kind of standard you think I have. Just be you. All I want is you. However you come."

He stared at me with a new intensity. Before I knew what was happening, he lifted me into his arms, slamming his mouth to mine, dropping everything he'd had in his hands. I wrapped my whole body around him as he carried me to the couch. He fell back onto the couch, situating me so I was straddled on his lap, all while continuing his yummy assault on my lips.

He pulled back, placing his hands on the sides of my face, stopping my own advances. "Where did you come from, princess?" he asked with a soft wonderment.

"New York." I smiled teasingly.

He laughed and shook his head, letting out an amused sigh. "You're going to ruin me."

"I'm scared you're the one that's going to ruin me." My smile slipped from my face with the thought.

His own lightheartedness slipped away with my words as he focused on my eyes with a stern expression. "I don't want to. And I'm going to try my hardest not to. You're special, Val. And I want to do right by you...but—" he stopped himself, his brows pinched with worry.

"But what?" I encouraged, hoping he'd continue. He didn't. "Talk to me...you can tell me anything. I want you to be able to tell me anything."

"There are things in my past...things I know would have you running straight out that door without even a glance back. And you should."

"Never. I'm stronger than you think. I can handle whatever it is."

He pushed my hair behind my ear. "I know you're strong.

It's one of the things I admire about you. But it's not something you should have to deal with. It's not something I want you to deal with."

"Liam...I know what it's like to worry that people are stereotyping you, making assumptions about who you are as a person. I promise I won't do that. I won't push you to tell me. I just hope someday you will."

He leaned in, placing a gentle kiss on my lips before locking his eyes with mine. "I'm sorry, Val."

"For what?"

"For whoever hurt you. Whoever it was didn't even deserve to have the opportunity."

"It doesn't matter now. It made me a stronger person, opened my eyes to the truths of the world. I was naive for a long time. I'm not anymore."

I dropped my eyes down to my hands, remembering that eye-opening experience. His hand slipped under my chin, bringing my eyes back to his.

"You amaze me, princess. I'm sorry if I made you feel otherwise by pushing you away before. I was just trying to protect you."

"And now?"

"Now...I'm just hoping I don't fuck this up."

"I won't let you." I grinned reassuringly, threading my fingers through his hair, reuniting our lips with my determination.

I knew it was a reckless promise. There was an incontestable connection between us that was so strong I continued to ignore all the warnings he'd given me. I felt as if I was making the best and worst decision of my life.

We spent the rest of the night relaxing in each other's

arms on the couch, learning trivial little facts about each other. As insignificant as they were, it helped me understand who he was. He told me more about his friends and how they met and became Derailed. His eyes would light up with boyish happiness as he spoke about them and music in general. We joked and flirted with a natural banter.

My stomach growled, interrupting our conversation. I hadn't realized how late it'd gotten, and apparently, I was starving.

"Shit, Val. I'm sorry. I should've thought about dinner. Do you want me to order something?"

"No, it's okay. I'll be fine with just something small. Do you have anything to eat in that kitchen of yours?"

"I can make a mean batch of mac n' cheese." He grinned proudly.

I laughed. "Mac n' cheese it is."

He kissed my lips before releasing me to head into the kitchen to prepare our dinner. I stood from the couch, stretching my legs, and took a mini tour around his mini home. The place was mostly scattered with automotive and music magazines, clothes, guitars, and typical manly para-phernalia.

A small keyboard sat on a stand at the end of his bed with a stool. There was a small table beside his bed that held a picture frame and a lamp. It was the only picture in the whole place, so naturally I was curious.

I walked to his bed, taking a seat on the edge as I picked up the frame. It was a young couple with a small, smiling boy who couldn't have been more than two or three years old. I would know those grey eyes and grinning dimple anywhere. It was a picture of Liam, and what I assumed to be his parents. He hadn't mentioned them once in our conversations. In fact, beyond Frankie, he never brought up his family.

It made me wonder where they were and why he hadn't mentioned them. I wondered if they weren't close. *If that's the case, then why does he keep a picture of them beside his bed?* Lost in my thoughts, I hadn't realized he'd approached. He snatched the picture frame from my hands and placed it back on the nightstand.

"The food's ready," he said, a little colder than I expected.

I peered up at him, concerned I'd overstepped some kind of line I wasn't aware existed. "Liam?"

"I don't want to talk about it, Val." He turned his back on me, walking back into the kitchen, where he dished up two bowls of mac n' cheese.

I remained on the edge of the bed, feeling insecure with my hands under my thighs, watching him. He grabbed the bowls and walked back to the couch, where he placed them side by side on the coffee table. He turned back to me with an impassive expression. I tried reading his eyes but only found hollowness.

"Do you still want something to eat?" he asked flatly.

I nodded my head and stood from the bed to join him on the couch. After a few minutes of uncomfortable silence, I decided to take a leap. "Liam...I'm sorry. I didn't mean to intrude."

He stopped his hand as it moved toward his mouth. He lowered his fork back down to his bowl, releasing the utensil with a clatter. The palms of his hands went over his face as he rubbed them harshly across it. Resting his elbows on his knees, he released a frustrated sigh.

"Don't apologize, Val. You didn't do anything wrong. I'm the one being an ass. I'm sorry." He rotated his head to look at me, the sincerity of his apology in his eyes.

I placed my hand on his arm, hoping my touch would soften his hardened body. Crawling into his lap, I ran my fingers through his hair as I massaged his head, hoping to relieve some more tension. He held his forehead against mine with his eyes closed. We remained silent. Just breathing.

He finally pulled away where I could study his face. I could tell he wanted to speak but wasn't sure what to say or maybe where to start. Maybe he truly wasn't ready to tell me about them. And I was okay with that.

"You don't have to talk about it," I said, offering him an out.

"I want to. I want to tell you. It's just not something I like to think about."

"The picture…it's of your parents?" I asked, trying to help lead the conversation for him.

He nodded.

"Are you close?"

"We were."

"You're not anymore?"

"As close as we can be."

I looked at him confused, unsure of what he meant by that. He took a deep breath, exhaling before he continued.

"My family is dead. They died in a car crash on the interstate when I was ten."

A tear welled in the corner of my eye and the rough pad of his thumb swept it away as it rolled down my cheek. "I'm sorry."

"It's okay, princess. It was a long time ago."

"So your uncle took you in after that?" I tried to connect the dots.

"Not exactly."

"What do you mean?"

He shook his head, then tilted it back to rest on the back of the couch, closing his eyes for a moment. When he raised it back up to look at me he had a stony expression. "I don't want to talk about this any further."

As much as I wanted to push him to continue, I didn't. It was obviously hard for him to tell me what he already had. "Okay." I planted a small kiss on his lips. "Thank you for telling me."

He pulled my head back to his, giving me a soft kiss, following it with another kiss and then another. Each kiss intensified until he was kissing me aggressively, as if he was trying to lose himself in me. I didn't mind. I wanted to be there for him. However he needed me.

He stood, carrying us to his bed, where we got lost in each other for the rest of the night.

CHAPTER 9

"How'd it go last night?" Lexie asked as she efficiently worked at making a couple of lattes for some customers.

"Good. Great, actually." I smiled, facing her after I rang up the last customer in the long line of people we had this morning. It had been a steady stream of crankiness, everyone in desperate need of their caffeine fix. Despite their less-than-friendly attitudes, the happiness I was feeling couldn't be ruined.

"I'm glad. You seem happier."

"How about you? Did you spend all day and night with Jake?"

"No. He had plans with his friends last night. Guy stuff."

"Sorry."

"It's fine. I was more than happy to miss out on watching them play video games. Plus, it gave me some 'me time' to veg out. We're all going to the beach to

128

camp out for Fourth of July. You should come. Bring Liam."

"That sounds fun, but…"

"But what?"

"Will Caleb be there? That could get kind of awkward."

She laughed. "I think Caleb has figured it out."

"Really?"

"Yeah. Jake bluntly told him when he asked about you yesterday."

"Oh. Well that makes me feel like a jerk. I should've probably told him myself."

"Don't beat yourself up over it."

I wouldn't. I knew Caleb was a player of sorts, but it never bothered me. I was never really interested in him beyond the physical.

"Do you think they'd be okay if I invited all the guys from Derailed? I'm not sure if they will come, but—"

"Hell, yeah! Everyone likes bragging about hanging out with them."

I shook my head as I laughed. "Okay. I'll send Liam a text when it gets slow again," I said, turning back to the newly forming line.

The rest of my double shift was long and exhausting. I, unfortunately, never had a chance to text Liam. By the time I got home and took a shower to wash away the coffee-bean aroma, I was barely able to hold my eyes open.

I crawled into bed, ready to watch some TV and pass-out for the night. I settled under the covers and picked up my phone. I had a new text from Ava, asking me to join them for dinner this weekend at their place.

V: Sure. Mind if I bring a friend?

A: A friend? As in Lexie?

V: No...;)

A: You've been holding out on me?!!

V: LOL...maybe. It's new.

A: Details!!!

V: Lunch tomorrow? Don't say anything to Rhett.

A: RME. See you then!

I grinned, giddy and excited to tell Ava about Liam. I knew I needed to get her on my side before introducing him to my overprotective brother. Rhett was not going to be easy on Liam. I just hoped he didn't have Liam running away from me by the end of our dinner. I also hoped Liam would actually agree to have dinner with my family.

I navigated through my phone to my text conversation with him. He'd been sending me texts all day on their drive. Texts that had me heated and missing him desperately. I opened the one I'd missed when I was in the shower.

L: About to go on stage...it's going to be hard to focus. All I want right now is for that wonderful mouth of yours to be on me.

I responded, even though I figured he was probably already on stage.

V: I'm sure you'll be fine. You'll have all those girls screaming your name. ;)

I sent the text as a joke, but if I was honest with myself, I was concerned about all the women who'd be throwing themselves and their undergarments at him. His response came immediately.

L: The only woman I want is you, princess. Going on stage. Call you soon.

I smiled sheepishly, setting my phone aside. I curled up in my blankets, snuggling into them as I watched TV, trying to stay awake for his call and ignore my insecurities.

～

I searched blindly for my phone that was ringing with the sound of Liam's lyrical voice. I'd downloaded one of my favorite Derailed songs and set it as Liam's ring tone. I dug through my covers in the pitch black of my room, grasping for the phone, connecting the call just before it rung off.

"Hello," I answered tiredly, my eyes remaining closed, barely registering my actions.

"Hey, princess. I woke you. Sorry. I needed to hear your voice." Liam's amped-up, sexy voice in my ear was like a dream.

"No. I'm awake," I lied with a yawn, cuddling back down into the warmth of my bed and the softness of my pillow.

He chuckled.

"How was the show?"

"Good. It would've been better if you were here to watch."

"I wish I was there," I whispered.

"Next time."

"Mmhmm...Liam?"

"Yes, princess?"

"Is it weird I miss you already? Does that freak you out?" I'm not sure what had me being so honest with him—maybe it was that I felt I was still dreaming.

"No." I heard the smile in his voice. "I miss you, too."

"It scares me," I admitted to the Liam in my dream.

"Why?"

"I guess cuz I've only known you a matter of days…keep my heart safe Liam…it's all yours."

There was silence as I drifted back into a deep sleep. I heard the soft timbre of Liam's voice one more time: "Sleep well, princess. I'll be back soon." Then it was gone.

~

"So, how long are you gonna stall before telling me about this new man in your life?" Ava asked with an anxious smile. We were having lunch on the patio of a little café a few blocks from her office.

I looked up from picking at my chicken salad and smiled at her mischievously. "I think maybe just a little longer. I like watching you squirm."

She rolled her eyes at me. "If you want me to help you with your brother, you better spill it. Now," she demanded.

"Okay! Okay!" I laughed. "Well…he works at the body shop where I got my car fixed." I decided to leave out the fact that we'd *first* met on the side of the road, when her car got a flat tire.

"Ooh…so he's good with his hands." She winked.

I blushed. "*And*…he's a musician in a really awesome band. He's the lead singer."

Her eyes widened. "And with his mouth. He sounds sexy already."

"I think your hormones are in overdrive right now." I raised an eyebrow at her.

She waved a hand at me in dismissal. "Just keep going. What's the name of his band?"

"Derailed."

"Oh! I've heard of them! Joce had me listen to some of their music the other day. Wow. They're really good."

"Yep." I smiled proudly.

"I can't wait to meet him. You're bringing him Sunday night for dinner then?"

"Yeah. Well, hopefully. He's been out of town for a couple shows the last few days, so I haven't exactly asked him yet."

"Well, I'll do what I can to keep your brother in check. But we both know how he is so…no promises."

I let out an exasperated sigh. "Yes. I appreciate any help you can offer. I really like him, and I don't want Rhett scaring him off. Don't tell him who he is either. I don't need him doing a stupid background check before he even meets him."

I was also kind of worried what he might find. Liam had already admitted he had some kind of past he wasn't willing to discuss right now. I didn't need Rhett getting in the middle of that and forming opinions on the matter. Whatever it was in Liam's past, I wanted to hear it from him. Not from some file my brother's security team put together.

She smiled at me knowingly. We wrapped up our lunch with discussions of her pregnancy and the nursery. She was nearing the end of her last trimester, and I was anxious to meet my little nephew.

"I'm so excited for you, Val." Ava hugged me outside of her office. "It's been a long time since I've seen you this happy about a guy."

I hugged her back. "Thanks. He does make me happy."

"I'll see you guys Sunday night. Love you."

"Love you, too," I said before she disappeared through the door of her office.

~

After dropping Ava back at work, I headed toward Frankie's body shop. Liam would be pulling into town soon and said he had to head straight to the shop. I figured I could kill two birds with one stone: pay Frankie for my car repairs *and* greet the sexy man I'd been missing for the last forty-eight hours. Texting and talking on the phone just wasn't enough. I needed to see him. I needed to touch him. I walked through the customer entrance of the body shop to the familiar dinging of the bell over the door.

Once again, I found it empty of all personnel, but this time I didn't have to wait for long. Frankie entered the room with a big smile on his face.

"Hey, hon! Must be my lucky day, seeing that pretty face of yours."

"Hey Frankie." I grinned back, wrapping him in a big hug. The short, stocky old man was becoming one of my favorite people. "I have a check for you."

"I leave town for two days and you're already moving on to my uncle?"

My heart skipped a beat at the sound of Liam's voice behind me. I turned to see his devilish smirk, and his thick arms braced on the open doorframe leading to the shop. He was leaning forward, his hands gripping the frame, looking like a sexy mechanic straight out of GQ magazine. I let my eyes roam, soaking in every bit of that rippled body.

"What can I say? He's a hard man to resist," I said with a smirk.

Frankie's deep, throaty laugh resounded behind me and was instantly joined by Liam's. He walked toward me with an effortless swagger.

"Princess, I don't know what I'm gonna do with that smart mouth of yours." He gripped my hips with his strong hands, connecting our bodies.

"I can think of a few things," I murmured, staring up at him as my body hummed.

Liam's eyes brightened as he bit his bottom lip, pressing closer to me, where I felt the pressure of his desire on my thigh.

Frankie coughed, pretending to clear his throat. "I'm gonna head back into the shop. Val, you can just leave the check with Liam." He shook his head with amusement, chuckling as he left us by ourselves.

"Tell me you're off the rest of the day," Liam commanded, never once letting his eyes drift from me, even with his uncle's interruption.

I nodded eagerly. "Yep."

His head tilted down, lavishing my neck with a series of delicate kisses before he placed his lips at my ear.

"Good. Because I'm taking you home. Now. I need to be wrapped up in you before my show. And tonight, after my show, I'm gonna take my time, savoring every curve of that sweet, sexy body…" His hands began to travel, roaming my body with the lightest touch, heavy with intentions. "I'm gonna slowly work my way all around it, saving the best spots for last. It's going to be painful, princess, so you need to prepare yourself."

I released a breathy whimper.

He growled, planting his lips on the back of my neck, burying his face in my hair. "I fucking love that sound. Those wonderful noises you make when I'm filling your body—the memory of those has been stuck in my head for the last two days." He moved so his face was aligned with mine. "We need to leave before I take you on that counter."

I couldn't agree more. I gave him a quick kiss on the lips and grinned. "Your place or mine?"

"Mine. It's closer." He grabbed my hand, hurriedly pulling me out of the shop, through the door and toward my car. "I'll drive. Give me your keys."

I handed them to him as we reached my passenger-side door, where he placed me inside, leaving me with a searing kiss before closing the car door. The man drove like an experienced NASCAR driver. He had us in his bed and naked in a matter of seconds.

Later that night, I relaxed on top of Liam with my arm and leg draped across him as we lay in my bed. As soon as they finished their last song of the night, Liam had rushed me out of the bar and to my house, not even bothering to stay for a single beer with his bandmates. I lifted my head, resting my chin over my hand on his chest.

"I have something I want to ask you, but I don't want to freak you out."

He flashed his dimple at me. "What's that?"

"And if you want to say no, I'll completely understand."

"Ask me, princess."

I took a deep breath and squeezed my eyes closed, afraid to see the expression on his face when I asked. I released the words rapidly in one breath before I lost my courage. "Will you have dinner with my family Sunday night?"

When he didn't respond I slowly opened one eye to look at him. He was watching me, expressionless. My already rapidly beating heart pounded harder.

It's too soon. I shouldn't have asked. He has to think I'm nuts. He's probably figuring out a way to escape right now, labeling me as a stage-five clinger. What was I thinking?

"That's a big step."

"I'm sorry. You're right. It's too soon. Forget I asked." I let the words spew out of my mouth before rolling over to hide my head below the pillow. I felt the bed shift beside me as Liam rolled onto his side next to me.

"Valerie."

I didn't respond. Instead, I tightened the pillow to the back of my head. I felt his hand glide up my bare back, followed by the heat of his kisses.

"Princess, look at me."

"No," I declined through the muffling of my pillow.

He yanked it away from my head and out of my grasp, revealing my distressed face and now frazzled hair. I lifted my head to look at him.

He was grinning. "I want to go."

"What? Really?"

"Yes."

"Why?"

He laughed. "Do you not want me to go now?"

"No! I mean yes, I do—I just don't want you to feel like you have to. I know this is all quick. It's just this thing we do.

Mostly because my sister-in-law loves to cook. Especially lately. My brother thinks she's nesting or something, but she's always been this way. She's a really good cook, although most of the food is high in calories," I rambled on.

"Val. You're confusing me. I can't tell if you're trying to convince me to go or not." He laughed, pulling me onto his lap as he sat back against my headboard. "Either way, I want to go. I want to meet your family." He brushed my hair with his fingers, helping to flatten it back down before pressing his mouth against mine, silencing me.

I stared at him in bewilderment. "You do?"

"Yes." He laughed again.

"You're sure?"

"Valerie. I'm not changing my mind, so I hope you're not changing yours."

"No, I'm not. I just...I need to warn you. My brother can be slightly overprotective. I don't want that to freak you out. He loves me dearly, and I know he means well...but it can be a little frustrating at times."

"I'm glad to hear you have someone who looks out for you like that."

I scoffed. "Yeah, it's not always a good thing..."

The pad of his thumb brushed across my cheek bone as he held my head between his hands.

"Thank you."

"Don't thank me yet. You may hate me after this."

"Impossible. I could never hate you, princess."

I draped my hands around his neck. "Since you're in such an accommodating mood, I have one more thing to ask you."

"Is this bigger than meeting the family?" He raised a quizzical brow.

"No"—I giggled—"I was curious what your plans were for the Fourth of July. Lexie invited us to camp out on the beach with Jake and his friends. They said you could invite the guys along. Interested?"

"Sounds like a good time. I'll ask them. Anything else?"

"Just one more thing…" I leaned in closer with a mischievous smirk, brushing my lips along his ear. "How fast do you think you can have me screaming your name?"

Within seconds of registering my words, he was flipping me to my back, causing me to squeal with laughter.

"You and that mouth."

His lips turned up into a smile as he peered down at me before beginning his delicious and deliberate meandering down my body, licking and sucking, wetting my body both inside and out. He followed the path of his tongue with a breath of air that he blew across my skin, sending a shiver through me.

His face hovered at my core, using the same methodical approach of tongue and air, forcing my hips to move upward on their own accord. He kissed below my navel, pushing them back to the bed.

"Liam," I pleaded for him to hurry. I needed him inside me.

"Not yet."

"I'm ready," I breathed.

"I know, princess." He kissed in between my thighs, before intensifying his manipulation of my body.

"Oh, God…Liam," I panted, feeling my body's release building. I clutched my hands onto his broad shoulders, preparing for the impending combustion. Just before my body exploded, he removed his mouth from me. I was tempted to push him back where I needed him most, but his imposing torso was already making its way up my body.

His eyes penetrated mine as he pushed inside me. I tilted my head back, closing my eyes, taking a moment to revel in the pleasure that now filled my body. His hand slid behind my head, threading his fingers in my hair, as he tilted it to his. He took my mouth roughly. Our tongues thrashed and our minds melded as our bodies worked together as one.

My body trembled and quaked as I screamed his name over and over. He wrapped me up into his arms, holding me against him as we both passed out for the night.

CHAPTER 10

I couldn't help the small giggle that escaped my lips when Liam opened his door to me Sunday evening. He was dressed in slacks and a button-up dress shirt with the sleeves rolled up above his elbows.

"What?" he asked, glancing down at his attire. "Should I change?"

I shook my head no, unable to speak. He looked sexy. The light gray shirt and black dress pants fit him in all the right places. It made me fall a little deeper, the thought of him making an effort to impress my family. I scanned his body, appreciating the full vision of him. It took everything I had not to jump him and strip him out of his clothes, so I could kiss every inch of that body that was hidden beneath them.

"I just...I've never seen you dressed up is all." I tried repressing the overjoyed smile on my face. "It's just different. You didn't have to do that. You can wear whatever you're comfortable in." I smiled, wrapping my hands around his waist to look up at him.

He lowered his head, dropping a kiss on my lips. "I'm good, princess...but you need to stop."

"Stop what?"

"You're giving me the 'look.' I love when you give me that look, but now is not the time, unless you want to skip dinner altogether."

I rolled my eyes at him. "Are you ready to go?"

"Yes. I'm driving," he stated firmly as he closed and locked his door behind him.

"What? Why?"

"You're a terrible driver, princess. I feel better being the one behind the wheel."

I smacked him on his shoulder as I pushed away from him. "I am not!" I crossed my arms with annoyance.

"You very much are." He laughed, pulling me back into his arms, giving me a platonic kiss on the top of my head. "After following you that first night and seeing the shape your car was in when it came into our shop, there is no doubt in my mind."

"First of all, the damage to my car was not my fault," I said pointedly. "Secondly, if I was driving terribly that night, it was your fault for distracting me from focusing on the road."

"Uh huh," he said, unconvinced.

"Whatever," I huffed. "It looks like you and my brother already have something you can agree on," I sassed. "Let's go, before I change my mind and leave you here."

I broke free from his arms, marching down the steps, leaving him to trail behind me. As soon as my foot hit the pavement below, I felt him scooping me up in his arms, planting a wet kiss on my lips.

"You're sexy when you're mad and all pouty."

"I'm not pouting."

He shook his head, a grin twitching on his gorgeous mouth as he carried me to my car. He placed my feet on the ground, opening the passenger door for me. I plopped into the seat, placing my keys in his hand without argument. He leaned into the car, giving me a quick kiss before closing the door and confidently strolling around to take his place behind the steering wheel.

I watched him, knowing there was no way I could stay mad at him for long. He looked entirely too good in that moment, and that damn dimple that was becoming a permanent fixture on his face got me every time.

The whole drive to Malibu Liam was talkative and relaxed, keeping his right hand tangled with mine as he drove. Occasionally, he'd drop kisses on the back of my hand, causing my body to ignite with each tender kiss. It wasn't until we pulled through the gates outside of my brother's home that he became quiet and tense.

He turned off the car, neither of us moving or talking. I waited a beat before squeezing his hand in comfort.

"Liam?"

He turned to look at me, giving me a weak smile. I knew the house, gates, and security could be intimidating for most people.

"I'm fine, princess," he assured me before releasing my hand to get out of the car.

I took a deep breath, praying that tonight's dinner would go smoothly. Liam opened my door, helping me out of the car. I linked my arm through his, guiding him up to the door. The massive wooden front door swung open just before we made it onto the porch. Ava stood there with her big, bright, blue eyes and a welcoming smile.

I felt Liam's body relax, making me thankful for Ava's naturally friendly demeanor. She stepped onto the porch, enveloping me in a big hug, calming my own nerves.

"Val! So glad you guys made it!" She released me from her arms, turning to Liam. "And you must be Liam." She gave him a big smile in greeting.

He nodded at her, reciprocating her smile.

"Liam, this is my sister-in-law, Ava," I introduced them.

"Ava, it's good to meet you." He put out his hand to greet her.

She bypassed it, giving him a hug. He gave her a one-armed hug, trying to avoid her protruding belly and maintain his hold on my hand.

"Where's Rhett?" I asked.

She rolled her eyes, turning to walk back into the house. "On the phone," she sighed. "Come on in," she said, waving for us to follow her. "He promised it'd be a short call. Dinner is almost ready."

We followed her into the house, through the entryway and toward the open living- and dining-room area.

"Can I get you two something to drink?" she offered.

"I'll take a glass of wine," I replied. We both looked at Liam expectantly.

"Whatever you have is fine," he responded, trying to be as little trouble as possible.

"We have everything. You're going to have to be a little more specific," Ava teased him.

He smiled, revealing his dimple. "I guess I'll take a beer in that case."

"One wine, one beer. Coming right up." She turned to walk away, glancing over her shoulder at me, giving me a corny smile and a thumbs up. Thankfully, Liam's back was to her as he glanced around their home.

I turned to Liam, hugging him to me, nervous energy radiating from him. "Just be yourself."

He nodded, dropping his nose to mine as he inhaled a deep breath. We silently breathed each other in, letting our bodies calm each other. The clearing of a gravelly throat made Liam instantly step away, putting unwanted distance between us. I watched his body harden, standing at attention, staring behind me. I turned to my brother, who looked as intimidating as always, grinning at him, hoping to diminish his unapproachable disposition.

"Rhett!" I smiled the biggest smile I could.

Despite everything, I was always happy to see my big brother. His own charming smile spread across his face as he focused on me. I gave him a hug, silently pleading that he'd take it easy on Liam. I pulled away from our hug, giving him a final pleading look before turning back to Liam.

"Rhett, this is Liam. Liam, this is my brother, Rhett."

The two stared at each other for a few uncomfortable seconds before Rhett offered his hand and a tight smile to Liam. But a smile, nonetheless. Knowing my brother, it was the closest thing he'd give to a peace offering.

"Liam, it's a pleasure to meet you."

I let out some air in relief as Liam instantly gave him a firm handshake.

"Same. You have a beautiful home." Liam glanced around the space.

"Thank you. It's mostly Ava's doing."

"That's right. Val mentioned she was an architect."

Rhett nodded. "Can I get you something to drink?"

"Already have them covered," Ava said, coming back into the room with our drinks in hand. She handed them to Liam and me, before sidling up beside Rhett. He put his arm around her, pulling her in protectively. "Dinner is ready when you are. I set it up on the patio, since it's a beautiful evening."

"Well, let's eat then," Rhett said, extending his arm for Liam and me to go first.

I took Liam's hand in mine, leading him out to the patio that overlooked the ocean. Ava was right; it was a beautiful evening. The warm, salty air—with just the perfect amount of breeze—felt good on my skin.

The conversation at dinner started off slow and slightly tense between Rhett and Liam, but Ava and I worked our charm, easing the two men into conversation. By the end of the meal, Rhett was more welcoming toward him, and Liam was more relaxed.

"So Liam, Ava tells me you work at the body shop that repaired Val's car. That's where you met?"

"Yes, I do. But no, we actually first met—"

"At a concert!" I interrupted in a rushed panic as I elbowed Liam hard in the side.

He grunted in pain under his breath, clutching his side.

"We first met at a concert. Then again at the body shop," I continued, building on my lie, securing my hands firmly underneath my thighs.

They were all staring at me as my cheeks began to flush— Liam with a look of confusion, Ava with narrowed eyes, and Rhett with a raised eyebrow. I turned my eyes down, focusing on my plate, deciding it was best to avoid their stares.

"Right...I must've been confused and told you wrong," Ava said, coming to my rescue, despite knowing I'd told her a small lie. "Must be the pregnancy brain." She smiled up at Rhett as she took the blame.

God, I love her. I knew she'd probably make me pay for it later, but I didn't care.

"A concert?" Rhett asked, still eyeing me suspiciously, his tone incredulous.

I grimaced. My brother could read me like a book most of the time. "Liam's band was playing that night." I glanced over at him, hoping he wouldn't refute me and would follow my lead.

"They're really good," Ava added. "You should listen to some of their music. Your voice is awesome, Liam."

"Thanks, Ava. Maybe sometime you two can come watch us play." Liam shifted uncomfortably in his chair.

I wasn't sure if it was because of the lie he was now letting slide, or because he felt self-conscious about Ava's compliment. Knowing him, likely the former. I felt terrible for making him take part in a lie to my brother, but it was really inconsequential. I'd make it up to him later.

"Oh! I'd love that. Maybe after the baby comes?" Ava looked over at Rhett.

"Sure, beautiful," Rhett agreed. I don't think he was truly convinced by our ploy, but he let it go.

I started to relax, now that the attention was off of me, and I mouthed a silent thank you to Ava when neither of the guys were looking.

After dinner, we all continued to visit a little longer. Liam and Rhett remained on the patio to have a nightcap outside, while Ava took me inside to see the latest additions to the nursery.

"Are you going to tell me what that little outburst was about?" Ava prompted me when we were alone in the safety of the nursery.

"No?"

She narrowed her eyes, cocking her head to the side, throwing her hands on her hips. It was a very motherly look, the one that told you you were minutes away from suffering the consequences if you didn't fess up now. My poor nephew wouldn't stand a chance against that look. The same way I had no chance right now.

"Keep it between us?"

"Depends..." she said, taking a seat in the oversized, wingback glider next to the crib.

"On what?"

"On whether you agree to babysit for us whenever I want for a year." She put her feet up on the stool in front of her, relaxing back into the chair with confidence, like she was a savvy business woman, laying out the terms of a deal. Rhett was unfortunately rubbing off on her.

"Are you seriously trying to blackmail me?"

A wide grin slid across her face.

"Unbelievable. Why do you need that anyway? Won't you guys have a nanny?"

"No. I already told Rhett absolutely not. I don't want a full-time nanny. We'll just have one here during the day while we work."

"You don't even know my secret yet. How can you think that it's even worth me agreeing to this?"

"Something tells me it is…" She winked.

I let out an exaggerated sigh. "Fine."

It's not like the terms were something I wouldn't do for them anyway. I planned to spoil that little nephew of mine rotten.

"We met the day I picked up your car. I got a flat tire on the way to my audition. He pulled over to help me."

"I thought my tires looked different. Wait…*a* flat tire? As in single?"

"Yes, but I had them all replaced, hoping you guys wouldn't notice."

She laughed at my absurdness. "So you didn't meet at a concert or the body shop?"

"Well…"

I went on to tell her about the first few frustrating days of our encounters, leaving out his warnings and the fact that he had a mysterious past he wasn't willing to tell me about just yet. I wasn't going to share that information when I wasn't even sure what it was he was warning me against.

"Wow…well, I'm glad you guys ended up together. I really like him. I think he'll be good for you, Val."

"Thank you. And thank you for your help with Rhett."

She shrugged. "I didn't do much. Just made him promise to give it a chance and to stay out of it. I know it may not seem like it, but he trusts your judgement, Val. He just worries. He wants to protect you."

"I know. I love him, even the craziness that comes with him." I smiled.

Ava and I rejoined the guys on the patio. There was an awkward silence between them that had me feeling a little uneasy when we first approached. We had obviously interrupted a serious conversation. As soon as they were aware of our presence, they both quickly changed their expressions. I worried about what had been said between them, but when Liam put his arm around me, relaxing me into his side, I let his touch banish any negative thoughts.

I rolled onto my back, my head on my pillow, basking in the afterglow. After leaving Rhett and Ava's house, we ended up at my place for the night. On the drive home, I had to embarrassingly explain why I lied about our first meeting. His only response was to shake his head with amusement.

Liam rolled onto his side, sprinkling my neck with kisses as I tried to slow my heartrate and heavy breathing. He pulled his face from my neck, giving me a soft, rare smile.

"What?" I asked.

"Nothing. Just trying to figure out how I got so lucky to be here with you right now."

"This is where you belong," I assured him.

His smile faded as I watched the doubt spread through his eyes.

"Liam." I spoke his name softly, reaching my hand to his jawline, letting his scruff grate the pads of my fingers.

"Let's not talk, princess. I just need to hold you right now."

He pulled me onto my side, so my front was pressed against his as he held me close. I cuddled into his body, closing my eyes. As much as I wanted to push, the idea of cuddling with him won, allowing him to escape any probing questions I had.

I tried to force my mind to shut down and sleep, but it was running rampant with unsettling thoughts. Every time Liam would avoid the topic of his past, my imagination would take over. I had no idea what to think. I knew in my heart there was nothing that would make me look at him any differently, but he seemed to have the same level of confidence that it would.

I felt his breathing slow. I glanced up to look at his beautiful, sleeping face, resisting the urge to touch it. He looked so at ease. I didn't want to wake him. I took a deep breath to clear my mind, and I let sleep overtake me.

CHAPTER 11

The warm water ran over my body as I tried to wake my sleepy brain. I had snuck out of bed to ready myself for work, letting Liam continue to sleep. I resented that I had the early shift and wished I could stay in bed having a lazy morning with him.

Liam and I had spent every free hour we had together over the last three weeks, which weren't as many as I'd have liked. His full-time job at the shop, evening practices, and late-night shows left him with very little spare time. My own schedule wasn't any better.

I'd seriously contemplated quitting my job at Sweet Beans. It wasn't as if I needed it, and it would make it easier for me to make my auditions. Regardless, I couldn't bring myself to actually do it. I loved working there and cherished the friendships I'd made. Sweet Beans had been a place of growth for me, both emotionally and professionally. It taught me what it meant to work for something I wanted, giving me a sense of accomplishment. I'd just have to figure out a way to balance my work life and newfound love life.

To top it off, surprisingly, I'd already gotten a response from a new agent last week. She'd picked me up as a client, despite the warnings she'd heard from Donna. I thanked her a million times over for taking a chance on me and promised her I'd do everything I could to prove Donna's less-than-stellar review of me wrong.

I stepped out of the shower, drying off and throwing on my robe. I leisurely got ready for work, before cracking open the door to my dark bedroom. I could see the silhouette of Liam's body sound asleep in the bed. I stumbled in the dark toward my bed, trying my best to be quiet. I reached for my phone on the nightstand. Strong hands grabbed me by the waist. I squealed through my laughter as Liam pulled me back onto the bed with him.

"What time is it?" he mumbled into the back of my neck.

"Too early," I said, breathing him in. "I have to go to work."

"Call in sick," he demanded. He leaned forward, running the tip of his nose along my jawline. "Stay with me, princess," he whispered. His hand ghosted along the side of my body, spreading tingles in its wake.

"I can't," my brain said as my body fought to stay. "It's Friday, and we'll be ridiculously busy this morning." Breathy words left my mouth. "I can't leave Ethan to fight that crowd by himself." I gasped, holding in a whimper as his unrelenting manipulations of my body continued. "Besides, you have to go to work also." I was struggling to find reasons not to give into Liam's seductive tactics.

"Frankie won't care."

I laughed, knowing that was true. "As tempting as that sounds, I really can't." I sat up, finding an unknown inner strength, breaking free of Liam's hypnotic hands that had a hold of my body.

He groaned. "Give me a few minutes, and I'll be ready to go."

"No. Stay. Sleep." I brushed my hand along the side of his face. "Leave whenever you're ready. Lexie stayed at Jake's last night, so just lock up when you leave."

I leaned down to give him a kiss goodbye. He took advantage, cradling my head, pulling me back to him as he plunged his tongue into my mouth, causing me to release the whimper I'd been holding in. I broke free from the kiss before I was lost for good.

"Calm down, rock star." I laughed while trying to hold him at arm's length. "We'll finish this later."

He slapped my butt as I stood. "I'm going to make you beg for it tonight," he threatened.

"I have no doubt you will."

I smiled as I sauntered out of the room, loving the way it felt to have his eyes follow my every move. I was pretty much always begging for it after one of his concerts. Every time I watched him sing, I became an impatient, needy mess. But after tonight, I'd have all his time and attention for the next few days.

Tomorrow we'd be celebrating his Uncle Frankie's birthday. Neither one of us had to work. Plus, it was the first Saturday that Derailed didn't have a concert. Sunday was Fourth of July, and we'd be spending the night on the beach, watching fireworks. Knowing all that made it a little less painful to walk away from the beautiful, half-naked man lying in my bed, begging for me to stay. Only a little, though. A very miniscule amount, actually. *Why am I walking away again?*

I turned around at the doorframe, taking one more look at his grinning face before blowing him a little kiss and forcing myself to leave for work.

~

"Knock, knock," I hollered as I opened the screen door to Frankie's house, balancing his birthday cake in one hand.

"Come on in, darlin'!" Frankie hollered from the kitchen.

I walked through the old, cluttered living room toward the back of the house, where the kitchen was located. Frankie was at the stove, turning a pot on his ancient gas-burning stove to simmer.

"He's making you cook on your own birthday?" I joked, giving him a one-armed hug before placing his cake on the worn metal-and-teal retro table in the corner of the kitchen.

Everything about Frankie's made me feel like I was stepping back in time. Most of his belongings were things he'd had for years and probably never planned to replace, even if they broke. Frankie was one of those guys who would make every effort to fix or rig something so that it still functioned well enough before he'd dream of replacing it. He was your "they don't make them like they used to" kind of guy.

His home had all kinds of interesting memorabilia and clutter. It was organized chaos at its best. I'd never be able to find anything, but he always knew exactly where something was hiding below a pile of papers. It reminded me a lot of the shop's customer-service area.

"Nah, he's out back grillin' up some burgers. I'm just manning the beans. That cake looks tasty." Frankie nodded toward the cake I'd placed on the table. "Chocolate's my favorite. Did you bake that just for me?"

I laughed. "As much as I wish I could take credit for this, I can't bake to save my life. This one is from the bakery near my house. I can make you a mean cup of coffee to go with it, though."

"It's the thought that counts, sugar." He chuckled, putting his arm around my shoulders. "Come on...Liam's out back."

Frankie led me outside to the backyard. The smell of grease and charcoal burning, the sound of hamburgers sizzling on the grill, and the heat of the summer sun all hit my senses at once, creating a euphoric comfort I hadn't felt before. Liam was at the grill with the lid open, flipping the patties with his back to me. Frankie took a seat at the patio table on the back porch and popped open a fresh beer.

I watched Liam's taut back muscles ripple through the fitted, white T-shirt he was wearing. There was something so sexy about watching him at the grill. It was a masculine act that I hadn't realized could turn me on. I snuck up behind him, wrapping my arms around his waist while placing a kiss on his shoulder.

"Hey there, rock star," I greeted him with a seductive tone.

Between the delicious smells coming from the grill and the smell and vision of Liam, my body was in overdrive. He closed the lid of the grill, setting the long spatula aside. He swiveled in my arms, enclosing me with his own.

"Hi, princess." He flashed that dimple at me, and my

already-overheated body melted some more. "It's about time you got here."

"Were you missing me?" He'd only left my place a couple hours ago to get a head start on grilling.

"Every minute." He placed a kiss on my lips, before dropping his arms from me. He picked up a bottle of beer that was resting on the side apron of the grill before taking my hand to lead me to the table where Frankie sat.

I took a seat with the two men who were growing on me faster than I could have ever imagined. Frankie had a natural ability to make me feel like a part of the family, the same way Ava had when I first met her. He had an infectious positive outlook on life. Even though, from the things he'd told me, his life hadn't been easy or full of happiness, considering he lost his wife early on, and never remarried.

And then there was Liam. I couldn't begin to understand the connection I felt with him. It was instantaneous and beyond explanation. I felt bound to him. It was a hold I couldn't break free of even if I tried. I'd never try, though. I knew if I cut that tie, I wouldn't be setting myself free; I'd be losing the one person who made me feel like there was a purpose for my life. He was my purpose, my strength, my everything. And I wanted to be that for him.

The sun began to set as we relaxed into the evening, talking and laughing as we ate burgers and chocolate cake topped with vanilla-bean ice cream. The string of patio lights lit up the dark sky above our heads as a comfortable silence fell over us. I smiled at Liam. He gave me a light squeeze just above my knee. He glanced over at me with an adorable smirk as his fingers began to trail up my inner thigh.

Frankie sat forward, clearing his throat. "I guess I should

start cleaning all this up," he said, making an excuse to give us some privacy. He slid to the edge of his seat, bracing his hands on the armrests as he slowly struggled to stand.

"Let me help." I stood to gather some of the paper plates and trash from the table. Liam stood with me.

"You don't have to do that, hun. I got it covered," Frankie said feebly, with a weary look in his eyes. It was obvious he was feeling worn out.

"I insist. It's *your* birthday."

"We got it," Liam added firmly, staring at Frankie with a determined expression, not allowing him to argue any further. Frankie nodded with a weak smile, patting Liam fondly on his arm as he walked past him to go inside.

Once Frankie had disappeared into the house, I turned to Liam. "Is he okay?"

"He's fine." Liam busied himself, gathering the empty beer bottles on the table.

"Liam?"

He didn't respond.

"Please, tell me what's going on."

"Nothing. I told you he's fine." His harsh and dismissive tone caused my back to straighten.

His avoidance of the conversation infuriated me. I turned away frustrated, aggressively clearing the table. I was tired of him always deflecting my questions and not opening up to me.

"Shit," he huffed under his breath, "...Val, I'm sorry."

"Why won't you talk to me?" I clipped, anger still coursing through me.

He grabbed my arm, stopping my movements. "I just don't want you to worry."

"Well whether you tell me or not, I'm going to worry." I yanked my arm from his hand. "I can tell you're worried, so just knowing that is going to make me worry."

"You're right." He hugged me to him, trying to calm us both. He breathed me in, taking a moment before he continued. "He had a heart attack a little over a month ago. Just before you and I met. It was a small one. And he is on medication now, but I still worry about him working too much."

"I'm sorry... I know how much he means to you."

"He'll be fine. He's a tough old bastard." He half-smiled.

I nodded my agreement, standing on my tip toes, planting a kiss of support and comfort on his lips. "Thank you for telling me. I'll take care of the dishes inside. You take care of finishing up out here."

"Thanks, princess." He kissed me on my forehead before releasing me.

I walked through the back door into the kitchen. Searching through the cabinets, I looked for containers to store the leftover food before working on the dirty dishes. After scrubbing the third pot of lacquered-on baked beans, I made a mental note to look at purchasing Frankie a dishwasher. And maybe a maid.

After the last dish was washed, I drained the sink and hung the damp towel I'd been using to dry. Liam hadn't come back inside yet, so I walked into the living room to check on Frankie. He was lying back with his feet up in his old, tan recliner. The room was dim, with only a lamp and the glow of the TV illuminating it.

He was morbidly still. A tiny wave of panic got caught in my throat. His chest finally rose and fell slowly. He was breathing. I laid my hand over my chest, exhaling my relief. I walked farther into the room, taking a seat on the end of the couch closest to him.

His eyes flitted open. I flinched guiltily.

"I'm sorry. I didn't mean to wake you," I apologized.

"Nah. You didn't wake me, sugar. Just restin' my eyes for a moment," he lied. He focused his eyes on the TV, watching the animated weather man forecast the temperatures for the holiday weekend.

I let my eyes wander around the living room, cataloging all the details of the space. The TV sat on a stand directly across from the couch, blocking a large window that looked toward the front yard. Perpendicular to the TV was a red brick fireplace flanked by wooden bookshelves that rose from floor to ceiling. They appeared to be original to the house and were filled with books, random veteran paraphernalia, and photos.

There was one particular photo my eyes focused on. It was a picture of Liam and Frankie, standing outside his shop with smiles that stretched the full width of their faces. The photo looked recent, like maybe it was taken in the last year. I scanned the other photos, expecting to find some from an earlier time. The only other ones displayed were of Frankie and who I assumed to be his deceased wife, Evelyn.

I swiveled my head a fraction to Frankie, unable to completely remove my gaze from the photo. "How long has Liam lived with you?"

"I believe it's been about three years." He turned, looking at me with curious eyes.

Three years? I'd just assumed that Liam had moved in after his parents passed. Frankie continued to watch me closely as I processed the tiny bit of information he'd given me.

"He didn't move in with you after his parents passed away?"

Frankie shifted uncomfortably in his chair, looking away from me. He didn't respond immediately. I watched as he thought hard about how to answer my question. His gaze fell back on me with an expression of regret.

"I didn't know him at the time. We first met when he started working for me at the shop."

"I don't understand. I thought…I mean…how did you not know your nephew?"

He tilted his head down, his chin pressed to his chest, giving me a look that told me I already knew the answer to that.

"You're not his uncle," I said under my breath to myself, remembering his words to me the first evening we met. He nodded once, confirming my response.

Realizing this only stirred up more questions. They swirled in my head, directionless, causing my brain to desperately crave more information about Liam. There was so much in his past I had no idea about. So much I wanted to know. Needed to know.

"Who raised him after his parents passed away? Does he have other family?" The questions came flying out of my mouth uncontrollably. I gave Frankie a pleading look, desperate to know more.

"That's not my story to tell, darlin'."

I could see the remorse in his eyes. He wasn't going to tell me. His loyalty was with Liam. As much as I hated that I wouldn't get answers from him, I respected his decision not to divulge any more details.

We both turned back to the TV, letting our silence fill the room. Liam walked in through the kitchen with a joyous expression that clashed with everything I was feeling.

"Hey, old man. You up for seein' your birthday present?"

Frankie turned his head to look at Liam with a teasing expression. "You making me get out of my chair?"

Liam laughed. "Get up you lazy bastard. It's outside."

Frankie lowered his legs as he sat up in the recliner, grunting and mumbling under his breath, but with a hint of a smile as he moved to stand. I stood to help him out of his chair. The three of us walked through the kitchen and out the back door, following Liam to the garage.

Liam gripped the handle of the garage door, yanking it upward, rolling the door open. There in the middle of the garage was a motorcycle with a big red bow. Liam turned back toward us with a contagious grin on his face as he watched for Frankie's reaction. I did the same. I didn't know much about motorcycles—okay, I knew nothing at all—but from the expression on Frankie's face, I could tell this one was special.

"Liam...son...Well, shit." Frankie threw his hands on his hips, shaking his head slowly in disbelief, lost for words. "Does it work?"

Liam laughed, crossing his arms firmly over his chest. "You think I'd give you a broke-down motorcycle?"

Frankie chuckled. "I wouldn't put it past ya."

He stepped forward to stand beside Liam and admire the cruiser a little more closely. Watching the two of them silently bond over the bike, shortly after finding out what I had, made me view their whole relationship differently. I admired it more. They were so close; I never would've guessed they weren't family, or that they hadn't known each other for many long years.

"I did have to replace a few parts. Don't get me started on what a pain in the ass it was to find them, either."

"Thanks, kid." Frankie clapped Liam's shoulder. He moved to stand next to the motorcycle, running his hand over the body of the bike before squatting to admire the chassis.

Liam and Frankie boisterously discussed the bike and what Liam had to replace to get it running. I listened to the two of them. Beyond understanding that it was a 1977 Harley Davidson lowrider, I was lost throughout the whole conversation, as if they were speaking another language.

It was a nice-looking bike, with black trim and a black leather seat that scooped upwards, connecting to a seat for a second rider. The motorcycle had been shined and polished to look brand new with a bright, reflective, silver frame.

Liam looked over at me as Frankie continued to gaze at the bike. I moved to stand beside him. His arm clutched me into his side. I splayed my hand across his abs, cuddling against him. The garage fell silent as we watched Frankie, who seemed lost in his reverie.

"Reminds me of Evelyn," he said with a quiet fondness and a hint of sadness in his eyes.

"Do you want to take it for a ride?" Liam asked Frankie.

He shook off the sadness that had momentarily possessed him. "Nah. Not tonight. Why don't you take Val for a ride? Evelyn always loved ridin' at night." Frankie stared over at me with an encouraging smile.

"What do ya say, princess?" Liam gave me his own coy smile. "You want me to take you for a ride?" He danced his eyebrows up and down playfully.

I gave him a meek grin. "I don't know…I've never been on a motorcycle before."

"Don't worry. I'll take it easy on ya." He winked.

Frankie laughed, patting Liam on the back. "I'm turning in for the night. You kids be careful."

"Happy birthday, Frankie," I said, giving him a hug as he moved to leave.

He glanced back at the bike one more time before disappearing back into the house, leaving us alone in the garage. Liam walked over to a table, pulling two helmets out of a box. I stood by the bike, running my hand over the smooth frame.

"This may be a little big. I got it for Frankie," Liam explained as he stepped closer to me, holding both helmets in his hands.

He laid one on the seat, grinning excitedly. His eyes dropped the length of my body as his teeth captured his bottom lip.

"Fuck, princess…having that tight little body wrapped around me on this bike is going to do things to me. This may be a short ride."

He used one arm, tugging my body so it was pressed firmly against him. His heated stare and the thought of being wrapped around him on the bike had me feeling like a bundle of nerves. He kissed me fiercely, putting me in a heady trance, only adding to my frenzied state of mind. I moaned my pleasure, suddenly thinking we should skip the ride altogether, preferring to take a different kind of ride.

Liam promptly ended our kiss, closing his eyes, taking a deep breath before opening them back to look at me.

"Pull your hair back," he commanded gruffly.

I did as I was told, pulling it back into a low ponytail at the base of my neck. I smiled knowingly at him. It was obvious he was trying to control his own urges. He lifted the helmet above me, slowly sliding it over my head until it was snug and secured. He lifted the face guard, so he could see my eyes.

"Does that feel okay?" he asked softly.

I nodded, unable to verbalize a single word. His innocent movements felt more sensual than they should. My chest tightened as the pulsing in my body increased.

"Okay. I'm going to climb on first. You'll climb on after me. Keep your feet on the pegs. You're going to want to hold onto me. *Tight.*" He smirked. "Just follow my lead. When I lean, look over my inside shoulder. Okay?"

I nodded again.

"Don't worry. I won't let anything happen to you, princess," he assured me, interpreting my silence as fear. "Do you trust me?"

"With every part of me." I nodded. He smiled, but his eyes flashed with something I couldn't comprehend.

Liam pulled on his own helmet before taking a seat on the bike. He tilted the bike into an upright position, lifting the kickstand with his foot. He looked back at me and nodded for me to get on.

I hesitated a moment, trying to figure out my footing before lifting my leg over the bike while holding onto his shoulders for balance. I straddled the seat behind him, sliding forward until my front was pressed to his back. He moved my hands from his shoulders, guiding them around his waist, where I squeezed him tight.

He lifted his face guard, glancing over his shoulder. "Lower the guard. Keep it down while we're moving."

I nodded again, lowering my face guard.

He cranked the key and the engine roared. The bike vibrated between my legs, sending a shiver down my spine with excited anticipation. Liam raised his feet as the bike began to roll forward out of the garage. I instinctively gripped him tighter and felt his firm stomach beneath my palms rumble with laughter.

Turning onto the residential street, my heartrate tripled its pace. The thrill of the powerful machine below me and the powerful man in my arms had me feeling exhilarated and alive. Liam drove the motorcycle skillfully through the streets of L.A. As he increased our speed, the wind bristled against my skin, sending goosebumps up my arms.

The miles passed by in a flash. The motorcycle slowed as we pulled up to Angel's Point. Liam killed the engine, leaning the bike slightly to the side, onto the kickstand. He removed his helmet, hanging it on the handle bars. I removed my own helmet and rested it behind me, shaking out my hair.

Liam twisted at his waist, pulling me onto his lap. I burrowed my cheek into his chest. The whole ride had constantly plagued my hormones. The blood in my veins was ignited by the ride like a trail of gunpowder, making my body combustible. I tried to slow my breathing as I stared out at the view before us.

The twinkling lights of Los Angeles glowed, contrasting with the black sky, creating a breathtaking view of the city. I felt his lips touch the crown of my head. I lifted my head to stare up at him. His painfully beautiful smile inched across his face as he tucked my wild hair behind my ear.

"What did you think?"

"I loved it. Best ride of my life."

He raised a cocky eyebrow with a smirk.

"Well...besides the one I hope you'll be taking me on later tonight." I grinned slyly.

His head fell back with a short stint of laughter. I loved seeing him laugh. I loved hearing his laugh. I wanted to be the one to always make him laugh.

"God, princess..." He let out a breath as he looked back down at me. His eyes dimmed with unexpected grief. "You make me so happy," he whispered as he rubbed his thumb across my bottom lip.

My heart sunk with the tone of his voice. He spoke the words as if he didn't deserve to feel that way—as if he didn't deserve me. The thought killed me. It made me want to dive into the depths of his pain, discover his secrets, and take away the anguish they caused him.

I moved in slowly, caressing my lips against his throat. His grip on my hips tightened as his body became tense with desire. I ran my hands up the contours of his chest, sliding them over his broad shoulders, linking them behind his neck as I worked my way up his jawline.

My movements were purposefully unrushed, with the objective to make him feel every touch, every motion. I needed him to feel me, feel how much I wanted him, how much I needed him—feel that every part of me was his to keep. He groaned as my lips met his. I pressed my body to him, leaving no room for anything to ever become between us.

"Valerie," he pleaded against my lips, trying to resist everything I was giving him.

I didn't relent. There was no room for him to have any doubt about us. I wouldn't allow it.

He crushed his lips against mine, surging deeper into the depths of my soul, finally accepting everything my body was telling him. I twisted my legs around his hips, needing every inch of my body to be wrapped around him like a boa constrictor.

I ground my hips into him, releasing a moan. I needed more, and I could tell by his own aggressive ministrations he needed the same. He abruptly ended our make-out session, pulling his head back from mine.

"We need to go." His labored breathing matched mine. "I'm not doing this here."

I nodded my agreement, not wasting any time resuming my position behind him on the motorcycle. I clung to his body as he drove us back to his place, unwilling to release him for the rest of the night.

CHAPTER 12

"Frankie, are you sure you don't want to come with us to the beach?" I asked as Liam loaded my car with the items we would need for our overnight camping trip.

Frankie shook his head. "Nah, I'm too old for that shit. You kids have fun, though. While you're sleepin' in the sand, I'll be sleepin' like a baby in my own bed."

I laughed. I couldn't blame him. The idea of sleeping on the ground in a tent didn't sound too appealing to me either.

Dax came up behind me, throwing his arm across my shoulders. "You sure old man? You're gonna be missing out."

Frankie grinned. "Watch who you're callin' old," he warned with a humorous tone.

"And get your arm off my girl before I break it," Liam said with less humor, coming up behind us.

"Shit, Val...how do ya deal with these two grumpy bastards?" He winked, removing his arm from my shoulders.

Liam quickly replaced it with his own arm, pulling me in possessively. It made me curious if he was ever made aware that mine and Dax's previous flirtations were all a ploy.

A loud honking and a raucous group distracted us all before I had a chance to respond. We turned, looking down toward the street to Blaine's SUV, pulling up at the end of the drive already packed with a carload of people. Trent was hanging out the window, hollering and pounding his hand on the side of the door.

I laughed at their rowdy excitement. Liam and Dax, on the other hand, seemed less amused with their behavior.

"Hey, Dax," a blonde girl seductively purred, hanging outside the rear passenger window, revealing way too much cleavage.

Dax gave her a quick lift of his chin in acknowledgment before turning his back to her. "Shit," he scowled under his breath.

"Aren't those the girls you guys took home a couple weeks ago? Liam asked, squinting his eyes toward the car.

"Yeah, and the blonde is fuckin' nuttier than shit. Hot as hell. But fuckin' crazy." He smirked in dismay. "Assholes probably invited them cuz they're angry about me taking all their money in poker the other night. Bunch of sore losers."

Liam and I laughed at his obvious distress.

"I'm riding with you guys," Dax decided.

"Like hell you are," Liam retorted.

I rolled my eyes at Liam. "You can ride with us Dax."

Liam glowered. "You keep your fuckin' hands to yourself."

He raised his hands up in the air with his palms out. "Promise." He grinned, his eyes full of mischief.

I shook my head, walking toward Frankie to give him a hug goodbye.

"Good luck, darlin'. I don't envy you having' to ride with the two of them," Frankie teased me.

I started to think his idea of staying home was a good one. *Maybe I will just hang with Frankie.*

"Let's go, princess," Liam called behind me.

I swung around to look at my man, who was smiling ear to ear. I scanned his masculine body, dressed casually in baby-blue board shorts and a fitted white T-shirt, looking like sex on legs. *Never mind.* I couldn't pass up an opportunity to be pressed against *that* tonight.

"Coming," I hollered before turning back to Frankie. "Make sure you call us if you need anything. I left some of my sister-in-law's homemade lasagna in the fridge for you. She made way too much and insisted I bring some for you."

"Thank you, sugar. You don't have to worry about me. Go on. Get outta here." He patted the side of my face.

I gave him a kiss on his cheek and ran to Liam, who was waiting for me. Dax hurdled over the side of my convertible, jumping into the back seat. Liam lifted me into his arms and over his shoulder as he manhandled me into the passenger seat. He claimed my mouth with his. Blaine banged on his horn as the crazed group in his car hooted and whistled. We laughed through our kiss at the cheers around us.

Liam gave me one last quick peck before jogging around the front of the car and sliding in behind the steering wheel.

∽

The beach was crowded with people celebrating the holiday.

171

When we arrived, Lexie, Jake, and their group had already set up camp, having arrived earlier in the weekend. The guys took care of unloading everything and setting up our tents for the night as I hung with Lexie on her oversized and vibrant beach blanket.

"I feel like I haven't seen you in weeks," I said as I took a seat next to Lexie.

She was lying back on her elbows, watching the masses splash around in the water and lounge on the beach.

"You've been a little preoccupied," she said, dropping her sunglasses down her nose and eyeing me over the frames.

I removed my cover up to reveal my white, floral print, strapless bikini. "I could say the same for you," I smirked, pulling and twisting my long hair into a pile on top of my head.

I had barely been out here for thirty minutes and already I was starting to break a sweat. I leaned back on my own elbows to lay beside her.

She shrugged, raising her sunglasses back up to conceal her eyes. But she wasn't quick enough. I saw the expression she was trying to hide.

"What's going on?"

"Nothing." Her answer was short and tight.

I studied my friend, knowing damn well something was up. "Where's Jake?" I asked, looking back at the campsite, realizing I hadn't seen him or his buddies.

She nodded her head in the opposite direction, looking toward a game of beach volleyball. I followed her gaze, seeing Jake and his friends playing volleyball with a group of girls I didn't recognize.

It only took a few minutes of watching the game to

realize what had my friend upset. One of the girls was being overly friendly with Jake, and he wasn't doing anything to discourage her flirting.

"Ignore it, Lex. It's nothing. I'm sure," I tried to comfort her, even though my own anger was starting to surface.

She turned back to look out at the ocean, and I worried she was fighting tears back behind the cloak of her dark sunglasses.

Liam joined us a few minutes later, looking agitated as he crawled over me, covering my body with his.

"What are you doing?" I laughed, pushing lightly at his large frame. "You're blocking my sun."

"I'm blocking the rest of these assholes who are getting off just from looking at you," he growled as he pressed his sweaty body firmly to me. "Don't you have a one-piece or something? Fuck, princess."

"Maybe you should piss on her, that may help," Lexie said with a smirk.

I laughed, weakly pushing against his shoulder a little harder. "Stop being ridiculous. That'd give me awful tan lines. It's just too bad this isn't a nude beach," I goaded him some more. I loved when he went all alpha male on me.

He glared at me. "You better not be getting naked for anybody but me."

"Then I expect the same from you."

He smirked, giving me a kiss, grinding his hips firmly against my core in response. I gasped, forgetting where we were, and that my best friend was less than a foot away.

"Seriously you two..." Dax said, towering above us, shaking his head. "At least move inside the fucking tent, so we don't have to watch."

"Where's blondie?" Liam retaliated.

"Shut up, asshole," Dax frowned, taking a seat next to Lexie. He leaned forward, bending his knees to rest his forearms on. "Lex, how ya been?"

"Good," she said, perking up a little. "You?"

"Better now. Where's your man?"

"Busy...playing volleyball."

Dax looked over at the volleyball game, catching onto the situation immediately. He turned back to her. "His loss," he smiled wryly. "It's hot as fuck out here. You wanna go for a swim?"

She raised her sunglasses on top of her head, her eyes brighter than a few moments ago. "Sure," she smiled up at him.

He stood, helping her to her feet. Liam rolled off of me to his side, taking her place on the blanket beside me. The two of us watched them walk away, playfully touching and pushing on each other as they laughed.

"This is going to get interesting." I glanced over at Liam.

He shook his head with annoyance. "Dax needs to watch his back...I'm not helping him out if Jake tries to kick his ass tonight."

"Jake's a jerk. He doesn't deserve to be with Lexie."

"Regardless, princess. She's still his girl. At least for the moment."

"Well, you wouldn't know it with the way he's acting right now."

Liam's face softened as he looked at me. "I didn't say he wasn't being an asshole. Whatever happens is between them. I don't want to get tied up in everyone else's bullshit. I want to spend the day with my girl."

He leaned down, caressing my face, pressing his lips to mine, slipping his tongue into my mouth. I ran my fingers through his hair, pulling him back over me.

"I think we need to cool off." He released a heavy exhale.

"I disagree."

He chuckled. "Let's go for a swim."

"No way."

He pulled back farther, his face contorting into confusion. "Why?"

"Unless there's a pool of crystal-clear water around here, there's no way you're getting me to go for a swim."

He grinned with wide-eyed amusement. "Are you afraid of the ocean, princess?"

"Terrified."

"You're telling me you've been living here for how many years? And you've never stepped foot in that ocean?"

"Three. And I've put my toes in the water, but I've never gone deeper than my ankles. I'm not about to give some man-eating shark the opportunity to make me his dinner."

He rolled to his back. A deep laugh erupted from him, reverberating around me.

"It's not funny," I huffed, aggravated that he found my biggest fear humorous.

"It is. And you're getting in that water," he demanded.

"No, I'm not."

He crawled to a crouching position with an evil gleam in his eyes, ready to pounce.

"Don't even think about it," I warned, sitting up, readying my own escape.

He inched his crawl toward me. With every movement of his, I made one of my own. I braced my palms on the ground, ready to jump and run. My heartrate picked up with anticipation as I held his gaze.

"Liam," I warned again.

His grin grew wider. My anxious brain couldn't handle it. My nerves were wired. I could feel my pulse in my throat. I jumped to my feet, turning to run as fast as I could. I heard his laughter behind me as he closed in on me within seconds, scooping me into his arms and over his shoulder.

I screamed and laughed, flailing my arms and legs as he carried me toward the ocean. My mind and body whirled with confusion—excitement, fear, lust, and anxiety, all mixing chaotically.

"Liam! No! Please!" I begged as he neared the water's edge. "Oh my gosh! I'm gonna die! Put me down! I'm gonna die!"

"You're not gonna die," he laughed, walking us into the water. He was now knee deep.

My breathing became erratic. I clenched my eyes closed as he slid me down his body once he was thigh high in the water. I clung to him, refusing to allow him to put me down now. I tightened my arms around his neck and my legs around his hips, hanging on for dear life, burying my face in his throat.

"Princess," he said softly. "Look at me." I lifted my head at his encouraging tone. "I'd never let anything happen to you. You trust me, right?"

"Yes. But I don't trust the sharks in the water."

He chuckled. "I'm going to go deeper now. I won't let you go."

"Okay," I said, releasing a deep breath, and feeling braver with him holding onto me.

He walked us farther into the water. I flinched at the coldness as the salty water lapped up my lower body. Once he was waist high, he kissed me. His kiss was strong but sweet, firm but soft, making me forget all my fears as he lowered us into the ocean water.

I was fully submerged from my chest down before he broke our kiss. His smile lit his face. He lowered his forehead to mine. "See? You did it. You're safe."

A smile crept onto my face, and I kissed him again. I was safe, as long as he continued to hold me. Something slimy brushed along the side of my foot. I screamed, the thought of safety long forgotten.

"Shit! There's something in the water! Get me out! Get me out!" I panicked, trying and failing to climb farther up his body.

He didn't move. He just laughed and held me tighter. "It's probably just a fish or seaweed. Calm down."

"I don't care! Get me out!"

"Okay!" His amused laugh was unceasing. "We'll move closer to the shore, but we aren't getting out."

I agreed. I'd agree to anything right now, if it meant he'd get me closer to the safety of the sandy beach. I'd just make another run for it once we got to shallower waters.

When the water was at his calf I loosened my grip, preparing to run. He loosened his own grip, sliding me down his body. As soon as my feet were submerged in the water and touching the ocean floor, I twisted from his arms, bolting for the shore.

I heard Liam's laughter from behind as he splashed through the ocean, chasing me. I screamed with laughter as he closed his arms around my chest, wrestling us both down into the sand.

"You're evil!" I laugh-yelled, struggling to free myself.

"I told you, we're staying in the water."

His laughter weakened my resolve. He rolled us into the shallow water, inches from where the waves rolled onto the shore. He pinned me to my back as he straddled my hips. He stared down into my eyes with a carefree expression. His eyes shimmered with happiness.

I relaxed, no longer able to struggle as I gazed up at him. His skin glistened in the sunlight as the salt water dripped down the ripples of his strong, tan body. He released one of his hands from my wrist, running it through his wet hair to brush it back from his forehead.

My heart fell deeper. An emotion I'd never felt before flipped and tumbled in my stomach. Words formed on my lips that scared me. I choked them back.

"You're giving me that look, princess."

Afraid of what would come spilling out of my mouth, I didn't respond verbally. I reached my one free hand up to his body, urging him. He lowered his body to mine, kissing me. I clung to the kiss, kissing him desperately hard, letting all the emotions within me filter through my lips.

For the rest of the day we alternated between splashing around in the water and laying on the beach, soaking in the sun and each other while enjoying the company of our friends.

The tension between Lexie and Jake continued to grow,

but Dax kept her distracted. I tried a couple times to talk to her and make sure she was okay, but she would pretend that everything was fine, and there was nothing for me to worry about.

As the sun started to set, Ethan and his buddies showed up to join us for the rest of the evening. They'd spent the day surfing the waters. We now had a loud and rowdy group spread throughout our little campsite. I hung near Liam, Dax, Lexie, and Ethan. We all visited and drank around the campfire while we waited for the fireworks to start.

When the first burst of bright red, white, and blue scattered across the sky, the hordes of people on the beach began to whistle and holler with excitement. Liam clasped my hand as our small clique flocked down the beach to get a better view of the show.

The booms of the fireworks echoed around us. We all stood silently, watching the breathtaking display of color. Liam's strong, tall body was folded over me from behind. I held onto his forearms, lolling my head back onto his chest. This moment...this day would forever be one of my most cherished memories.

The fireworks ended and the crowd dispersed. Liam and I remained. The smoke cleared, leaving the sky lit by only the stars and the moon. Liam's lips pressed against the top of my head. I closed my eyes, tightening my grasp around his arms. I breathed in the salty air around me that was mixed with the comforting smell of Liam.

"Are you ready to go back?"

I shook my head no.

Liam loosened his grip, moving to sit down on the sandy beach. He pulled me down with him, settling me between his bent legs. I leaned back into his chest as he held me close. We sat in a comfortable silence, just watching the waves roll onto the shore.

"Princess?"

"Hmm?" I responded lazily.

"Will you tell me something?"

"What do you want to know?"

He waited a moment before he spoke again. "Who hurt you? What did they do?"

Confused by his question, I twisted in his arms. I could see a heaviness in his eyes. He was struggling with something.

"It doesn't matter anymore," I said timidly.

"It does to me." He ran his fingers behind my ear, through my hair.

I sighed, turning back to face the water. I waited a moment, deciding how much to share with him as I watched the moon reflect across the black sea.

It wasn't that I didn't want to tell him everything. It was more that I didn't know what he was struggling with. I didn't want to tell him anything that might persuade him to distance himself from me. I inhaled deeply, gathering strength and courage, hoping that opening up to him would prompt him to open up to me.

"My ex-boyfriend and my ex-best friend," I paused, closing my eyes, fighting back the resurfacing pain. "Our senior prom...I slept with him for the first time. He was my first. I...I thought I was in love with him, and I thought he loved me. He'd tried many times before, but I always insisted I wanted to wait.

"The night after prom, a classmate of ours threw a big

house party. I didn't go; it was one of those parties where everybody was there, getting wasted, celebrating the pending end of our high school careers—wasn't really my thing.

"But, it was my boyfriend's and my friend's thing. They were both there. They ended up hooking up and having sex that night."

Liam's hold on me tightened.

"Pictures of them making out were blasted all over social media. People tagged me, so I was sure to see it."

I could feel the rage start to roll off of him. I wished the story and pain had ended after that night, but they hadn't.

"It turned out I meant nothing to either of them. She was my friend since grade school, and I dated him for two years. He'd pursued me for a year before that, so to find out they only wanted to be seen with me to raise their own social standing, hurt. I wouldn't have believed it if I hadn't seen the hurtful things they tweeted about me afterwards. They never once apologized."

"I'm sorry, babe."

I shook my head. "I still don't understand it. I mean...it was one thing for him. But she was my best friend. It's hard for me to believe that our whole friendship was a lie. We went through a lot together. It just...it doesn't make sense to me. Still."

He kissed my shoulder. We both sat speechless for a little longer. I tilted my head up to look at him.

"Liam...will you tell me something?" I asked nervously. Worry passed briefly through his eyes. "It can be whatever you want. Whatever you're ready for."

He let out a heavy breath and nodded. "What do you want to know?"

"Will you tell me who raised you after your parents died? Frankie told me he isn't really your uncle." I bit my lip with concern and anxiety. I didn't want Liam to be angry with Frankie.

"I was in foster care. My parents were both only children. My grandparents had passed away when I was younger."

"Were you adopted? Do you have adopted family?"

"I was an older kid. Angry with the world after their death. Nobody was going to adopt a kid with issues."

I glanced down momentarily. My heart broke a little, knowing he had no family in his life. At least, not until Frankie. I looked back up at him, forcing the tears back that were forming in my eyes.

"Don't look at me like that, princess."

"Like what?" My voice cracked.

"Like you feel sorry for me. I'm fine. I have Frankie now. I don't need legal documents or our blood to be the same. He's my family."

"I know. And I'm glad you have him…but Liam—" I rotated further in his arms, moving to kneel between his legs. I took his face between my hands, locking my eyes on his. I needed to make sure he heard me. That he saw me. "You have more than just Frankie. You have me."

He placed his hands over mine, removing them from his face. He held them in my lap. "Val, I have a lot of shit to work through still. I want to be someone who can take care of you."

"I don't need you to support me. If you haven't noticed, my family has basically set me up for life." I grinned sheepishly.

He released a quiet chuckle. "I'm not talking financially,

princess." He paused. His intense eyes pierced mine. "I want to be able to take care of you—mind, body, and soul."

My heart resounded in my chest. His words washed over me, clarifying all the unrecognizable emotions I'd been feeling. *I love Liam Stone.* I loved him with my whole being—mind, body, and soul.

The realization scared me, yet it made me feel safe. There were still things about his past that were a mystery to me. But somehow those things didn't matter. I trusted him. I trusted him more than I'd ever trusted anyone.

Needing him to feel me, I demolished the inches between us, throwing myself on top of him. He fell back into the sand, wrapping his arms around me, kissing me with a new determination.

CHAPTER 13

The rest of the summer was consumed by my auditions, work, and Liam's concerts. I went to as many of his shows as I possibly could, knowing that when school started I'd have less time to attend. The start of my last semester of school was only a week away.

Liam and I had planned to spend the next couple of days together. Just the two of us. He had somewhere he wanted to take me for a short getaway. He refused to tell me where, which drove me completely nuts—*how's a girl supposed to know what to pack?* But I tried to hide that fact.

The only detail he gave was that it was one of his favorite places to go growing up. He was sharing another small piece of his past with me. It made me believe he was beginning to heal from whatever plagued him.

We were leaving as soon as my shift was over at work. He'd be picking me up from Sweet Beans. The only downside of the trip was leaving Lexie alone for the next couple days. She and Jake had broken up recently. Again.

She assured me she was fine, that this time was different. She did appear to be handling this breakup better. For once, it was her who had broken things off with him. It seemed she'd had enough of his mind games.

"Okay," I said, walking back behind the counter, "all the tables are cleaned and the condiments are restocked." I untied my apron, folding it up before setting it below the counter.

"Thanks. Liam's coming to pick you up, right?" Lexie asked.

"Yeah, he should be here any minute. Are you sure you don't want me to stay? We could have a girls' night. Eat sushi and get drunk off martinis while we watch chick flicks."

She rolled her eyes with a shake of her head. "I hate chick flicks. I only watch them because you love them," she smirked.

It was my turn to roll my eyes, knowing that was a lie. She just refused to admit it.

"And I told you. I'm good. I don't need you to babysit me."

"I'm not saying you do. I just thought I'd throw it out there…since we hadn't done that in a while."

She turned away from me, moving to wipe down the coffee bar counter. "We can do that when you get back. Besides, I know you've been looking forward to this trip with Liam." She glanced over her shoulder at me, giving me a small smile. "Plus, I have plans."

"What plans?"

"I have a date." She shrugged an apathetic shoulder.

My eyes widened. "With who?!"

"Doesn't matter. The point is, you need to quit worrying about me," she said, avoiding my eyes. Which only made me more curious.

Before I could demand she tell me who, Liam walked through the door. "Looks like your ride is here." She gave me a big smile, knowing she just dodged my interrogation.

As happy as I was to see the gorgeous man walking toward me dressed in his standard ensemble of jeans and a T-shirt, I was wishing I had a few moments longer alone with Lexie to force information out of her.

"Hey, Liam," Lexie said cheerfully, relieved by the interruption.

"What's up, Lexie?" He leaned his forearms on the counter across from her as I grabbed my purse from under the counter.

"Not much. Just trying to make sure your girlfriend doesn't back out on this trip you have planned for her."

His brow furrowed. "Back out?"

"I wasn't trying to back out." I threw her an annoyed glare as I stepped up beside Liam. "I just felt bad for abandoning my roommate all the time. Excuse me for trying to be a good friend."

Liam stood, straightening his tall frame, putting his arm around my shoulder. "Do you want to stay? We can do this another time."

"No!" Lexie yelled abruptly. "You two get the hell outta here. I have plans. I don't need you around ruining them." She threw her hands on her hips.

"She has a date."

"A date?"

"Yes, a mystery date she refuses to tell me about."

Liam's brow furrowed deeper in thought before some kind of understanding passed across his facial features.

"Seriously, you two. Leave now. Before I throw you out," Lexie demanded.

"Fine. We're going," I said, grabbing Liam's arm, pulling him with me toward the door. "I'll see you in a couple days, and I expect details when I get back."

She shook her head, laughing. "You two have fun." She waved us off.

~

"Are you going to tell me where we're going yet?" I asked Liam as I catalogued another road sign as we passed it on the 210.

I was trying to determine our mystery destination by our route. Besides the fact that we were heading east, I had no idea. The state of California was huge, especially compared to my tiny home state of New York.

His mouth twitched with a smile. "You can't stand it, can you?"

I shrugged, feigning disinterest. "Just trying to make conversation to kill the time."

"I can think of other ways to kill the time." The corner of his mouth lifted, his hand sliding up my thigh, under the summer dress I'd chosen to wear.

"Focus on the road, rock star." I smiled smugly. "There will be plenty of time for that later."

He laughed. "Is that a promise?" He glanced between me and the road.

"I think we both know it's a guarantee."

"You're right. I don't plan on letting you leave the bed, other than for necessities. I've had dirty thoughts all day long and every one of them has been inspired by you."

I blushed. I loved that he thought about me when we were apart. I was more than happy to see his plan through.

"Don't pretend you haven't been having the same thoughts, princess," he teased me some more.

I grinned, shaking my head in dismay. The need within me was growing. His hand was moving dangerously close to exactly where I needed him. I intertwined my fingers with his, stopping his progression.

"Focus," I commanded again.

"Oh, I'm focused," he said mischievously, glancing to the side as he tried to move his hand north again.

"On the road!" I laughed, nodding my head toward the road in front of us.

He lifted our locked fingers to his mouth, kissing the back of my hand, chuckling to himself.

After about an hour of driving, we changed directions and roads, headed north into the mountains. In less than an hour we were pulling into Big Bear Lake. Liam turned onto a narrow, winding, dirt road with no road sign that was shaded by the canopy of the tall trees lining the roadway.

The sunlight filtered through the forest, creating an enchanting ambiance. My stomach fluttered with the suspense. The trees opened up as we neared the end of the road, reaching our final destination. My eyes widened. A modest but well-kept secluded log cabin sat facing a piece of the lake.

The cabin was wrapped with a covered wooden deck that gave you breathtaking views of the lake and mountains beyond. It was a little piece of serenity within the forest.

Liam slowed the car, pulling it under a carport before putting it in park. He glanced over at me, studying my expression carefully. I locked my eyes with his.

"We're here," he finally said, breaking our silence.

"Where's *here*, exactly?" I didn't have to explain that I wasn't asking geographically.

"My family's cabin—my cabin." His face dropped as he corrected himself.

Reaching across the console, I rested my hand on his thigh in comfort. "It's beautiful."

He gave me a weak smile, laying his hand over mine, squeezing it lightly before opening his car door to exit. I sat back, taking a deep breath, knowing this was a big step for him. I needed to be the strong one this weekend. I needed to be strong for him. Being here was likely going to stir up some memories. It meant a lot that he was sharing this with me.

He moved around to my side of the car, opening my door for me. He helped me out of the car before grabbing our bags to carry them inside. I walked a few feet ahead of him, stopping to take in the view and breathe in the fresh mountain air. The sun glistened and reflected over the gentle rolls of the rippling water.

Liam disappeared into the house. I walked up the stairs of the porch and strolled along the wooden deck, running my fingers across the railing. I halted my progression as my fingers passed over a rough spot in the otherwise smooth railing. I stared down at the four sets of carved initials. I studied them, tracing my finger over each. The only one I knew for sure was the LES—Liam Edward Stone.

I didn't have time to contemplate the other initials for long. Liam was suddenly behind me.

"Come on, princess." He smiled as he lifted and cradled me into his arms.

I squealed with a giggle, wrapping my arms around his neck. He walked me toward the door, carrying me over the threshold as he kissed me. He gently lowered my feet back to the ground, steadying me as our kissing continued. His dimple graced his face when our lips separated.

"I need to get the food and other stuff out of the car. And then we'll finish this."

"Do you mind if I take a tour?" I asked nervously, not wanting to overstep or pry.

"Of course, princess. Make yourself at home." He brushed his hand down my cheek, giving me one more gentle kiss before leaving out the front door. I slowly spun around to face the interior of the cabin. It was a simple rectangular layout with a minimalist design, but it had all the necessities.

To my far right was a small wooden dining table with four chairs that sat opposite the kitchen. The only separation between the two rooms was a breakfast bar with barstools. There was a narrow staircase that started in the dining area and rose to an open loft area above the kitchen. The open loft housed a couple of children's twin bunk beds.

To the left of the door was a seating area with a moderate-sized TV that hung over a stone fire place with a thick, rustic, wood mantel. An old, patterned, fabric couch of dark forest green was placed opposite the fireplace and accented with brown leather throw pillows. A single brown recliner flanked one side of the couch, with an end table separating them.

Beyond the seating area was a wall lined with crowded bookshelves and a door that led into a master bedroom with the only bathroom in the whole cabin. I walked toward the wall of bookshelves, drawn to the photos of his family, needing to see the people who were tragically ripped from his life.

There were tons of photos, most of which appeared to have been taken during times they spent at this cabin. It was a timeline of their lives. The first few showed younger, vibrant versions of only his parents. There was one of his mother pregnant, standing on the deck outside, staring out at the lake. She looked content, as peaceful as the view that surrounded her. I glided slowly along, following the story.

His parents were always smiling. They seemed happy and in love. I stopped at the last picture, picking it up to study it closer. It no longer displayed a family of three, but a family of four. Liam smiled from atop his father's shoulders, and looked to be a little older than he'd been in the photo I'd seen in his place in L.A. His mother held a small baby dressed in a pink and white floral onesie.

I forced back the sob and tears that were rising. The realization he'd lost not only his parents but also a little sister in that car accident had my heart aching. Hearing the rustle of Liam returning, I suppressed my sadness for the man I loved, trying to maintain the strength I was determined to have for him.

I hastily placed the frame back on the shelf. I forced a smile before swiveling to face him. His hands and arms were full as he struggled to maneuver everything through the narrow door opening.

"Do you need any help?" I choked out with an unnatural cheerfulness.

"Nah, I got it, princess. This is everything."

He walked toward the table, setting it all on top. Unable to remain idle—where the sad thoughts would have free rein over my mind—I moved to help him anyway. We both unpacked the grocery bags, putting away the food he'd purchased for our stay. Once everything was stored away, Liam made us a quick bite to eat before carrying me off to bed, caveman style.

~

Liam rolled to his side, resting his head in his hand as he gazed down at me. I watched my finger as I traced it along the black lines of his tattoo, lost in my thoughts.

"Will you tell me about your tattoo?"

"What do you mean?"

"Well…most people choose tattoos for a reason, right? Is there a reason or story behind yours? Or did you just get drunk one night and choose it at random?"

He released a small chuckle. "No…it means something to me."

I watched his face before focusing on his indicative eyes. I waited for the hard, distant Liam to appear, but he didn't.

"Will you tell me?" I asked cautiously.

"The symbol stands for strength," he said, grazing his hand through my hair.

"And the numbers?" I asked, looking at the tiny 4:13 that was interwoven into the symbol.

A heaviness darkened his eyes. He closed them for a moment before opening them to respond. "It was the official time they were pronounced dead." My breath caught in my chest. I expected for him to end his explanation there, but he continued.

"After their funeral, the pastor who performed the burial service found me hiding from the crowd of people that attended. My parents had a lot of friends. They were well loved, but I barely knew their friends. Most I didn't know at all, so the last thing I wanted was to be surrounded by them and their grief-stricken faces.

"I'd been sitting on the back steps of the church, tracing the numbers over and over with a black pen on the back of my hand. I'm not even sure why I was doing it. I guess I was just wishing somehow, I could go back before that time and change the events that led to that moment. Like if I engraved them on me, they'd magically take me back in time, where I could keep them from getting into that car.

"The pastor didn't speak when he first sat with me. He remained quiet for a long time, just sitting there, watching me with the pen. When he finally spoke, he told me those numbers were some of his favorite numbers. When I asked him why, he said because they reminded him of the words of Philippians 4:13... 'I can do all things through Christ who strengthens me.'

"He asked why I was writing them on my hand. I told him

it was their time of death. He waited a few moments before he spoke again, but his words have stuck with me since that day. He told me maybe there was a reason God took them at that moment. Maybe God was telling me that I could endure the pain I was currently suffering, that I needed to find strength in Christ.

"At the time, his words of comfort meant nothing to me. I was ten. All I wanted were my parents. I was angry with God for taking them. It took me many years to find that strength and move forward from my pain and anger. It was around that time that I got the tattoo."

Unpreventable tears had welled in my eyes by the time Liam finished speaking. One slipped from the corner. He rubbed his thumb along my skin to catch it.

I didn't know what to say. I could barely form words. I was afraid I would release a sob when I was trying to be strong for him. I was failing miserably. I hated he had to go through all of that at such a young age. And all alone. My heart broke for ten-year-old Liam.

"Liam, I...thank you... Thank you for telling me."

He nodded, giving me a frail smile, barely visible on his face. "I think that's enough history lessons for the night."

I nodded my agreement. He pulled me to his chest as he rolled us, laying back onto the bed. I pressed my cheek against his heart, listening to its rapid beats. He kissed the crown of my head. His heart slowed to a strong, steady rhythm. I inhaled a deep breath, releasing it in synchronization with his.

I closed my eyes, feeling stronger. Feeling stronger in us. In our future. I knew every time he shared a piece of himself with me, was another step he was taking to show me how much he trusted me. It showed me how much he was in this with me—that he was finally accepting that he could be happy. That he could be happy with me. He deserved happiness. He deserved a loving family. And I hoped I could be the one to give him that.

CHAPTER 14

The following morning, I woke before Liam. I'd been working a lot of early morning shifts over the last few weeks, which set my internal clock to wake earlier than I liked. I watched Liam's handsome face as he slept peacefully. After so many minutes had passed that my act of love and adoration seemed just plain creepy, I decided to get up and make us some breakfast.

I eased myself out of the bed, being careful not to wake him. I slipped into the bathroom, quietly brushing my teeth and pulling my hair into a ponytail. I tiptoed out of the room, closing the door softly behind me before walking into the kitchen to dig through the ingredients that Liam had brought.

After setting the coffee to brew, I pulled out the eggs, bacon, and bread. I scoured the kitchen cabinets in search of the necessary pans and utensils to prepare breakfast.

Liam usually did all the cooking for us. I'd never been a

cook until Lexie moved in with me. I hadn't needed to; growing up, I'd had personal chefs at my disposal. I'd always eaten at Rhett's or out at a restaurant after I moved to California. But Lexie had taught me how to make a few basics.

As I wrapped up the scrambled eggs, Liam sleepily walked into the kitchen with his exposed abs and only a pair of black, mesh athletic shorts on. His hand rubbed over the top of his head, further messing up his already-ruffled hair. He looked so devastatingly handsome I completely forgot about the bacon I was now burning.

"Crap!" I yelped, removing it from the pan, ripping my eyes from his Greek god-like body.

"You're cooking?" He raised an eyebrow.

The state of shock on his face and humor in his voice was almost offensive. In fact, had a wide grin not accompanied it, revealing his delicious dimple, I may have truly been upset.

"Well I was trying until you walked in here, distracting me," I huffed, pulling the last of the bacon from the pan.

He wrapped his arms around my waist from behind and buried his face in my neck.

"The burnt bacon is your fault," I blamed him.

He released a quiet laugh, dropping a line of kisses down my shoulder. "Do you need help, princess?" He nipped at my ear.

"No," I breathed.

"I don't mind." The tip of his nose ran back up my neck.

I tilted my head to the side. "It's already ready." My voice came out strained.

"So am I." His hands splayed over my hips, pulling them back to press against the ridge in his mesh shorts. My breath hitched.

"Liam," I pleaded. I wasn't sure if it was for him to continue or stop.

"Yes, princess?"

Unsure of what I actually wanted, I didn't respond. His hands rotated my hips, so I was facing him. One slid to the small of my back, as the other brushed down my jawline.

"Come back to bed."

"We need to eat."

"We can eat later," he continued to persuade my body.

"It'll be cold by then...plus, I have a feeling once we go back, we won't be getting back out."

He grinned. "You're right. And you'll need your energy. Eat and then bed," he agreed.

He cupped my face between his hands, planting a firm kiss on my lips, leaving me lightheaded. He snuck a piece of bacon before turning to make a cup a coffee.

"Hey!" I laugh-yelled, smacking his butt for his thievery.

"Extra crispy. Just how I like it." He winked.

It was a little more than extra crispy, but I accepted the compliment anyway. I dished up two plates of scrambled eggs and bacon. I retrieved the toast from the toaster, buttered them, and placed one on each plate. Liam took a seat at the head of the table, sipping on his coffee. I set a plate in front of him before taking a seat with my own. Liam pulled my bare feet into his lap, needing constant contact.

"I think this is the first meal you've ever cooked for me." He stared down at his plate.

"You're the first guy I've ever cooked for."

"So I'm taking your cooking virginity?" His eyebrows raised.

I laughed. "You're terrible. Just eat."

I watched him as he took a bite of his eggs, grinning roguishly. His chewing came to a stop with the sound of a crunch between his teeth. My face dropped as he brought his napkin to his lips, removing the food from his mouth.

"What? What's wrong?" I stared at him anxiously.

"Nothing. Just a little bit of egg shell."

"Oh my gosh. I can't believe I messed up the eggs, too." I hid my face with the palms of my hands. I thought I had retrieved all the pieces that had accidentally cracked off when I was cooking them earlier.

He laughed lightheartedly. "It's fine, princess. It happens to even the most seasoned chefs." His lie was sweet, but we both knew that to be untrue.

He leaned forward, removing my hands from my face, placing a kiss on my lips. "It's good," he assured me. When I didn't move to pick up my fork, he tilted his head demandingly. "Eat, princess. I want you back in bed, sooner rather than later... Just beware of egg shells." He laughed.

A grin snuck onto my face. I playfully pushed against his shoulder, forcing him to sit back in his chair.

We finished our breakfast with our usual playful and flirty banter. Liam cleaned up the dishes while I went to freshen up and check my text messages. I crawled back in bed, pulling the blankets over me, grabbing my phone from the side table. I sent Lexie a quick text, inquiring about her date.

Liam walked into the room with lust and mischief seeping from every inch of his body. He moved forward, his body full of swagger. I set my phone aside. My eyes remained locked on him, mesmerized.

"No blankets this time, princess. I want to see every bit of that gorgeous body."

His voice floated over me like cool silk. My body instantly responded. The heat cascaded down me from head to toe, waking a carnal desire. He lifted the blankets from my body, tossing them back to the foot of the bed.

"Strip."

His one-word demand would have normally triggered a rebellious reaction from me. But the strong, firm delivery had my body and mind submitting to his every command.

I gripped the hem of my tank top, pulling it over my head, exposing my bare chest. I dropped my shirt over the side of the bed to the floor. I scooted forward, lying back, sliding my shorts and panties down my legs, discarding them also.

I lay completely bare to Liam. The heat and appreciation in his eyes as they moved up the length of my body turned me on as much as his touch. Liam removed his shorts, standing gloriously over me.

He crawled onto the bed at my feet. "Raise your hands and grab onto the bed."

Once again, I complied without thought or argument, clenching my fists around two of the iron spindles of the headboard. My eagerness had small spasms running through my keen body with irregular breaths.

"We're going to do this my way, princess. Keep your hands locked on the bed. If you remove them, I stop," he warned. "Understand?"

I nodded, even though I wanted to tell him screw that and this game. I wanted him inside me. Now. But for some reason, I was intrigued and willing to put myself through the delicious torture that awaited me.

His head ducked down as the tip of his tongue slipped through his lips, licking up the length of my inner leg. His scruff grated my skin as he went. I held my breath, clenching my fists tighter around the iron rods. My heart accelerated.

As his tongue came within inches of where I needed him most, my hips raised to guide him to the sweet spot. He forced them back to the bed, shaking his head in warning. He continued his mercurial manipulations. My body continued to spasm with desperation. Every second he kissed, licked, and caressed each inch of my body, felt like an eternity.

"God, princess," Liam groaned as the palm of his hand glided up my flattened tummy. "I love feeling your soft, silky skin against me."

He climbed up my body, aligning himself at my entrance. I held my breath, ready for the divine torture to end.

"Liam," I begged as he hovered over me. I was so wound up I thought I might die. I was losing the strength to remain clutched to the bed frame. I needed to touch him. Desperately. But I didn't want to risk him stopping. I wouldn't be able to handle it if he did.

"Tell me what you need, princess."

"You. I need you."

With the release of my words, he claimed me, pushing inside me with ease, reuniting us, my body accepting him as its other half.

"Liam," I moaned my plea. "I need to touch you."

"Okay, princess...let go," he gritted out between his forceful pumps.

The words had barely left his mouth before I desperately clung to his shoulders, digging my fingers into his skin. We slammed our mouths together as he deftly worked our bodies to their precipice.

My body hummed. He lifted his upper body to his hands, holding himself above me as he steadily continued to move inside me. I clutched his taut biceps as he watched me come unraveled below him.

"Liam." His name was barely a breathy rasp falling from my lips. I closed my eyes to conceal the vision of his strong body, trying to control my release, stretching it out longer.

"Fuck…" he grated. "I love watching you spasm below me, moaning my name."

His words were my undoing. The little bit of control I had over my orgasm was lost. A tremble rolled through me. Pleasure exploded. He growled his own release while helping to extend mine.

His tired, sweaty body fell over me, melting into me. When our breathing slowed, he rolled us into his favorite position, plastering me against his chest as he held me firmly to him. We laid in silence for a while, bringing our minds and bodies back down to Earth.

~

We spent most of our morning in bed. It wasn't until after Liam made me lunch that we ventured outside of the cabin, going for a hike along a trail that followed the edge of the lake. Liam told me more about the property and his family.

They owned a little over four acres where the cabin was situated. His family spent many long weekends together here. It was where they would go to get away from their busy city life. His dad was a plastic surgeon and his mom was an attorney. Most of the memories he still had of his family were from their time spent here. The property had been left to him in their will. It was the only thing he had left of them. Everything else he'd gotten rid of, but he couldn't bring himself to part with the cabin.

He didn't come out here as much anymore. But Frankie, Dax, and he would try to make it out to the cabin every couple of months for a fishing trip or to take care of maintenance issues to keep it in good shape.

By the time we returned to the cabin, I was exhausted. I relaxed on the porch swing, looking out at the shimmering lake. Liam was inside, grabbing us some snacks and beverages. He returned with a glass of wine for me and a bottle of beer for himself, along with a small plate of various deli meats and cheeses.

Liam held my hand as the swing swayed slowly back and forth. We watched the sun descend as we sipped our drinks with casual conversation. The sun departed, and the air cooled around us. A chilly breeze sent shivers through my body, and goosebumps prickled my skin.

"Are you cold?" he asked, pulling me closer to his side to warm me.

"A little," I admitted.

"I'll get you a blanket." He kissed my temple before releasing me to go inside.

I pulled my feet up onto the edge of the swing, wrapping my arms around my bent knees. Liam returned moments later with a blanket and my phone. He handed both to me.

"Your phone was blowing up in there," he explained when I gave him a questioning look.

"Oh." I swiped at my screen, unlocking my phone to find a multitude of missed calls and texts from every member of my family. "Oh my gosh!" I jumped up from the swing in a panic, the blanket falling to the ground. "We have to go! Now! We have to go back to L.A!"

Liam's face fell with concern. "What happened? Is everything okay?"

"No!" I spit out without thinking.

His eyes flashed with fear. His body went rigid.

"I mean, yes. Sorry. Ava's in labor. My nephew is coming!" I beamed excitedly.

He relaxed immediately, and a slow smile stretched across his face. "Okay, princess," he said calmly. "We need to pack up and then we can head back."

"There's no time! We have to get to the hospital."

He laughed. "I don't know much about having a baby, but I do know they don't just come flying out as soon as the woman goes into labor. Maybe call your family. See how she's doing. I'll pack."

He kissed my forehead before heading inside to pack up our things. I called Rhett and confirmed she was still in early labor. He assured me we had plenty of time. My parents and Ava's family were on a flight headed to Los Angeles. Ava's mom had arrived earlier in the week, anticipating that she would be going into labor soon.

Liam had us on the road within forty minutes of hearing the news. He drove us straight to the hospital. Rhett met us in the waiting area to give us a brief update. He seemed way calmer and more in control than I was. I had no idea how he did it. I was a hot mess. After giving us the latest, he rushed back to be with Ava.

My parents, Ava's sister, Emily, her husband, Jackson, and their grandmother, who we all called Nana, arrived. I hugged them all, giving them the latest and introducing them to Liam. The introduction to my parents was a bit awkward...it wasn't exactly how I'd planned for them to meet Liam for the first time. I hadn't even thought to warn Liam.

It worked out for the best, though. My parents were so overly joyous about the arrival of their first grandchild that my father didn't even think to give Liam the third degree. After another hour of waiting impatiently in the uncomfortable hospital chairs, Ava's mother, Sarah, came out to give us the most current update.

"She's starting to push. He'll be here soon!" She smiled gleefully. "She's doing great."

We all sat on pins and needles, waiting. Liam held my hand tight as everyone visited in hushed voices. After what seemed like forever, Rhett came out with the proudest smile on his face and a gleam in his eyes. Nathaniel David Blackwood had arrived, named after Ava's father. He was healthy and happy, snuggling in Ava's arms.

We gave Ava and Rhett a few more minutes alone with their son before we each took turns going to meet him. When it was finally my turn, Liam went with me. I walked into the room, peeking my head through the cracked door. My giddiness over meeting my baby nephew was obvious from the huge smile on my face.

Ava was sitting up in the bed, holding baby Nate as Rhett stood beside them, staring lovingly at his family. I watched for a moment before interrupting them. I looked back at

Liam with fondness. He smiled back at me. I opened the door farther.

"Hi," I said softly, not wanting to startle the baby.

Ava and Rhett looked up at me simultaneously.

"Val," Ava greeted me with a grin. "Come meet your nephew."

I walked with light footsteps into the room, with Liam following behind. He stepped off to the side as I approached the side of the bed.

"Oh my gosh...Ava...he's beautiful."

"Just like his mother," Rhett added, kissing her on the top of her head.

I smiled down at my baby nephew, taking in every little feature, from his tiny fingers to his tiny ears that were surrounded by a full head of dark brown hair. I stuck my finger out, letting him grasp his little hand around it.

"Hi there, Nate. I'm your Aunt Val." I leaned in, whispering to him as his big blue eyes landed on me.

"Do you want to hold him?" Ava offered.

I nodded eagerly. Ava shifted, sitting up to delicately pass Nate to me. I cradled him in my arms, pulling him close to my body, unable to remove the smile that was plastered permanently to my face.

I glanced over at Liam, who was standing awkwardly off to the side. "Come meet him."

Liam looked at Rhett, who gave a single encouraging nod. He walked to stand behind me, looking over my shoulder at him.

"Isn't he the cutest thing you've ever seen?"

"He's definitely a handsome guy." Liam smiled softly down at him.

"Do you want to hold him?"

He shook his head, "I'm good."

I giggled at his obvious nervousness. I wondered if he'd ever been around a baby besides his baby sister.

"Fine. More snuggles for me." I wasn't really ready to release him anyway.

After a few more minutes of bonding with Nate, I handed him to my brother. He held him closely to his chest as we all visited. Ava and Rhett each gave us their version of the moment Ava went into labor. Nate fell asleep, despite the conversation around him. Nana came through the door with Sarah.

"Where is that handsome great-grandson of mine?" she asked as she slowly moved farther into the room. Sarah supported Nana as she walked. It amazed me that the old woman was still kicking. She had a youthfulness about her, despite her aged body.

"He's right here, Nana," Rhett grinned at her.

He moved a chair one-handedly next to the bed for her to sit as he held his son in the other. Sarah helped Nana settle into the chair. Once she was situated, Rhett handed Nate over to her. She smiled proudly down at him.

"He's just as handsome as his father. He's going to be a strapping young man."

"Thank you, Nana...but I think all the best parts of him come from his mother's side." Rhett glanced back at Ava, winking at her.

"Maybe so...but he definitely has your cheeks," she reached up, patting Rhett's face with one hand.

Ava choked on her laughter, while the rest of us held in our own. The old woman adored my brother and had never been shy about letting him know it. As if his ego needed it.

We watched Nana coo at Nate a little longer before telling everyone goodbye. I promised to stop by the house after they were settled at home.

∼

Liam was oddly quiet on the drive back to his place. In fact, he had been oddly quiet since the moment we arrived at the hospital. I looked over at him, noticing the tenseness in his face for the first time.

"Is everything okay?"

He didn't respond.

"Liam?" I said as I slid my hand over his thigh. He flinched slightly before glancing over at me.

"Sorry. Did you say something?"

"Yeah...I asked if you were okay."

He nodded, giving me nothing else. He was closing himself off again, and I couldn't understand why. I removed my hand from him. I sat back, trying to process what possibly could have happened for him to turn cold. We'd come so far over the last few days.

I closed my eyes, needing to think. I was tired and drained from the long night. I opened my eyes when the car slowed and came to a stop. I looked over at him, confused. We were outside my apartment building.

"I thought we were going to your place?"

"It's been a long night, Val. You should get some rest."

"You're not coming up with me?"

He shook his head. I stared at him in disbelief. This was

worse than normal. He was pushing me away. Not just emotionally, but physically.

"I'll call you tomorrow," he said, reaching out to run his hand along my face.

I swatted it away. "Don't bother," I clipped.

I flung the door open, rushing out of the car, slamming the door behind me. My heart pounded hard in my chest, even though it was crumbling. I moved as quickly as my feet would carry me without breaking into a full-on sprint. I heard the slam of a car door.

"Damn it! Val! Wait!" Liam yelled from a distance. I ignored him, focused on getting inside my building and away from him. I was only a few feet from the main entrance when I felt a hand clasp around my wrist. I tried to yank free, but his hold was too strong.

"Val, stop!"

I whipped around. "Screw you," I screamed. Tears escaped from my eyes. I had no idea why I was crying; most likely it was simply the result of the emotional roller-coaster I'd been on for the last forty-eight hours. He crushed me to his body, trying to calm me down. I beat my fist on his chest, letting out every emotion through my punches.

"I'm sorry...I'm sorry. I'm a fucking asshole." He ran his hand down the back of my hair as he held me tight. I pushed against his chest forcefully, freeing myself. He loosened his grip, allowing me to step away.

"Stop it! Stop freaking apologizing and just tell me what's wrong!" I demanded through my tears.

"I..." he stuttered. "I don't know. I..." He raked his hands through his hair.

"I don't understand you. I'm trying really hard to. I want to be here for you. But you keep pushing me away."

"I don't want to hurt you."

"Then don't push me away. Talk to me. Let me be there for you."

He nodded, but his face remained hardened. I turned away from him. I needed to calm my nerves.

"Val." He grabbed at my wrist desperately.

"I'm not walking away. I just need a minute," I assured him. He released me. I took a couple of deep breaths, gathering the strength we both required.

When I turned back to him, his face was sunken with defeat as he stared at the ground, lost in his own head. I stepped toward him, cupping his face in my hands as I raised it to look at me.

"Liam...we're staying the night together. And you're going to talk to me." My determined stare and tone left no room for argument.

"Okay, princess."

"Okay," I reconfirmed. I took his hand in mine and led him into my apartment. I had no idea if Lexie was home, and I started to wonder if maybe it would have been better for us to go to his place. But at this point, I was too tired to make that drive, and too determined to get some answers as to what had spooked him and made him want to push me away.

When we walked into my apartment, the place was dark and eerily quiet. I got the feeling Lexie was probably not home. I just hoped that didn't mean she was back with Jake. I didn't let myself think about that for more than a second. In that moment, I needed to focus on Liam.

We walked into my bedroom. I released his hand, leaving

him in the doorway of my room. I switched on a lamp, illuminating the room with a dim glow. It was still dark outside, but the sun would be up in a few hours. I hadn't slept, but I was wide awake.

I slipped off my shoes and climbed into my bed. Liam stood, unmoving. I looked at him expectantly. He hesitated before moving, slipping off his own shoes and stripping out of his clothes. He crawled into bed beside me. His arms enclosed me as he pulled me down to my side to face him. We stared at each other for a moment before he spoke.

"I've only been in a hospital two other times. Once when I waited for my family to die, and once when I thought I was waiting for Frankie to die."

I closed my eyes as I realized what being there might have been doing to him.

"I'm sorry. I didn't even think—"

"Let me finish, princess." He brushed my hair from my face. I nodded.

"I'm glad I was there. I'm glad I got to witness life come out of there and not just death."

"Then why—"

He raised an eyebrow at me, silencing my question. *Right. Let him finish.*

"You have so many people in your life who love you. You have a great family. They're perfect. You're perfect. And I don't want to be the imperfect in your life. I don't want to be the one who drags you into the dark."

His face was pained with self-doubt.

"Liam...we are far from perfect. We just accept each other for who we are. We love unconditionally. And regardless of what you think of yourself, you are perfect. You're perfect for me," I told him with conviction.

"I wish that were true, princess. But there is so much you still don't know. Things that would change your mind."

"Nothing will change my mind, and I hope one day you will trust in me—in us—enough to tell me. But until that day, I'm going to do everything I can to make you believe it."

His feeble smile told me he was pretending to be hopeful. But I could see the anguish still in his eyes. I lifted my lips to his, pressing a firm kiss to his mouth. I burrowed into his chest, preparing to allow my sleepy mind to rest.

"Thank you for staying and talking to me," I whispered. He kissed the top of my head moments before I drifted off to sleep.

CHAPTER 15

My final fall semester was a whirlwind of school, work, and auditions. Liam and I mostly saw each other in passing, but we stayed as many nights together as we could. It was the week after Thanksgiving, and I was finally done with school, except for the graduation ceremony. Liam and Frankie had spent Thanksgiving with my family and Ava's. The day had been full of laughter, especially watching the repartee between Nana and Frankie.

It turned out Donna dropping me as a client was a blessing in disguise. My new agent, Amanda, was able to get me auditions for better roles that lead to greater opportunities. I had one earlier in the day for a small indie film that I knew I'd nailed. I was really hoping to get a call back. The script for the movie was great. With the right people involved, it could end up gaining a lot of traction—traction that could help my own career.

I was on my way to pick up Lexie from work. We were headed to do a little shopping for outfits to wear to the Derailed concert tonight. I hadn't been able to attend one in a while, which I hated. Liam understood. He was always supportive, telling me I needed to focus on school and my auditions, assuring me there would be plenty of shows for me to attend in the future.

Despite his best efforts to make me feel better about missing them, I still felt badly. I wanted to be able to support him and his music. I knew how much his music meant to him. Plus, I hated the thought of all the groupies getting their claws on him when I wasn't around. I had no doubt Liam would do everything to avoid their advances. I trusted him. It didn't mean I liked giving them the opportunity to try, though.

Lexie was already waiting for me outside of Sweet Beans when I pulled up. She jumped in my car, just as excited about the shopping trip as me. Or maybe she was more excited about going to the show. Either way, we were both in happy moods and happy relationships.

It turned out her mystery date from months ago was Dax. The two of them had been dating ever since. I was ecstatic for her. Dax seemed as into Lexie as she was him. Plus, it gave me someone to hang with in their reserved booth during the concerts as we privately glared at all the other girls ogling our men.

We decided to begin our shopping trip by getting our nails done. Tonight was a special night for Derailed. They had recently brought on a manager—a manager who had a lot of connections. He had arranged for the producer of a well-known record label to attend tonight.

After wrapping up our girls' day, Lexie and I returned to our apartment to get ready for the show. We both had picked out dresses and heels to wear. Lexie was more open to wearing stilettos, knowing it drove Dax wild when she did. She still needed a little practice walking in them, though.

I wrapped a towel around me as I stepped out of the shower. I curled my hair into big, loose curls and applied my makeup before walking into my room to slip on my dress. I picked up the burgundy velvet dress I had bought; it was a skin-tight number, with spaghetti straps and a scoop neck that showed enough cleavage to be sexy without being too revealing.

I sat on the cream bench at the end of my bed as I slipped on my black strappy heels. Lexie walked into my room just as I was standing to give myself the once-over.

"Wow, Lex," I said as I turned to face her. "Dax is going to freak when he sees you."

She glanced down at the fitted, strapless, black leather minidress she had her body wrapped in. "Well we both know how much he likes his women in leather," she said with a wink.

I laughed.

"Do you have heels I can borrow?"

"Of course," I said, walking into my oversized closet. Lexie followed behind me. "Which ones do you want?"

"You pick. I'm too overwhelmed by the selection. We'll be here all night if I have to pick," she laughed.

I skimmed my shelves in search of the perfect pair. My eyes landed on my golden gladiator-sandal stilettos. I pulled them from the shelf, turning toward Lexie. She eyed them skeptically.

"Those look scary. I'm going to kill myself in those things. How tall is that heel anyway?"

"I don't know…maybe two inches," I lied, keeping my fingers wrapped around the shoes. They were definitely three inches. I extended my arms, pushing them toward her. "Put them on. They'll look hot with the black leather. I'll grab you a pair of gold earrings to match."

She took the shoes from my hand, sitting on the round, tufted bench in my closet to put on the heels. "I already have earrings."

"Yeah, but they're boring studs. You need some dangly gold ones. Something that says, 'I'm a rock star's girl…'"

"My grandmother gave me these!" she shrieked, pretending to be offended as she placed her hand over her ear lobe.

"My point exactly…"

She rolled her eyes, laughing. I selected my twenty-four-karat gold, diamond-shaped drop earrings before walking over to her. "Here you go. Put these on."

"Anything else you want to change about me?" she asked with a hint of sarcasm as she switched out the earrings.

I laughed. "No. You look perfect now."

I offered my hands to help pull her up from the stool. I gave her a minute to balance herself in the heels before releasing her hands.

"I feel like I'm on top of the world up here."

"If you don't stop being a smart ass, I'm going to push you over."

She laughed. "Fine…are you ready to go? The Uber driver is probably close. And I'm going to need all the time I can get to make it downstairs in these things."

"Yes," I giggled, grabbing a black leather jacket for myself.

∼

There was a long line outside of the entrance to The Republic. It surprised me to see a crowd this size on a Thursday night. With the growing popularity of Derailed, it was becoming harder to get into one of their concerts. Luckily for us, we were automatically admitted and able to bypass the line. Joe gave a slight smile as we approached.

"Go on in ladies," he said as we passed by.

"Thanks, Joe," we both said before entering through the main door of the bar.

The place was already packed. We couldn't maneuver through the crowd without rubbing against random people as we pressed through to get to the band's booth. Derailed hadn't started, yet. There was currently another, younger band I'd never heard of opening for them.

When we arrived at the booth, Marcus, their manager, was already seated with who I assumed was the guy from the record label. Marcus smiled at our arrival.

"Ladies, how are you?"

"Great," Lexie answered for us as we slid into the booth opposite them.

"Aaron, these two beautiful ladies are Lexie *and* Valerie Blackwood. Ladies, Aaron Walker from Blue Light Records," James said, introducing us.

The fact that Marcus had name dropped my last name and not Lexie's wasn't lost on me. And as much as that would have normally angered me, I let it go. If it would help Liam and Derailed, I would put my own issues aside.

"Blackwood?" A slimy smile spread across Aaron's face. "As in Blackwood Industries?"

Lexie looked over at me with concern in her eyes. I plastered on an over-enthusiastic smile, "The one and only."

His own smile grew to a new level of sleaziness. He leaned his greedy body forward, resting his forearms on the table. "And what is your association with Derailed?"

"I'm dating the lead singer, Liam."

"I see," he said, sitting back as he processed this piece of information. "So, Rhett Blackwood is your...?"

"Brother," I answered his lingering question.

The crowd erupted into high-pitched squeals and cheers, interrupting any further conversation between us. We turned our eyes to the source of excitement. Derailed had taken the stage. The crowd continued to scream, wild with anticipation as they waited for the band to start playing the first song of their set.

Once the band started to play and Aaron and Marcus were distracted, I felt Lexie nudge my shoulder with her own. I turned to her questioning eyes. She was worried about me. I gave her a reassuring smile before turning my focus back to Liam.

As soon as he started to sing, everything that had just happened was forgotten. His insanely talented voice poured over me, warming me. I clenched the edge of the seat as I leaned forward. My body was drawn to him like a bee to the nectar of a flower. It was natural. Instinctive. As if it needed him to survive.

I barely registered the waitress who had brought us our preferred drinks. I remained focused on Liam the whole night, unable and unwilling to remove my eyes from him as he sang and played the guitar. Watching Liam in his element was my second-favorite thing to do. My first was watching Liam in my bed, whether it be him sleeping, or making me spin out of control as he manipulated my body.

Liam seemed to be having the same problem as me. He glanced over at me with his sexy grin more often than usual. Most of the time he focused on the crowd, drawing them in with his performance, driving the females mad.

We hadn't seen each other since yesterday morning. It was one of our longest stints apart, and likely the reason for his distraction. Dax had smiled and winked at Lexie when they first took the stage. A few times—when I was able to tear my eyes momentarily from Liam—I caught them making eyes at each other, too.

As the guys began the last song of the night, I looked over at Aaron to see if I could read his expression as he watched. For the most part his face was impassive, but his body language told me he liked what he was hearing. He listened intently and watched the crowd as the band interacted with them.

When the song ended, Derailed moved to leave the stage. Marcus slid out of the booth to retrieve the band members who were being detained by crazed fangirls. Liam and Dax broke free first, already headed toward us, while Marcus freed Trent and Blaine from their claws. I stood, allowing Dax to sit next to Lexie.

I remained standing, being drawn into Liam's side by his arm. Aaron introduced himself to Liam and Dax as the other guys came up behind us. Not wanting to distract Liam from any important business conversation, I excused myself to go to the ladies' room and signaled for Lexie to follow.

We took our time in the restroom. After seeing the guys were still in what looked to be a good conversation with Aaron, we decided to head to the bar to get ourselves another round of drinks

"Do you think he'll offer them a deal?" Lexie asked.

"He would be stupid not to. If he doesn't, someone else will."

"I almost hope he doesn't."

"Why?"

"I don't know...he just rubbed me the wrong way. He seemed very interested in you and your family."

"Most people are, Lex. It's why I tell you I prefer not to say anything."

"I know...I've just never seen that kind of reaction before. I know you said it happens, but it's the first time I've seen it myself."

I shrugged. I didn't want to think about it anymore.

"It made me want to punch him in the face," she added.

I laughed at her protectiveness of me. The bartender handed us our drinks. I glanced over at the booth, finding Aaron on his feet, shaking everyone's hand in departure.

"Looks like the coast is clear." I nodded my head toward them.

"Let's go," she said, waving her hand ahead of her for me to lead.

I began squeezing my way through the crowd. I glanced back toward Lexie, only to find she was no longer behind me. I stood on my tiptoes, trying to find her. I spotted her a few feet away, unmoving, with a troubled expression.

I retreated from my original destination, making my way back to her. As I drew nearer, the reason for her distress became clear. Jake stood in front of her with a tight hold on her arm.

"What the fuck, Lex?" I heard him yell at her.

"Get your hands off of me."

"Is this why you broke things off with me? So you could become a fucking groupie?"

"Fuck you, Jake."

"Let her go," I gritted out, moving beside her. I glared at his glassed-over, bloodshot eyes. He was drunk. Or high. Likely both.

"Stay out of this, Val. This is probably all your fucking fault. You're nothing but a stupid, spoiled bitch."

"Watch how you talk to my girl, motherfucker."

All of our eyes flung to Liam, who had just arrived to our shouting match. Dax stepped up beside him. Seeing Jake's hand on Lexie, he started to shove past Liam to get to her. Liam raised his arm, holding Dax back.

"Let her go, Jake," Liam's gruff voice demanded.

Jake's eyes narrowed as he glared at Liam and Dax. Realizing he was outnumbered, he pushed her toward Dax as he released her. "Fucking take her. She's nothing but a needy bitch, anyway."

Dax lunged for Jake. Liam moved quickly to stop his friend, but Dax had already gotten a swing in, connecting his fist with the side of Jake's face. I heard the crack even over the loud music.

Jake stumbled back, rubbing his hand along his jaw before lunging for Dax. Lexie screamed, moving to stop him. I grabbed her, pulling her away from the fight. Liam jumped between them, shoving his friend back. At the same time, Joe appeared and pushed Jake away from Dax. The two struggled to get at each other around the large bodies of their friends.

"Dax!" Liam yelled, trying to distract him from his rage. The tension and anger ricocheted between them. "Calm the fuck down. Take Lexie and cool off."

Dax breathed heavily, finally stopping his charge as he watched Joe force Jake from the bar. He nodded, moving his eyes in search of Lexie.

I had her wrapped in my arms as she sobbed. Dax moved between us. "Shit, Lex. Come here, babe." I released her as he pulled her from my arms, hugging her to him, kissing her sweetly on the top of her head. He guided her toward the back of the bar, near the emergency exit.

Liam's arms wrapped around me as I watched them disappear. Until now, I hadn't even noticed my own racing heart.

"Let's get out of here." Liam's gruff voice pulled my eyes from my friend.

"But Lex—"

"She'll be fine, princess. Dax will take care of her."

I nodded my head. We went back to the booth to grab my jacket and tell the others goodbye before we left. As we walked out of the bar, I pulled on my jacket. I scanned the parking lot for Liam's car.

"Where's your car?" I asked.

He gave me an adorable smirk, erasing the unpleasant emotions from moments before.

"It's not here."

"What?"

"I rode the bike." He nodded toward Frankie's Harley Davidson.

"Oh," I said, looking down at my dress and heels.

"Shit. I didn't think about you being dressed like that," he said, tracing the same path down my body with his own eyes. "Not that I don't love the way you look in that." His teeth gripped his bottom lip. His eyes ignited. "Do you want to call an Uber? We can meet at my place."

"No. I want to ride with you."

"Are you sure?"

"Yes."

"Okay. Don't worry. It's a short ride home, and I'll stay off the freeway."

He picked up the extra helmet. He kissed me before placing it on my head. He climbed on the bike, putting his own helmet on. I waited for his signal, then climbed onto the bike behind him. I snaked my arms around his waist and squeezed my thighs against his as he fired up the motorcycle.

I was glad I'd had the foresight to wear the leather jacket. The wind hitting my bare legs was cooler than it had been in the summer. Thankfully, the heat of the engine and Liam's body warmed me.

I remained tightly wound around Liam until we pulled into the garage below his apartment. He held the bike steady as I climbed off. I removed my helmet, shaking out my hair.

He silently grabbed my hand, pulling me along with him up the stairs and into his apartment. Walking through the door, he threw his keys to the side table, dropping my hand and making a direct route to the refrigerator. Within seconds, he had a beer open and on his lips as he took a long pull from the bottle.

I watched him, bewildered by his mood. He set the bottle on the counter, knuckling his fists as he used them to brace his body with his back to me. He dropped his head as he leaned forward. His muscles rippled in his shirt. His back raised and lowered with heavy breaths.

I wavered, trying to decide whether to approach him or give him a minute to work through whatever was running through his head. The urge to touch him won. I slipped off my heels and jacket and placed them beside the couch. I kept my footsteps light as I quietly walked toward him. I splayed my hands around his lean waist, pressing my body to his. I placed light kisses across his back through his soft shirt. His body straightened as he placed his large, rough hands over mine.

"Are you okay?" I asked.

He shifted out of my hold, rotating his body so he could lean against the kitchen counter. His hand rubbed over the back of his neck as he angled his head down, avoiding eye contact, hiding the emotions that would be revealed in his expressive eyes.

"No... I'm fucking pissed at Dax."

"He was just defending Lexie. Jake deserved it."

"It doesn't fucking matter, Val." He looked up at me, his eyes full of sorrow and regret. "He could have cost us everything. If the fight had gotten out of hand...he could have ended up in jail, or in the fucking hospital."

"Jake was provoking him. I'm sure he wasn't thinking about that."

"That's the problem. He needs to be thinking about that

shit. We have a chance to finally get a record deal. He can't be acting like a jealous asshole."

"And if it were me...would you still feel the same way?"

"Val," he warned sternly.

I raised my eyebrow at him with a knowing smirk. A grin tugged at his mouth. He shook his head, unable to argue with me. "Trust me. I wanted to punch the dipshit myself." He clenched his teeth. "What he fucking said to you—"

"It doesn't matter. It's nothing I haven't heard before."

"It does fucking matter. You aren't any of those things, Val. You're the kindest, most giving person I've ever met."

I stepped closer to him, running my hands under his shirt, up the planes of his abs. His skin was warm and smooth. I breathed in his manly scent as I lifted his shirt. He raised his arms over his head, tugging from the back to assist with removing it completely. My heart clenched. My breathing intensified.

I kissed along his chest. His hands cupped my bottom, lifting me into his arms. I crossed my arms behind his neck as he turned, placing me on the edge of the counter. His tongue slid across the seam of my mouth. My lips parted as his claimed me.

His hands drifted up my thighs, pushing my dress to my waist. His erection pressed between my legs where my body throbbed. Our kisses became desperate and wild, our lust overwhelming us. My veins thrummed as desire rushed through me.

Liam's hand pressed between my legs. He growled his approval at my readiness. He tugged at the thin lace separating us, pulling it down my body.

He removed his pants and kneeled between my legs,

locking his arms under my bent knees as he kissed up my thigh. His face disappeared between them. My head fell back with a sharp inhale. My eyes fell shut. I weaved my fingers through his hair as he continued his ministrations. My brain fell dark as my body soared toward the heavens.

"Liam," I let his name slip through my lips with a needy rasp.

I was on the verge and I needed him inside me. He ignored my plea. He gripped my body tighter to him as he continued to dance his tongue at my core. My panting came out shallow as an electrifying release rolled through me. He helped extend the pleasure as I rode the wave of ecstasy. I leaned back onto my hands, trying and failing to catch my breath as he stood.

He peeled my dress from my weak and satisfied body before he pulled me into his arms, carrying me to his bed.

"I hope you're rested…because we're just getting started, princess," he whispered in my ear in his husky voice.

"Shit," I cursed under my breath, unable to tame the profanity on my tongue.

He let out a light chuckle, laying me back onto his bed. He crawled over me, settling between my legs before fusing us together. We spent the rest of the night cherishing and memorizing every part of each other's body until we fell asleep from exhaustion.

～

I woke the next morning to Liam's large, heavy frame draped across me. I remained on my back, completely still, loving the way it felt to have the weight of his body securing me in place. I would have stayed there all morning if I hadn't heard my phone vibrating repeatedly in my jacket.

I gently squirmed out from under Liam's arms, falling over the edge of the bed with a thud. I bit my lip, holding in a small yelp. I glanced up from the floor at Liam. Thank God he wasn't a light sleeper. He rolled to his side, facing away from me, still sound asleep. I crawled from my hands and knees to a stand. I picked up Liam's T-shirt from the floor, pulling it over my head. I tiptoed across the room to my jacket and pulled out my phone. I had multiple missed calls from Lexie.

I padded softly to the bathroom and quietly closed the door behind me. I took a seat on the toilet, bending my knees up to rest on the edge of the tub before dialing to return Lexie's call.

"Hey," she answered with a hoarse voice.

"Hey. How are you?"

"I'm okay. About to leave to head back home. Are you at the apartment?"

"No. I'm at Liam's. What time is it?"

"A little past noon."

"Crap. Really?"

"Yeah."

"Do you need me to come home?"

She paused, not answering right away. "No...I—"

Her voice cracked as she choked back a sob. "Lex, I'm coming home. Liam's still sleeping, but I'll call for a car."

"No really, I'll be fine...I'm just a little shook up still...it's just...he was so angry. I didn't even recognize him. We've said some hurtful things to each other before...but...I've just never seen him like that. He's hurting badly, Val. I don't know what to do."

My heart dropped. "Lex...you aren't thinking about getting back with him, are you?" I held my breath, waiting for her answer.

"No. I'm just not sure if I can continue things with Dax. I don't want to drag him into the middle of all this drama."

I understood her fear and hesitance, but I wasn't sure I agreed with her. Dax had been good for her. He'd made her feel alive and worthy of love. He adored her; I knew from the way he looked at her, he would do anything for her. She needed someone like him in her life. Not someone like Jake.

"Don't decide anything just yet. I'm going to get dressed and call an Uber. I'll meet you at the apartment, so we can talk some more."

"Okay," she said weakly.

"I'll see you soon," I promised before hanging up. I stared down at my phone, worried about my friend. The bathroom door cracked open and Liam's sleepy bedhead nudged into the opening.

"Everything okay?" he asked, rubbing his hand over his face as he opened the door farther.

I shook my head. "No...but it'll be. That was Lexie."

He nodded his understanding, coming into the bathroom to pull me up from the toilet. He tugged me into him. "Do you want me to make you some breakfast? There's something we need to talk about."

The serious tone of his voice told me this was not going to be a light conversation. And at that moment, I wasn't sure

I could deal with any more turmoil than I already had waiting for me at home.

"Can it wait? I promised Lexie I would leave now to meet her back at the apartment. She needs me right now."

He hesitated answering. "Sure, princess." He paused. "Let me get dressed and I'll take you home."

CHAPTER 16

I spent the rest of the weekend with Lexie, talking her out of making what I thought would have been the biggest mistake of her life. Against my demands, she accepted a phone call from Jake. I was on the edge of my seat the whole time, waiting for the call to end. She had disappeared into her bedroom to talk to him privately.

When she finally came out of her room to join me in the living room, her eyes were brimmed with red, but her expression, resolved. She gave me a hint of a smile. I just hoped she was smiling because she had closure, and not because she was getting back with Jake.

She took a seat next to me on the couch. I stared at her expectantly, waiting for her to speak.

"Well?" I finally asked impatiently, unable to take it anymore. I was going to have a nervous breakdown. I was way too invested in my friend's love life.

"We're good."

My eyebrows shot to my hairline as my eyes widened. *What the hell does that mean?* She giggled at my distress, enjoying tormenting me. I did not find it funny. At. All.

"We're officially done. For good. We both agreed. He apologized for the other night. We care about each other a lot. But we both know it's time for things to end and for us to move on."

"Good. I'm glad. I'm glad you guys are ending it on better terms." I gave her hand a comforting squeeze. "So…where does that leave you with Dax?"

She shrugged her shoulders. "I'm not sure. I haven't talked to him since Friday. When I left his place, I told him I needed space and time to figure things out. It seems he was fine with giving it to me. He hasn't tried to contact me once."

"Lex, I doubt that's what he wanted. But knowing him, he would do whatever you ask. You should call him."

"It's Sunday. He's probably playing poker with the guys."

"Well, I'm sure they'll be okay if he skips out on it. Liam is. He's going to help me babysit Nate tonight."

"Sorry. I've been monopolizing all your time the last few days. Poor guy has to resort to babysitting just to see you."

I laughed. "Don't you dare apologize. You know I'm always here for you. He understands that. Plus, this should be fun…watching Liam change a diaper."

I gave a sly smile as she laughed. Her giggle ended with a deep inhale. She released her breath slowly as she stood.

"I guess I should get this over with. Hopefully, he didn't pick up a hot new groupie after their last two concerts."

"Not that you would ever need to worry about that, but I know for a fact he didn't. I had Liam keeping tabs on him for me. Dax left immediately after both their Friday and Saturday shows. *Alone.*"

A smile that I hadn't seen in days graced her face. She gave me a hug. "Thank you, Val. You're the best."

"I know," I teased.

Her spirited laughter rung out into the room as she shook her head, walking back to her bedroom.

~

"There are bottles in the fridge. All you need to do is heat them up in the warmer on the counter. Don't use the microwave. Make sure you test the temperature. He'll want one before he goes to bed."

"I know."

"Oh, and he has to have his binky to fall asleep. He prefers to be rocked. And make sure you turn on his turtle night light."

"Ava, I *know*." I rolled my eyes. "This isn't the first time I've put him to bed. Go," I demanded, trying to push her and Rhett out the door. "Joce and Riley are probably already waiting at the restaurant."

"She's right, beautiful. We need to go," Rhett added, also trying to persuade his overprotective wife out the door. Rhett had officially rubbed off on her.

"Okay. Fine. Call me if you need anything."

"I will." I wouldn't.

She needed this night out. They both did. It was only their second night out alone since Nate had been born. Despite her blackmailing me for a year of babysitting duties, she had rarely cashed in on them.

Liam stood behind me with Nate in his arms as we waved the two of them off. Once they were securely in the car and moving down the long driveway, I closed the door, locking it behind me.

I leaned my back against the door, staring at the hardcore rock star, holding the tiny, innocent baby. Nate babbled and smiled in his arms, pulling at his hair while Liam laughed. Both of their laughs only instigated the other to laugh harder.

I smiled fondly at the man I loved holding the nephew I loved. Liam glanced over at me, his dimple gracing me with its presence.

"You're giving me that look, princess."

"What look?"

"You know damn well what look, and there's nothing I can do about it when I have this guy in my arms."

"Well," I sauntered past him, "I guess we may just have to move up his bedtime." I turned, winking at him over my shoulder. His deep laugh echoed behind me off the walls of the entryway.

We spent most of the evening in the living room, playing with Nate on the floor. Liam helped me give him a bath, blowing bubbles into the air around him. Nate would giggle that cute little baby laugh, making Liam's dimple a permanent valley on his face. My heart exploded as I watched them interact. The two boys were smitten with each other.

I left Liam to dress Nate on his own while I warmed a bottle to put him to sleep for the night. When I returned, Liam was struggling to put the onesie pajamas on him.

"What on Earth? Is that two diapers on him?"

"Yeah, the little man has some explosive shits. What the

hell do they feed this kid? He blew right through the first diaper. It was everywhere." His eyebrows furrowed together as he focused on coercing Nate into his pajamas.

I looked down at the dirty diaper and the massive mound of used wipes piled on the changing table. Laughter burst through my mouth as I gripped my aching stomach.

"Let me do it," I said laughing as I moved to stand beside a disgruntled Liam. He let out a loud exhale, stepping aside. I removed the two misshapen diapers, replacing them with one new, securely fastened diaper. Liam watched as I masterfully diapered and dressed a grinning Nate.

"You make it look so easy."

"I've had a lot of practice as a little girl who played with dolls," I said, smiling up at him. "Now clean up that mess," I playfully demanded. I picked Nate up in my arms, scrunching my nose as he pulled at it. "Come on little guy..." I cooed at Nate. "We'll leave Uncle Liam to clean up this mess. Let's you and me get you to bed."

I smiled back at Liam, whose face had an expression I couldn't read. I caught his eyes, looking for some kind of understanding. Before I could interpret it, he turned away from me, cleaning up the dirty diaper.

I decided to let it go for now. I needed to get Nate to sleep. I turned on his turtle light before taking a seat in the rocking chair. When Liam finished cleaning up the mess, he turned off the other lights in the room. He walked over to me, placing a light kiss on a drowsy Nate. He followed the kiss with another one on my forehead before leaving the room, softly closing the door behind him.

I continued to rock Nate to sleep as I mulled over my thoughts. When I couldn't make sense of what had passed through Liam's face, I pushed them aside, focusing on the tiny, sleeping man in my arms. I let his peaceful aura seep into my body.

When I was sure he was out for the night, I stood. I sidled up to the side of the crib, cautiously laying him down to sleep. I crept out of the room, taking the baby monitor with me.

I found Liam relaxing on the couch with his arms stretched across the back of it. He was focused on the sports channel he was watching on the oversized TV. I took the now-empty bottle to the kitchen sink, grabbing my phone from the counter before joining him on the couch.

I curled into his side as he draped an arm around me. I was exhausted. Watching Nate somehow always made me feel more exhausted than running a marathon. I had no idea how Ava and Rhett did it on a daily basis.

"Is he out?"

"Yes. Hopefully, for good," I said, glancing at the baby monitor I had set in front of us on the coffee table. I turned, looking up at Liam. "Is everything okay?"

He briefly dropped his eyes to me before looking back at the TV. "Yes."

I could read nothing into his one word. And frankly, due to the mental exhaustion I felt after the last two days, I gave up on trying. I looked down at my phone. I had a missed call and voicemail from my agent. I opened up my voicemail to listen to Amanda's message.

I let out an excited gasp. Liam turned to look at me as a big smile overwhelmed my face.

"What?"

I dropped the phone from my ear. "I got a call back!"

Whatever sullen mood Liam had previously been in instantly disappeared as he pulled me onto his lap to kiss me firmly on the lips.

"That's awesome, princess!"

I grinned. "It's only a call back. It's not like I got the part, yet. But still, it's more than I've ever gotten in the past."

"You'll get the part," he said adamantly.

His confidence in me made the butterflies in my stomach take flight. Or maybe it was that sexy dimple he had on display for me. I ran my hand over his shoulder, down his arm, an unpleasant thought overpowering the happiness I was feeling.

"If I do...I'll have to go to New York for a few months."

"New York?"

"Yes. That's where they'll be filming it."

"How long is a few?"

"Two to three months. Normally."

He nodded.

"You could come with me," I offered. I wasn't sure how I was going to handle being apart from him for three months, but I had a pretty good notion: terribly.

"Val—"

"You could see New York. We could stay at Rhett's condo. It sits empty pretty much year-round. I could show you all my favorite things in my home city. It would be great. There's so much to do," I rambled on.

"Val, slow down." He brushed his hand down my cheek. I knew it was a longshot to get him to agree to come to New York with me, but the thought of not seeing him was too much to bear.

"You don't want to go?"

"You know that's not it. It's just there's Frankie, and the shop. The possibility of us getting that record deal. If we do, they want us to go on tour immediately…and there's something we still need to talk about. Something you need to know."

"I know what I need to. That I want to be with you. That I'm not sure I can go months without seeing you."

I was being reckless with my thoughts, not able to think clearly. My emotions spun out of control. He shook his head, disagreeing with everything I was saying.

"Do you not want to be with me?"

"Shit, Val. Don't say things like that. I want to be with you more than I want anything in this world. I never thought I'd want what we have. Being with you…with your family…it makes my dark world a little brighter. It's pulled me temporarily out of the hell I've been sentenced to."

"Stop it. Stop talking like things are going to end someday."

"Val—"

"No. You don't get to make that decision for me. I'm telling you whatever secret you have that you think has deemed you unworthy of me, doesn't matter. I don't care what happened in your past and part of me doesn't even want to know anymore. It's in your past. Maybe that's where it should stay."

He closed his eyes, shaking his head slowly. I boxed his face between my hands, impeding its movement. I wasn't going to allow him to argue this.

"Liam…please," I begged. "Let me be your future."

I didn't care how desperate I sounded. I *was* desperate. I needed him. Forever. I never wanted to let him go. I would beg and plead and fight to keep him. Even if it meant fighting against his own internal demons.

"I want you to be my future, princess. I do. I just don't want you choosing to have a future with me blindly."

I started to argue with him more but was interrupted by the sounds of the front door opening and footsteps coming down the halls of the entryway. Liam's body tensed, and he effortlessly removed me from his lap to sit beside him on the couch. Seconds later Ava and Rhett appeared.

We booth stood nervously from the couch, as if we were two teenagers caught making out. Rhett's eyes focused on our body language. My brother was a perceptive bastard. It's what made him a great business man. That and his killer instincts.

"How was he?" Ava asked.

"A perfect angel. You should stop worrying so much."

"I see the house is still in one piece," Rhett remarked as they walked farther into the living room toward us.

"Anything that isn't is Nate's fault." I grinned.

Rhett chuckled quietly at my quip, shaking his head in disbelief.

"What? I never had a little sibling to blame anything on. Unlike you," I accused him teasingly.

"So you're taking it out on my son, now?"

"Karma." I laughed, looking up at Liam, who was being painfully quiet.

Rhett turned his attention to Liam. "You want to join me for a nightcap?"

"He'd love to," I answered for him. "I need to talk dresses with Ava for the party next weekend," I lied.

Liam squeezed my shoulders. "Sure. What did you have in mind?"

"I just got a new bottle of bourbon, if you want to give it a try," Rhett said, moving toward his study off the living room. Liam followed behind him. I watched them leave. As soon as they were out of sight, I turned back to Ava's prying eyes.

"What?"

"You going to tell me what's going on?"

"As soon as you get me a glass of wine." I dropped my hand that was twisting in my hair.

She released a soft chuckle, turning toward their kitchen. "Come on. It sounds like we're both going to need one."

I curled my legs up under a blanket on a lounger as Ava and I both took a seat out on their patio next to the gas fire pit. I watched the blue and orange flames whip in the breeze as I sipped my glass of wine.

"So…what's going on?" Ava asked.

"I got a call back."

"That's great news, Val!" Ava exclaimed. "Wait…why don't you look happier about it?"

"It's just a call back. Not an actual part, yet."

"And?"

"And…the filming will be in New York."

"You love New York."

"I do. But it's for at least three months and Liam will be here in L.A. or on tour. I don't know…"

"I see. I'm not going to pretend like that will be easy for you guys."

"No. It won't…"

"Why do I get the feeling there's more?"

"Because there is." I took a deep breath before turning to

239

face her. "There's something I haven't told you. Mainly because, I don't know what it is. But I don't want Rhett to know either. I need you to keep this to yourself."

"You're starting to make me feel like a terrible wife... keeping so many of your secrets from your brother."

"I'm sorry...I just...I don't know what it even is."

"I'm so very confused right now. Why don't you tell me what it is you don't think you know?" she said with a smirk and a raised eyebrow.

"There's something in Liam's past. Something he struggles with. I have no idea what it is. He's sure when he tells me, it will end our relationship. At first, I wanted to know. But now I'm not sure I do."

"Do you think he's right?"

"No," I stated firmly. Because I knew it didn't matter.

She nodded her head, quietly processing what I was telling her.

"I'm not sure what to tell you, Val. All I know is what I see. I can see you've fallen for him. You're happier with him. You seem stronger with him. And beyond the changes he's helped you make, I genuinely like him. So do Rhett and your parents."

"I love him, Ava."

She smiled. Her eyes filled with understanding. "Have you told him?"

"Not yet."

"Maybe you should. Maybe that will help make him understand."

I nodded. I wasn't sure I actually agreed, but I nodded anyway. We sipped our wine in silence for a few more moments before Ava lightened the subject with talk of the party next weekend.

It was a holiday party that Blackwood Industries was hosting for their employees and business associates. It was a pretty big annual event. They flew in all the staff from New York to attend. My parents normally flew in for it, also, but were unable to attend this year since they were off exploring Europe. Being a small shareholder of the company and a Blackwood, I was always expected to attend.

Normally, I didn't look forward to it. It was a stuffy black-tie affair that always bored me to tears. But this year, Liam was joining me as my date. The idea of seeing him in a tuxedo had me more than willing to put up with some of the pretentious idiots who would be there.

We had moved on from discussing the party to discussing the latest with Joce and Riley. Riley had finally proposed to Joce, after moving here three years ago to be with her. They were planning the wedding for next summer. Ava was giving me the details she knew when Rhett and Liam joined us on the patio.

Rhett crawled in behind Ava on the lounger while Liam took a seat next to me, pulling me into his arms. "We should go, princess. It's late."

I nodded, setting my empty glass aside. Liam helped me up from my chair. "Thanks for the wine," I said to Ava, leaning over to give her a hug. "We'll see you guys next weekend."

I hugged Rhett. Liam followed behind me, giving Ava a hug and shaking Rhett's hand.

~

I fell asleep on the way home as Liam drove silently, holding my hand. I woke up when I felt the car come to a stop. I opened my eyes to the view of my apartment building.

I rotated my head to look at Liam. "You're coming up."

I wasn't asking.

"If you want me to."

"You know I do. Always."

His hand drifted down the side of my face.

"Okay, princess."

He shut off the ignition before opening the door to step out of the car. He moved around the front, opening my door and helping me out. He held my hand as we walked quietly through my apartment building into my apartment.

Neither of us spoke. We went through the now-familiar motions of alternating brushing our teeth and getting ready for bed. I crawled into bed, waiting for Liam to join me. He walked out of the bathroom, stripping out of his clothes before crawling in beside me.

He pulled me to him, and I snuggled into my spot in his side. He played softly with my hair. I closed my eyes.

"Val?" Liam whispered.

"Hmm?" I moaned sleepily.

His chest rose and fell beneath me with a deep inhale and exhale. "Never mind. Sleep, princess," he commanded gently.

So I did.

CHAPTER 17

"Come in!" I yelled, popping my head outside of my bedroom doorframe, to the person knocking on my front door.

I assumed it was Ava here to pick me up. I was running late getting dressed. I had overslept. I hastily threw on a pair of skinny jeans and a loose, silky, black, buttoned blouse. Ava was picking me up this morning so we could hit the spa before the party tonight. We would be getting our nails and hair done. And I hoped to squeeze in time for a massage.

Ava walked into my room, with two to-go coffee cups in her hand. "You know your brother would have a nervous breakdown if he knew you left your door unlocked like that."

I rolled my eyes. "He would die at a young age if he knew half the stuff I did. Besides, this place is like a high-security prison. Nobody is getting past the front desk without a background check, courtesy of my brother," I joked.

I sat down on the bench to slip on my sandals. Despite it

being the middle of December, I didn't want to run the risk of messing up my pedicure. Winters in L.A. were basically like an early summer in New York, anyway.

"Then I guess it's best we *do* keep secrets from him. I'm too young to be a widow and single mother."

She shoved the coffee at me as I stood. "Here."

"You're the best sister-in-law in the world."

She smiled. "Let's go. We're going to be late for our appointment."

I grabbed my phone and purse, following her out the door, locking it behind me.

～

We spent the rest of the day rejuvenating at the spa. It had been a long time since I had allowed myself to be this pampered. It was long overdue and much needed. I'm pretty sure they had to bring out the heavy-duty nail file for my toes. I cringed.

It's not that I had let myself go; I'd just tended to self-pamper over the last few years. And by self-pamper, I mean I would make Lexie paint my nails. She was much more talented at it than myself.

After feeling so refreshed and relaxed after our spa day, I decided I may have to reconsider my previous determination to watch my spending and stay away from my trust fund. I had made it through college, after all. It was time to reward myself.

Ava dropped me back at my apartment before heading home to get dressed. I had only a few hours to get ready before Liam would be here to pick me up. He ran to the shop to help Frankie while I spent the day with Ava. He would be getting dressed at his place before heading to mine.

I went to my closet, removing my gown from the hanging bag to air out. I hung it on the back of my closet door, then perused my jewelry for the perfect accessories. Lexie entered my room in search of me.

"You're home."

"Yeah, just got back."

"Wow. Is this the dress?" she asked, skimming her hand along the silky fabric.

"Yes, isn't it gorgeous? Wait until you see it on me." I grinned confidently. It had to be my favorite dress I currently owned.

The strapless dress was a long train of emerald silk fabric that dipped into a sweetheart neckline. The mermaid silhouette clung to my body, trumpeting around my knees into a sweeping train. It wasn't necessarily the easiest thing to walk in, but the graceful look of the dress was worth the effort, even if my walk wouldn't be as graceful. At least tonight, I had Liam's strong arm to hold on to.

"It almost makes me wish I was your date this year, instead of Liam."

I laughed. Lexie had been my plus one the last few years. She had kept me entertained at on otherwise bland event. We would both gorge on the unlimited expensive champagne and food.

"You know, you still could've come...you *and* Dax. My brother wouldn't have cared."

"I'm not sure it'd really be Dax's thing."

"And you think it's Liam's?" I raised my eyebrow.

That made us both laugh.

"I think we'll just 'Netflix and chill' tonight," she grinned. "He should be here in a little bit. What time will Liam be here?"

"Less than two hours."

"I'll leave you to it then, princess. I know it can take you at least an hour just to do your makeup," she goaded me.

I tossed a shoe toward her as she ducked out of my closet, laughing. After finding the earrings and tennis bracelet I'd planned to wear, I took a seat at my vanity and began plastering on my makeup for the night. It would not take me a full hour...it would only take forty-five minutes. Fifty-five tops.

I had just finished dressing, pulling on my silver stilettos and clasping my bracelet around my wrist when Lexie knocked outside my door.

"Liam's here," she said with a grin, running her eyes over me. "I have to admit...you were right. You look gorgeous, Val."

"Thank you," I beamed

"It'll be a tough call on which of you looks hotter tonight... Wait until you see Liam."

The mischief danced in her eyes, making me more anxious to see him than I already was. I hastily grabbed my clutch, dropping my phone inside as I walked out of my room.

My steps faltered as my eyes scanned the backside of Liam. He was facing Dax, talking in a low voice. I didn't need him to turn around to know how devastatingly handsome he looked in that tuxedo. I could already tell it hugged him perfectly.

Dax's eyes widened as they fell on me, looking over

Liam's shoulder. He knocked the back of his hand on Liam's chest, nodding his head toward me to signal Liam to turn. It was like watching a film in slow motion, as he turned painfully slowly to face me. My heart tightened in my chest and my breathing became nonexistent.

Lexie was wrong. It was not a tough call. Liam was definitely the hottest one in the room.

If the tuxedo didn't have me feeling faint, the breathtaking smile plastered across his face did. He stood casually, hands in his pockets, as if being in a tux was the most natural thing in the world for him. My eyes traveled repeatedly up and down his body before finally landing on his mesmerizing eyes.

I could feel the heat of his own stare doing the same to me. Tingles prickled through me. I suddenly wondered how upset Rhett would be if we just skipped the event altogether.

"Princess," Liam spoke through his sexy smile as he prowled toward me.

I remained unmoving, still unable to get my brain to function. He closed the distance between us. He ran a hand through the long hair that fell down my back and over my shoulders in soft waves.

"You look beautiful," he whispered in my ear as he leaned in, placing a soft kiss on my cheek.

"You don't look half-bad yourself, rock star." I grinned, wishing his lips had landed on mine instead of on my cheek.

"Aww, look at them, dear. They look so grown up," Lexie joked as she swiped at a fake tear, holding onto Dax, who was laughing under his breath with her.

I rolled my eyes as Liam's chest rumbled with a chuckle.

"Okay, get together. We need a picture!" Lexie demanded,

pulling out her camera phone. We played along, doing typical prom poses before taking a more natural one.

I felt my phone vibrate with a text from Jim. He was waiting with the limo downstairs. He had already dropped Rhett and Ava at the party and had just arrived to take Liam and myself.

"We have to go," I told them.

"Wait, just one more!" Lexie begged. We gave her one more silly pose before heading toward the door.

"Now son, you better have her home by midnight or I'm hunting you down," Dax said, playing the protective father. Liam playfully punched him in his shoulder as we walked out of the apartment.

"You kids have fun tonight!" Lexie yelled behind us before closing the door. We both laughed, shaking our heads at our ridiculous friends.

As soon as Jim had closed the limo door behind us, Liam moved in a rush, instantly landing his mouth on me as he gripped my head in the palm of his hands. His kiss was fierce, bold, and demanding. I deepened the kiss, thankful he had finally given me what I had so desperately wanted from the moment I saw him. He pulled back, both of us breathing heavily.

"This is going to be a long and fucking painful night," he said, adjusting himself.

"We could always just make a quick appearance and leave," I said, grinning.

I was more than happy to stay less than thirty minutes at the party. As much as I liked seeing Liam in that tuxedo, I would prefer to see him out of it.

The limo stilled to a stop outside of the Alexandria. The valets opened the door. Liam exited before rotating and offering his hand to help me out of the limo. The flashes from the paparazzi's cameras were going off like strobe lights as I stepped out of the car. Liam held our arms tightly locked together. His face remained devoid of emotion, but the tension in his body told me he hadn't been expecting this kind of welcoming.

"You better get used to it, rock star," I smiled up at him, trying to ease his discomfort as we walked into the building. He grinned back down at me, all terseness gone.

I was used to being in the spotlight, but this was the first time I was in it with the man I loved. With that thought, I stood taller, ready to stake my claim in front of the world.

We entered through the private entrance of the grand hall, which led to the historic ballroom where the event was being held. We walked through the cocktail lounge, stopping to pick up our drinks before entering the main ballroom. The room had been extravagantly decorated with silver and gold holiday décor. It was tastefully done, as to not overpower the natural elegance of the white-trimmed ballroom, with its high arched ceilings and enormous, original, shimmering chandeliers.

The room was already filled with elitists, but it only took a minute for me to spot Rhett. My brother could easily command a room, dominating it with just his presence. Ava was by his side, looking as beautiful as ever. As we edged closer to them, I realized Riley and Joce were the couple they had been talking to.

I greeted them all, introducing Riley and Joce to Liam. Riley shook Liam's hand firmly, giving him an unnecessary protective brotherly glare. Rhett chuckled and Ava smacked his chest in warning, rolling her eyes. Liam seemed unbothered and accepting of it, as if he wouldn't have expected anything less from the two men.

After the awkward introduction and visiting for a few minutes, I pulled Liam onto the dance floor. We swayed together naturally. He held me close as we moved through each song, singing softly into my ear to the songs he knew, his voice stimulating the hunger within me.

We continued dancing through the night, laughing and joking as he teased my body, giving me private kisses on my neck when he thought nobody was watching. I repaid him the favor.

Needing a break from dancing, he dragged me from the dance floor. I searched the room for Ava and Rhett, so we could join them while we rested.

"There they are." I pointed across the room to where they were standing with a couple I didn't recognize.

Liam followed my gaze as we walked toward them. As we neared closer, his body came to a sudden halt, stiffening as he clutched my hand painfully tight. Startled by his grasp, I looked up at him. His face had darkened, the fun and light-heartedness gone.

"Liam?"

He didn't respond.

"Liam," I said more firmly. He gave a slight jolt, as if being knocked out of a haze by the sound of my voice. He looked down at me blankly.

"I'm going to get another drink. Do you want anything?" he asked.

"Sure...another glass of champagne...I'll come with you," I offered, getting an uneasy feeling. I was suddenly afraid to leave his side.

"No. I'll just be a few minutes. I'll find you."

I nodded, despite everything inside warning me not to let him go. He released my hand. I watched him walk out of the room while trying to figure out what had caused his sudden change in mood.

I turned back to where Rhett and Ava had been standing only to find Rhett and the couple were gone. Ava was now standing with Joce. Riley was nowhere in sight either. I maneuvered through the crowd. Ava smiled as I approached them.

"Where's Liam?"

"Getting us drinks. Rhett and Riley?"

Ava rolled her eyes with annoyance, "Said he had some business to discuss. He should be back in a little bit. Riley went with him."

"Who was the couple you guys were just talking with? I've never seen them before."

"Oh. The guy is a potential business associate of Rhett's. His name is Scott Lewis, and that was his wife with him. Her name is Tessa. Sweet girl. I really liked her. Kind of timid, though."

Joce nodded in agreement before changing the conversation to Nate, asking how he was doing. Ava spoke animatedly, telling Joce various stories. I pretended to pay attention as their conversation went on, periodically searching the room for Liam. He had been gone longer than I would have expected. Rhett and Riley hadn't returned either, but Ava and Joce didn't seem to notice. They were too enthralled by their conversation of weddings and babies.

I waited another few minutes before excusing myself to search for him. I scanned the main ballroom, knowing it was unlikely he was in there. I quickly moved out into the cocktail area, since that was where he had claimed to be going. He wasn't there.

My pulse quickened and my lungs tightened as a feeling of dread fell over me. I pulled out my phone, sending him a text, inquiring where he was. He didn't respond. I dropped my phone back into my purse and headed toward the hall where the restrooms and coat check were.

He wouldn't just leave me, would he? I knew something had startled him. I knew he was shutting down—shutting me out—but I didn't believe he would just walk away from me without saying anything. I couldn't believe that.

I started to turn the corner into the hallway with the restrooms but was distracted by voices coming down the hall in the opposite direction. It was a male and female voice. The male voice I knew all too well. I walked slowly toward them, my heart now pounding at an ungodly speed. I clenched my clammy hands into fists of nervous tension.

I could tell by their tones they were in a heated argument. As I drew closer, I saw him. Liam was standing with the woman who had been with Rhett and Ava earlier. Tessa. And she was beautiful. Petite, with long blonde hair that stretched to the middle of her back. There was a familiarity about her. I watched her body language and flinched when she reached to touch him. He didn't remove her hand from him, but he wasn't staring at her with desire either. He was angry.

I snuck closer, staying out of sight. They were too invested in their argument to notice me spying on them.

"You need to leave," she demanded. "He knows you're here. He saw you."

"I don't give a fuck."

"Liam, please. If you ever cared about me, please leave. You know what seeing you is going to do."

He glared at her. "That's not my problem anymore," he gritted.

She flinched, as if his words stung, and removed her hand from him. "I'm sorry, Liam. I'm sorry for everything. If I could take it all back, I would."

"That's not good enough, Tessa. Leave him. Let me take care of you."

"It's not that easy."

I choked back a sob in my throat. Tears welled in my eyes. *What was he talking about? Who the hell was she?* I backed away, unable to listen to this.

My feet were carrying me backwards, protecting me from the destruction that was sure to happen to my heart. But my eyes didn't leave them. I stumbled backwards, knocking into a console table along the wall that held a glass vase. The vase teetered off the table, crashing to the floor, shattering into a million tiny pieces. Just like my heart.

My eyes widened when their heads whipped around to search out the noise I had created.

"Shit." Liam's eyes focused on me.

I stood there like a frightened deer in headlights. Tessa glanced between me and Liam, looking just as frightened. She gave Liam a pleading stare before dropping her head and rushing past me. The motion of her leaving sent a signal to my body that it needed to do the same. I turned to leave.

"Damn it! Val. Wait!" Liam yelled behind me.

Thanks to my freaking dress there was no way I would be able to get away from him. I couldn't outrun him even in workout clothes and running shoes, so instead I turned to face him, planting my feet firmly on the ground, hardening my exterior appearance while my insides crumbled and fell apart.

"Who is she?" I demanded answers.

"Nobody," he said cautiously, moving in toward me.

"Not good enough Liam. Tell me. Now."

"She's nobody important."

"That's not what it looked like and it sure as hell didn't sound that way when you were begging her to leave her husband for you."

His eyes narrowed as his own face hardened. "You don't know what you're talking about, princess."

"I heard you Liam! And don't fucking call me princess. Not right now."

"Val. Listen to me," his eyes pleaded with me, his voice trying to calm me. "We need to go. We can talk about this somewhere else."

I shook my head while I tried to process everything I heard and everything he was saying. I tried to force my brain to think rationally, but my emotions were stabbing through me. I knew I needed to get them under control. I needed to hear him out, but the anger and hurt took me back to high school. Back to the pain. Back to the darkness. I knew Liam wasn't that guy, but I had heard him with my own two ears. I was lost. Lost to my thoughts and emotions.

"Val, please. Please come with me." He was now standing dangerously close to me, adding a new level of complexity to my already-frazzled thought process. Now my body was charging with his touch. His hand was on my face, halting my shaking head.

"Let's go home. We can talk there. I'll tell you everything."

"Take your hands off her," Rhett's gruff, demanding voice rumbled from behind me.

Liam looked over my shoulder at my brother, dropping his hand. I swung around to find Rhett fast approaching us with Jim, Eric, and Riley in tow.

"Rhett?"

"Go back to the party, Val."

"No. What's this about?"

"Now, Valerie."

"I said *no*. This is between me and Liam. I don't need you and your attack dogs getting in the middle."

They stopped a few feet away from us, all looking pissed and ready to fight. *What the hell was going on?*

"Circumstances are different now. Go back to the party."

"What circumstances?"

I glanced back at Liam, who was standing rigidly behind me, fists clenched, ready to fight. His expression was stern... but his eyes confused me. His eyes held pain, and defeat—as if he'd been expecting this.

"Rhett?" Ava pushed through the bulldogs to her husband's side. "What's going on?"

"That's what I would like to know," I said, throwing my hands on my hips.

"Ava, take Val and go back to the party."

"No! I am not a child, Rhett! You all need to leave. I'm

going home with Liam. This is between us," I retorted before Ava could respond.

"You're not going anywhere with him." He pointed a demanding finger at me. He turned his dark, narrowed eyes to Liam, "And you. You're going to stay the hell away from my sister and my family."

"No!" I screamed at Rhett. I was at my breaking point with my brother.

"She doesn't even know, does she?" Rhett growled, a sudden understanding crossing his expression.

Liam didn't respond. He just held his own angry glare on my brother. The rage was radiating from him.

"Know what?" I asked, glancing at Ava, who looked remorseful and angry at the same time.

"He has a record, Val! He was convicted. Pleaded guilty. He was in prison for two years." I shook my head incredulously. "For domestic abuse. Are you listening to me? He put someone in the hospital."

"Rhett, you promised me," Ava finally spoke up.

"I didn't break my promise, Ava. I was tipped off by someone who knows him."

Liam turned to me, gripping my arms in his hands, while Rhett was distracted by Ava.

"Val. I'm sorry."

I stood, unresponsive, looking at him, and searching his face for answers. I needed to hear him out. I promised him many times before I always would. That I wouldn't run. I wouldn't run from his past. None of this made sense. Liam wasn't abusive. He wouldn't even let his friend fight.

"Get your fucking hands off her!" Rhett stepped forward to forcefully remove Liam, his attention back on us.

Liam dropped his hands, not giving him the chance. He gave me one last, longing look, before stepping to leave.

"Liam? No!" I cried. The tears overflowed from my eyes. I fumbled, grasping for his hand to stop him. But he was too quick, pushing past everyone as they held me back from him.

"Let me go!" I screamed at my brother and his stupid goons. "Let me go!" I pounded my fists against my frustrating brother's chest.

"Let her go!" Ava screamed desperately for me. "Damn it, Rhett." She pushed his arms from me, wrapping her own tiny arms around me as I crumbled to the floor.

"Rhett?" Jim gripped his shoulder. He gave him a single nod and they all left, leaving me alone in the hallway with only my family.

I sobbed in Ava's arms as she sat with me, stroking my hair, shushing me. "What the hell were you thinking?" She turned her anger on Rhett.

"You can't seriously be angry with me right now? What did you expect me to do, Ava? I wasn't waiting for him to hit her for the first time."

"Do you truly believe he would do that?" She paused. "We both know how misunderstandings can come between two people. You should have talked to him first, given him the opportunity to tell you what happened."

I choked back my sobbing, silencing my cries at hearing Ava's words.

"He had plenty of opportunity to come clean, and he didn't," Rhett responded. "He hadn't even told Val."

He'd been trying. But things kept happening, preventing him... and then I told him I didn't want to know. This was my fault.

"I don't know what to tell you, Rhett...I just know what happened here was not the way to handle it."

I pushed up from her chest, staring at the two of them. A clarity washed over me. I struggled to my feet. I needed to go after him.

"What are you doing?" Rhett asked.

"Leaving. And I swear, Rhett, if you stand in my way, I will never speak to you again."

Rhett's head dropped, his hands rubbing down his face. He looked back up at me, his eyes acknowledging my threat. I pushed past him, leaving the two of them to work out their own argument. I needed to fight for the man I loved.

I hiked my dress up, kicking off my heels before breaking into a full-on sprint. I flew through the hotel entrance, spinning every which way to find him. I wasn't sure if he would even still be here. I ran down the concrete steps to the main sidewalk.

My heart dropped. He was still here. He stood from a sitting position on the side of the curb as a pair of headlights pulled up to him.

"Liam!" I screamed, running toward him, just as he grabbed the door handle of the car, opening the passenger side door.

He looked over his shoulder at the sound of my voice, watching me as I barreled toward him. He dropped his hand from the door handle, rotating to face me.

"Liam," I breathed as I came to a stop in front of him. "Don't leave... Please," I begged through my short breaths.

He didn't respond. I reached for him and he jerked back, dodging my touch. My heart hit my chest with one forceful beat, like I'd been sucker punched. I searched his eyes. I choked back a sob at the emptiness I found there.

"Liam?" I struggled to speak through my shaky voice.

"Go back inside, Val."

"No. I'm going with you."

He shook his head firmly, his eyes determined.

"Liam, listen to me. I don't care what was said in there. I love you. Do you hear me...? I. Love. You." I repeated each word with certainty.

A sliver of hope flashed through his eyes for a split second before it was replaced with more hollowness.

"Go back inside, Val," he growled.

"No. Did you hear what I said? I love you, damn it. You don't have to say you love me back. Just say you won't leave."

"I can't do that, Val. Those people in there...I don't fit with them. I will never be them. I never want to be them. I don't belong here."

"Those people? What do you mean by *those people*...you mean like me? You don't belong with me?" My voice quaked. My anger surfaced.

"No, Val. Shit..." He threw his hands in his hair, roughly running them through it as he struggled to explain himself. "You're not one of them..." He flung his arm out toward the building. "They're a bunch of arrogant assholes who think they can push everyone around. You're different...You're special."

"Then why are you pushing me away? Let me come with you."

He shook his head. "I can't. This is what I've been trying to tell you. This will never work. Your family will never allow you to be with me. And they shouldn't."

"Hey, buddy. I can't sit here all night. Are you two stayin' or goin'?" An irritated driver interrupted our conversation.

Liam glanced over at the man I wanted to punch in the face right then. He gave him a harsh nod before turning his gaze back to me.

"Go inside, princess." His words were sharp with regret.

"Liam," I pleaded.

He ignored me, getting into the car. I stood frozen by his rejection that I had felt one too many times before. He closed the door, not even giving me another sideways glance as the car drove away. As the man I loved drove away. As my world drove away.

He left me alone…desperate, angry, and hurt. Again. Desperate for his touch. Angered by his self-doubt. Hurt by his rejection. The tears poured from my eyes as my body gave into the gravity of my reality. The weight of my pain too much to handle, I fell to my knees, bending forward as I cried into the palms of my hands.

I'm not sure how long I'd been there when I felt large, strong arms around me. They lifted me into the air, cradling me against a firm, hard frame. I buried my face in their chest as I continued to sob. I was placed inside a limo, where I curled into a ball on the seat.

"I've got her. I'm taking her home," I heard Jim's deep voice say from somewhere near me. It was the last thing I remembered hearing from that night before my mind shut down, blacking out the world around me.

CHAPTER 18

The days after Liam left me were a blur. I spent the whole time locked in my room, falling in and out of sleep between fits of crying. I called in sick to work, pretending to have the flu. I couldn't deal with being around anybody. Not even Lexie.

By day two of me pushing her away and locking her out, she called in for backup. Ava showed up, trying to get me to come out of my room, if not to talk, at least to eat. I refused. She threatened to call my brother to break down the door. In turn, I threatened to never speak to any of them again. Not that I was really speaking to any of them at that moment, anyway. After spending hours trying to tempt me out of my room, I heard her tell Lexie she would check back later. She had to get home to Nate.

The next day, Dax showed up. Hearing his voice through the door almost had me opening it, if only to inquire about Liam. I wanted to know how he was doing so badly. *Was he suffering an unbearable pain like me? Or had he moved on with his life as if I never existed?*

My hand wrapped around the doorknob, ready to turn the lock. But then I dropped my hand, realizing I didn't really want to know the answers to the questions in my head. The idea of either one of those being true would just hurt and anger me more. If he had moved on, I would be devastated. If he was suffering, I would be infuriated at his stubbornness.

"Val, please come out," Lexie pleaded for the hundredth time through my closed door.

My head shook no with my forehead pressed to the door, even though she couldn't see it.

"We don't have to talk about anything. I just want you to eat. You need to eat something."

"Come on, sweetheart," I heard Dax's smooth voice. "You're not going to be able to kick his ass later if you don't eat. You need food to get that fight back in you."

I turned, pressing my back to the door as I slid down it. I landed on my bottom, pulling my bent knees to my chest, hugging them to me.

"I'm done fighting, Dax," I gave my weak response.

"I don't believe you, sweetheart…he needs you."

"He doesn't want me."

"I know you don't believe that."

I didn't know what I believed anymore.

"Don't make me break down this door. If I have to, I may injure my hand. I wouldn't be able to play the guitar after that…you wouldn't want that on your conscience."

I heard the humor in his voice and somehow his words provoked a small, snotty, snorted chuckle to release through the tears that were running down my cheeks. I grasped onto that little bit of light, knowing I needed to pull myself out of the darkness. I stood, unlocking the door. At the sound of the click, the door flew open and Lexie pushed through.

"Thank God," she gasped, throwing her arms securely around me, pinning my arms to my side. "Dax, get your tools."

Tools?

Dax entered the room, hugging us both and kissing me on the top of my head. "Glad you're still alive, sweetheart." He released us, leaving us alone in the room.

"Where's he going?"

"To get his tools. We're removing your doorknob," she said, pulling back to look at me. I would have thought she was joking if it hadn't been for the serious determination on her face.

"What? Don't be ridiculous."

"I'm not allowing you the opportunity to lock yourself in here again. Now come on. I'm making you something to eat, and you're going to eat it. No arguments. You've been scaring the living shit out of me for the last few days. It's the least you can do." She grasped my hand in hers, pulling me out of my self-defined prison.

I watched lifelessly as Lexie prepared me something to eat and brewed some coffee. She placed a plate of fruit and a glass of water in front of me while she scrambled some eggs and toasted a bagel for me. I stared at the assortment of fruit. My hands slowly moved to put a strawberry in my mouth.

She took a seat next to me, placing my coffee and the rest of the food in front of me. We both sat quietly, sipping our coffees. She took a deep breath.

"Val, I know you're hurting. I know you want to stay locked in that room forever...but I can't let you. Just like you would never let me." She turned to look at me. "You have to start living again..."

I kept my eyes down on my plate, pushing the food around with my fork. "I know..."

I turned to look at her. Her eyebrows slowly rose to her forehead, as though she were unsure she'd heard me right. "Well, that was easy." A cautious smile turned up on her face.

The moment I had unlocked the door, I knew I needed to at least try to function. Even if only out of necessity. Even if I felt like a shell of a person.

Despite my insistence that I would not lock myself in my room again, at least not in the near future, Lexie still made Dax replace my doorknob with an unlockable one. I rolled my eyes at her, but let it go. I had put her through a lot over the last few days.

I took one more day to pull myself together before going back to work. The following week, I was able to put on a good front during the daytime. It was easy during the day, with the distraction of work and going to my call back audition. At night, it was impossible. The loneliness I felt at night was hard to ignore. I would cry myself to sleep, wishing Liam was lying beside me.

∾

Graduation came and went. Christmas came and went. New Year's came and went. And still no word from Liam. Beyond stalking the Derailed website and hearing little bits of information from Dax, I had no idea what he was doing or how he was coping. Dax tried a few times to get me to talk to Liam, but I'd refused. I had already tried the night he left me. I was still trying to heal. I wasn't strong enough to go through another rejection. I couldn't handle that.

Today was my last day of work at Sweet Beans. It was a bittersweet departure. I would be leaving tomorrow to head for New York. I was offered the part in the small-budget indie film. I took it without a thought.

I worked the register one last time while Ethan and I chatted and playfully insulted each other. He snapped a bar towel toward my leg in retaliation for my last quip. I dodged it, laughing, just before it made contact on my hip.

"You've got a customer, smartass," he laughed, pointing his head toward the front of the register.

I turned around giggling, but my laughter came to an abrupt halt as my eyes landed on the person in front of me. The pulse in my body increased as I tried to calm my shaky nerves. I cleared my throat, forcing myself to speak.

"What can I get you?"

I watched her as her eyes scanned the menu. She was just as pretty as I remembered. Her frame was petite and delicate. I felt like I could break her with just my touch, but there was also a hardness about her. She momentarily studied the list of espressos before looking back at me. "I guess, I'll take just a plain decaf coffee."

I nodded, deftly ringing up her order before turning to pour her coffee into a to-go cup. I didn't even bother asking if she wanted it for here. I didn't want her here. I wanted her to leave.

I gave her the cup and started to turn and walk away.

"Valerie." The sound of Tessa's desperate plea stopped me in my tracks.

I took a deep breath, turning back to face her. I stared at her, waiting for her to speak again. When she didn't, I raised my eyebrow, crossing my arms over my chest. My stern stance outwardly appeared strong, but inside I was weakening. Crumbling into a pile of rubble. *What the hell did she want? What was she doing here? Of all the coffee houses, why had she chosen to come to this one?*

"I..." she stuttered, her eyes looking from side to side, avoiding my harsh stare. "I'm not sure what I'm doing here."

That makes two of us.

"I don't even like coffee," she smiled weakly, looking down at the cup in her hands. "Do you have a minute to talk?"

I waited a second before nodding my head. I walked back toward the register, standing directly across from her again. Luckily for her, we were slow at the moment and there wasn't a line forming behind her.

She took a deep inhale before she started to speak. "I'm sorry. For the night at the party. I didn't mean to come between you and Liam. Honestly, I was in complete shock to see him there. I never thought I would see him again. I came here to ask you not to give up on him. He needs you. I could see that in the moment he saw you in that hallway. I know Liam, and I know he is probably trying to shut you out right now. Push you away. It's what he does..."

"Why?"

She shook her head, unsure. "I think he comes by it naturally. I think it's his way of protecting himself and the person he is pushing away." She looked away from me toward the

266

front windows of the coffee shop. She shifted nervously before turning her eyes back toward me. "I know you don't owe me anything. But promise me you'll fight for him. He needs someone in his corner."

"Who are you to him?"

I could see she cared about him. But for some reason she was no longer part of his life. I wondered if he had pushed her away the same way he had me.

"I'm nobody. Nobody that matters anymore." The pain in her words broke me.

She gave me one last pleading look before turning and rushing out of the coffee shop. She was gone as quickly as she had appeared. I stared after her, my mind wandering uncontrollably, not knowing what to focus on or which way to go.

I needed more answers. All I had was bunch of puzzle pieces that were slowly going together. But there was still some missing that would complete the mystery of Liam's past.

"You okay?" Ethan's voice interrupted my internal struggle.

"Huh? Yeah…sorry." I shook the thoughts from my head.

"Who was that?"

"I wish I could tell you…"

He gave me a confused look before turning back to wipe around the fancy espresso machines.

"Well, your final minutes of working here are approaching. Do you mind cleaning off the tables before you go? I know you're going to miss that. I wouldn't want to deprive you of living your glory days one last time." He gave me a wicked grin.

I shook my head, laughing at him. "Sure. Only because I'm seriously going to miss you Ethan...not because I will miss cleaning up people's dirty dishes."

I finished clearing the tables and then went around to start saying my goodbyes to the regulars and staff at Sweet Beans. I removed my apron for the last time, folding it up and putting it under the counter. I gave Ethan one last hug before walking out the front door.

∾

I sat behind the steering wheel of my car, gripping it so tightly my knuckles were turning white. When I got into my car and started driving away from work, I had no intention of coming here. But somehow, I'd still ended up here.

I had already put my car in park and shut off my ignition, but I couldn't manage to remove myself from the vehicle. I stared up at the sign of Frankie's shop, wondering if I had seriously lost my mind. *What the hell was I doing here?*

I took a deep breath through my nose, closing my eyes, releasing it through my mouth. I opened the door of my car before I changed my mind. My body floated across the parking lot to the customer entrance of Frankie's.

I opened the door. The bell rang above my head. I felt my pulse racing, but I still couldn't even be sure I was breathing. I expected to find the customer area devoid of personnel, but Danny had come walking in just as I crossed the threshold.

"Hey there, darlin'. Didn't expect to see you back here so soon," he said grinning. "Did ya get in another accident?"

"Um...no," I said, caught a little off-guard by his presence and still unsure of what I was doing here.

Normally, his jab at my driving ability would have gotten a rise out of me. But right now, I was too preoccupied forming some kind of plan in my head. "Is Liam here?"

"Yep. I think he just returned from lunch. I'll get him. You wait here," he added unnecessarily. Or maybe it was necessary. Part of me did want to turn and run.

"Wait!" I panicked as he started to leave me alone. "Don't tell him it's me...please." Confusion took hold of his face. "It's a surprise." I tried to smile widely.

He nodded, returning my smile before he walked out. I paced in the small room while I waited for Liam to appear. As the minutes passed, I started to think he wasn't going to come—that he'd figured out I was here and refused to see me.

My back was to the opening of the shop bays when I felt a familiar electric current course through me. I slowly turned to stare at the man who held my heart in his hands.

"What are you doing here, Val?"

He stood tall with his mask firmly in place, his hands crossed over his broad chest. But I knew him now, and I knew how to see through that mask. His eyes gave him away. He was happy to see me, despite his rigid body and the harsh firmness of his words, which attempted to portray otherwise.

"I came to tell you goodbye," I lied.

I wasn't here to tell him goodbye. I was here to beg him to come with me, or at least give us another chance. His brows pinched together.

"I got the part. I leave for New York tomorrow."

His arms dropped to his sides and his body softened

slightly. "Congratulations, princess." His words were soft and genuine.

I nodded my thank you. The words were caught in my throat by the deceptive hope that he may actually still want to be with me.

"Come with me."

His head lowered in a shake, forcing his eyes to the ground. I slowly stepped closer to him.

"Why not?" I asked as I continued my progression.

"Val." His warning was a plea for me to stop.

"Is it because of the girl from the party? Tessa?"

"No."

"She came to see me…"

His head snapped up. His eyes widened with fear and worry. I pressed for answers.

"Did you love her?" I choked on the words as they came out of my mouth. They felt like knives slicing through me.

He nodded once. I felt the air around me disappear as I began to suffocate. My arms twisted around my stomach in pain. Liam moved instinctively to comfort me but stopped, holding himself back.

"Do you love her still?"

"Val… It's not what you think. I love her, but not the way you think."

"Then explain it to me!" I demanded. "Quit leaving me in the dark to imagine what could possibly be keeping you away from me."

"I warned you from the beginning. I told you I have shit in my past. You made me believe it didn't matter. And the moment I thought maybe it didn't, it came right back to fuck with me again. And now…now I have to fucking deal with it.

And worse, I have to deal with the fact that I hurt you. I never should have let things happen between us."

"You don't mean that. Let me help you. Tell me what happened. I don't believe that you could hurt someone like that."

"I did. I was guilty. And I did my time."

"No."

"You need to leave, Val."

"I know there has to be more. Don't push me away."

"It's for your own good. I don't want you anywhere near this fucked-up mess that's forcing its way back into my life. I need to take care of some things. You can't be around for that. I don't want to be worrying about you."

"Don't do that. Don't try to make this out like you're protecting me. This is about you. You're walking away for you. Not me." I glared at him.

"Leave, Val," he demanded once again. But I could see he was struggling with his own words.

I put an end to the last few inches of physical separation between us. I cupped my hands on his face, making him remember the feel of my touch. I locked my eyes with his.

"Make sure you really mean that, Liam. Because if I leave, I'm not coming back. I'm done. I'm done fighting for us. I can't do it anymore."

I'm not sure how I found the strength to form the words I spoke. But I meant them. Maybe it was the self-preservation I had instilled in me. I couldn't keep doing this. I had bared my heart and soul to him, given him everything I had. If he was going to choose to let me leave, I would have to find the strength to heal, no matter how impossible the task seemed.

His hands came to my hips and his forehead pressed

against mine as the air around us became toxic with anguish. We closed our eyes, reliving a familiar crossroads. I just hoped he would make the right decision this time. If he didn't…I would have to figure out how to live without him.

His hands glided up the sides of my body, sending a shiver up my spine. They landed on my face as he lifted both of our heads. His eyes scanned over every feature of my face, as if he was memorizing it for an eternity. My breath hitched, realizing this was the end. A tear fell out of the corner of my eye. He swiped it from my cheek and then ran his thumb over my parting lips.

The tip of his nose skimmed along my cheek. My eyes fluttered closed, wanting to feel every sensation of his touch. His lips pressed softly and firmly against my mouth. His tongue pushed inside, rolling with mine. The kiss became our last-ditch effort to convince each other. He fought to tell me goodbye, while I fought for him to stay.

Our kiss broke apart. Our labored breathing made it hard to speak. He pressed one firm kiss on my cheek before whispering in my ear, "Goodbye, princess."

His hands instantly fell as he turned and walked away. My eyes shot open to watch him turn his back on me for the last time.

∾

I'm not sure how I managed to carry myself out of Frankie's. I'm not sure how I managed to drive home. I'm not sure how I managed to finish packing that night. I'm not even sure how I managed to make it to the airport to get on my brother's private jet the next day. But I was here.

I checked my phone one last time, expecting to find a message from Liam begging me not to leave. It was an unrealistic expectation. But I had it, nonetheless. I turned it off just as Sarah came to tell me we were getting ready to depart.

I leaned my head back against the seat, closing my eyes, knowing that when I opened them, I would be in New York. I would be starting the next chapter of my life, hoping once again to heal from the previous.

EPILOGUE

LIAM STONE....

I knocked on the doorframe as I walked into Frankie's office. He'd been poring over the books for the shop the last three hours. I was pretending my reason for interrupting him was to let him know we just got a new car in the shop. The truth: I worried about him. Every fucking day I worried I would walk into his office or come home to find him dead.

The old, stubborn bastard didn't know how to take it easy. Especially when it came to the shop. It was his life. After his wife passed, he threw every waking hour into running the place.

"Come on in, son..." He barely glanced up, looking over the top of his reading glasses that sat low on his nose to briefly acknowledge my presence before looking back down at the paperwork on his desk.

"We got a new car in," I said, taking a seat in the old, orange, plastic bucket chair across from his desk.

He'd had them for so long, I was pretty sure the ugly things were actually back in style. I smiled inwardly at the thought. Nothing ever changed around Frankie's. Not at the shop and not at his house. It was the one constant I could depend on.

He nodded, mumbling something incoherent, not looking up from his accounting book.

"You know they have computers and programs that will help with that shit."

"I'm fine doin' it this way. It's how I've always done it." He continued to scribble in the book after adding some numbers together with his calculator.

"Maybe so…but it would make things easier for you. Take you less time…so you're not stuck workin' all the time."

He lifted his head, eyeing me over his glasses, before dropping it back down again.

"I don't see how learnin' a new way of doin' it would take me less time. Don't you know that sayin' about old dogs and new tricks? I'm too old for that shit…"

I chuckled, shaking my head. *Stubborn bastard.* "Maybe we should hire someone then. Someone who could do the books, greet customers, that kind of thing…"

Frankie laid his pencil down, finally looking up to focus on me as he leaned back in his cracked, brown leather chair. He crossed his broad arms over his belly, which had grown over the years I'd known him. He studied me for a moment, making me drop my gaze.

"Why don't you tell me what's really on your mind, son? Stop pussyfootin' around it."

I looked up, focusing my eyes on him, leaning forward to rest my forearms on my legs as I clasped my hands between them.

"I leave in a week, Frankie. You're gonna need the help. I'd feel better about goin' on the road, if I knew you had additional help around here."

He removed his glasses, letting out a deep sigh as he leaned forward, resting his arms and glasses on the desk in front of him.

"Kid, you gotta stop worryin' about me. Live your life. I've lived mine. I'm gonna die someday. It's part of the circle of life…like they say in that Lion King bullshit."

"You quoting Disney movies now?" I smirked.

He chuckled, shaking his head at me. "My point is, whether it be tomorrow from a heart attack, or in ten years from some other cause…I'm gonna die."

I turned my head to stare at the wall in his office. I knew everything he was fucking saying was reality. It didn't mean I fucking liked it. I'd lost everyone I'd ever called family in my life. He was all I had left. I wasn't ready to lose him, too.

"If anyone should worry, it should be me," he added, interrupting my thoughts. My brow furrowed as I looked back at him in confusion.

"What's that mean?"

He raised an eyebrow at me. When I didn't catch on to whatever it was he was implying, he continued.

"Do you want to know what made this life worth livin' for me?" He paused, waiting for me to answer what I thought was a rhetorical question. "Evelyn. I loved that woman more than anything in this world. More than that motorcycle. More than this shop. And I would give anything to have her back in my arms. You don't have a love like that come around more than once…unless you're lucky. But we both know I don't believe in luck."

I knew what he was getting at now. Valerie. He hadn't brought her up since the day I'd told him things had ended.

"Frankie," I shook my head in warning. "You know we can't be together."

"Honestly, son, I don't. And it pisses me right off watching you act like a stubborn fuckin' bastard."

Ditto old man.

"Tell me how ya really feel," I scoffed.

"I always thought you were a smart kid until the day you let her leave."

My pulse thrummed through my veins. His words triggering a suppressed rage to rise within me. *How could he not know why we couldn't be together?* My life was too fucked up. I was not drawing her into that shit. I never should have allowed things to go on the way they did. I should have told her the first day. Laid it all out there for her, so she would have gone running and never looked back. But I didn't. Because I wanted her. I wanted her in my life, even if only for a short time. Because I'm a selfish asshole. Another reason we shouldn't be together.

I stood from my chair, running a hand through my hair as I struggled to calm my breathing and anger. I didn't want to go off on Frankie. He had been the closest thing I'd had to a father since mine died. I was leaving in a week to go on tour with Derailed, and I didn't want any bad blood between us before I left. I didn't want to say anything I would regret.

"I appreciate the concern, Frankie, but we'll have to agree to disagree. I'm gonna get back to work."

He gave me a nod, accepting my dismissal of the conversation before picking up his glasses to refocus on his ancient books. I felt his disapproving eyes on my back as I walked out.

~

I went back to work on the car I had been repairing over the last few hours. I cranked up the music in the shop to drown out everything around me. Music had always been my escape. Whether I was composing, playing, singing, or just listening to it.

"Stone!" Danny yelled from behind me. I ignored him, finishing up the last touches around the rim.

"Stone! You got a visitor!"

My heart slammed in my chest. The last time he told me that I found Valerie waiting for me. A hope welled up in me at the thought of seeing her gorgeous face again. A hope I shouldn't be having, but for some reason I always did. I smothered any chance of her returning the last time she was here. I knew it wouldn't be her. She was in New York now. But I asked anyway.

"Who is it?" I glanced over my shoulder.

He shrugged. "Beats me. Never seen 'em before."

I wrapped up what I was doing before heading to the customer-service area. When I walked through the door, I thought someone had fucking punched me in the gut at my sudden loss of breath. They were the last two people I expected to see.

"What the fuck are you doin' here?" I addressed her first. I narrowed my eyes as I crossed my arms.

"Liam, hear us out. Please," Tessa begged, her voice clogged with anguish, but her stance full of determination.

"Give me one damn reason I should."

"I'm leaving him...I'm leaving Scott." The words quaked on her lips.

"I don't believe you."

"I'm pregnant," she said in a rush.

My eyes widened. Her eyes were full of remorse and fear.

"Does he know?"

I knew there was no way he would let her leave easily. And if he knew she was pregnant with his kid, he would never stop hunting them. Not because he would want her or the kid, but because he was an arrogant prick. Nobody took from him without paying the price.

"No..." She shook her head. "I need to leave him before he finds out. I can't raise a baby in that house...with him. I'm scared to even be pregnant around him. I'm scared of what might happen."

I glanced between the two of them, trying to control my anger and wrap my mind around what she was saying. This was more fucked up than before. Now there was a baby involved.

"Why the hell is he with you?" I nodded toward Rhett, not making eye contact with him. Seeing him only reminded me of Valerie and of what I couldn't have. He stepped forward, answering for her.

"I'm here to help."

"I don't need your fuckin' help." I glared at him. "I can take care of this on my own," I gritted through my teeth.

"Liam, give him a chance to explain. We both know when I leave Scott, the first place he'll look is with you."

As much as I hated to admit it, she was right. Scott would show up at Frankie's looking for her. The last time she'd tried to leave him, I helped. He showed up in less than twelve hours to convince her to come back to him. Filled her with every fucking lie in the book. That he would change, that he would never hit her again. And she believed him. Or she at least chose to go with him for some fucking insane reason, despite what I'd had to say.

Also, I was leaving in a week, which would leave her unprotected for months. I would bring her with me, but life on the road was no place for her while she was pregnant.

"Liam, I need to apologize. I was wrong. I should have talked to you first, instead of taking Scott's word. I know now you were trying to protect Tessa. She came to me. Explained everything that happened. It's not you who should have been in jail. It was Scott. I would have done the same thing, if…" He glanced away from me, as if the thought alone enraged him.

He didn't need to finish his statement. I knew if it were Valerie, he would have done the same thing. It was one of the reasons I respected him. He would do anything for Valerie. Anything for his family. The same way I would mine. Tessa was my baby sister. Standing by, watching Scott beat the shit out of her, wasn't an option.

I nodded my understanding and accepted his apology. "So what's the plan?"

They looked between each other before Tessa spoke.

"Scott's been trying to negotiate a business deal with Rhett. He wants to go in on a joint venture, purchasing a company in Texas. Rhett is going to suggest a business trip to get him out of town for a few days, so I have time to get my things and leave."

"My security team is working on getting her an alias. We'll relocate her, so he can't find her. They'll help her get her things and get her moved. As soon as they have confirmed she's out of the house and safe, I'll decline the business deal. I'm setting Tessa up with a bank account in her new name with plenty of money to get her on her feet."

"You don't have to do that, Rhett. I can take care of the money."

"It's not up for discussion. It's already done. It's only enough until she's settled. From there, I'll let you two figure it out."

I nodded. "I'll repay you every dime."

He shook his head. "How about you repay me another way?"

"What did you have in mind?"

He rubbed a hand across the back of his neck, releasing a heavy sigh. "Fight for her. I won't stand in your way. I never should have gotten in the way to start with."

Air clogged my throat as I fought to swallow. He was telling me to be with Val. Something I would have never expected from him. Had all this happened weeks ago, maybe I could have been with her. But it was too late now.

"She's done with me. And it's for the best. She doesn't need to be getting tangled up in this fucking mess."

Tessa flinched with guilt.

He nodded. "This will all be handled soon enough. Once it is, you need to fight for her. I know my sister. She may have told you she's done, but I can see she loves you. She's just hurt right now."

I shook my head. "I don't know..."

"I do. Look, I'm going to give you the same advice Jackson gave me: stop being a fucking idiot and get your girl back." A smile tugged at the corner of his mouth, despite the heaviness of our conversation.

I shook my own head with a small chuckle. But it faded quickly as I came to terms with my situation. "I leave for our tour next week," I said, knowing it was a lame excuse.

"You have a stop in New York, don't you?"

I nodded. It was almost a month away, though. By then she may have moved on. Forgotten about me. She'd already been gone a month. I could already be too late. The thought of that fucking killed me.

"I know what you're thinking," he said. "I had the same thoughts myself when it was Ava. You need to reach out to her before then."

"And if she won't take my calls?"

"You keep calling," he said firmly. "You fight."

Tessa shifted uncomfortably as she glanced down at her vibrating phone. She forced on a strong face, but I could see the fear in her eyes. "I'm sorry. I have to go."

I nodded my understanding. Scott was looking for her and if she wasn't home soon... I stepped closer to my little sister, pulling her against me as I hugged her protectively. I didn't want to let her go. I didn't want to allow her to walk back into that house with him.

But I knew I had to. No matter how bad it fucking hurt to let her walk out, I had to let her go. I kissed her on the top of her head before releasing her. This would all be over soon.

She gave a nod to Rhett with a weak smile, before turning for the door. Rhett put out his hand, and I shook it.

282

"I'll take care of your sister," he promised. "You take care of mine."

I nodded my agreement before he turned to leave with Tessa. I walked back into Frankie's office to let him know I was leaving for the day. That I needed to figure out a way to get my girl back. He smiled and wished me luck. I laughed …*Damn hypocrite.*

THANK YOU FOR READING!

I sincerely hope you enjoyed reading this book as much as I enjoyed writing it. If you did, I would greatly appreciate a short review on Amazon, Goodreads or your favorite book website. Thanks again!

VALERIE AND LIAM'S STORY CONTINUES IN

Forever Yours

REDEEMING
Lottie

Now Available

Click Here!

Subscribe for updates on my blog!

Website:

www.melissaellenwrites.com

ACKNOWLEDGMENTS

This acknowledgement is long overdue. I have to start out this book by thanking my husband. He has been my rock and the biggest supporter of everything I do. Whether it be to leave my comfortable, cushy job to set out on my own to begin a start-up company or to decide on a whim that I am going to start writing. If you know my husband, you know this is a big deal for him to relinquish that kind of financial security. But he does. He does it for me, and I can't thank or love him enough for it. Not only does he allow me to follow my crazy dreams, but he looks after our son to allow me the time to write in the evenings at a coffee house while he takes care of putting our son to bed. I hope every one of my readers have a man that will put his fears aside to support the woman they love. Because that is what I have, and I am the luckiest woman in the world to have that.

And of course, a big thank you to my readers. You are the reason I keep writing. Without you, my writing might have stopped at one book, but with you, I have the drive to keep writing just to put a smile on your face and happy tears in your eyes.

And as always, my support team! You know who you are. I love you all and love sharing this journey with you.